B

Kate Hoffmann

"...the talented Kate Hoffmann tickles our funny bones with hot romance and sparkling wit...."
—*Romantic Times*

"Ms. Hoffmann dishes up a luscious entertainment spiced with tangy sensuality."
—*Romantic Times*

Jacqueline Diamond

"Jacqueline Diamond is a master at creating humorous stories with witty dialogue...."
—*Romance and Friends*

"With an emphasis on fun and frolic, Jacqueline Diamond delivers sheer romantic amusement...."
—*Romantic Times*

Jill Shalvis

"Jill Shalvis pens an unforgettable story filled with extraordinary characters."
—*Romantic Times*

"Author Shalvis succeeds in gracefully combining...sparkling energy and humor for a fantastic read."
—*WordWeaving*

Kate Hoffmann started reading romance when she was an elementary school music teacher. She began writing romance when she was an advertising copywriter. And in 1993, the year her first Temptation novel was published, she quit the nine-to-five world and became a full-time romance writer. Since then, Kate has published more than thirty stories with Harlequin, including Temptation, Duets, continuity series and anthologies. Kate lives in Wisconsin with her three cats and her computer. When she's not writing, she enjoys gardening, golfing and genealogy.

USA TODAY bestselling author **Jacqueline Diamond** began her career as an Associated Press reporter and television columnist in Los Angeles, and has interviewed hundreds of celebrities. Now a full-time fiction writer, she has sold over sixty novels that span romance, suspense and fantasy. Though she was born in Texas and raised in Nashville and Louisville, home is now in Southern California. She and her husband are the parents of two sons.

Jill Shalvis has been making up stories since she could hold a pencil. Now, thankfully, she gets to do it for a living, and doesn't plan to ever stop. She is the bestselling, award-winning author of over two dozen novels. She's hit the Waldenbooks bestsellers list, is a 2000 RITA® Award nominee and a two-time National Reader's Choice Award winner. Jill has been nominated for a Romantic Times Career Achievement Award in Romantic Comedy, Best Duets and Best Temptation.

Kate Hoffmann

Jacqueline Diamond

Jill Shalvis

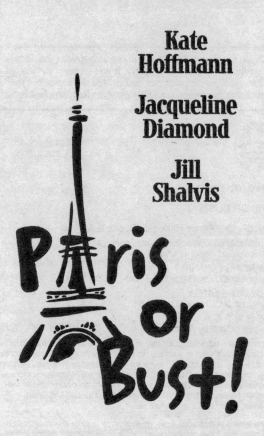

Paris or Bust!

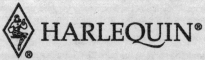

HARLEQUIN®

TORONTO • NEW YORK • LONDON
AMSTERDAM • PARIS • SYDNEY • HAMBURG
STOCKHOLM • ATHENS • TOKYO • MILAN • MADRID
PRAGUE • WARSAW • BUDAPEST • AUCKLAND

ISBN 0-373-83573-6

PARIS OR BUST!

Copyright © 2003 by Harlequin Books S.A.

The publisher acknowledges the copyright holders
of the individual works as follows:

ROMANCING ROXANNE?
Copyright © 2003 by Peggy Hoffmann

DADDY COME LATELY
Copyright © 2003 by Jackie Hyman

LOVE IS IN THE AIR
Copyright © 2003 by Jill Shalvis

All rights reserved. Except for use in any review, the reproduction or
utilization of this work in whole or in part in any form by any electronic,
mechanical or other means, now known or hereafter invented, including
xerography, photocopying and recording, or in any information storage
or retrieval system, is forbidden without the written permission of the
publisher, Harlequin Enterprises Limited, 225 Duncan Mill Road,
Don Mills, Ontario, Canada M3B 3K9.

All characters in this book have no existence outside the imagination of
the author and have no relation whatsoever to anyone bearing the same
name or names. They are not even distantly inspired by any individual
known or unknown to the author, and all incidents are pure invention.

This edition published by arrangement with Harlequin Books S.A.

® and TM are trademarks of the publisher. Trademarks indicated with
® are registered in the United States Patent and Trademark Office, the
Canadian Trade Marks Office and in other countries.

Visit us at www.eHarlequin.com

Printed in U.S.A.

CONTENTS

ROMANCING ROXANNE?

Kate Hoffmann

ROXANNE PERRY ...

... to dream about ...
... on ... her prince

PROLOGUE

There is only one person I know who deserves to be named "Mother of the Year" and that's my sister, Roxanne Perry. When we were little girls, Roxanne used to dream about getting married and having a large, happy family. We'd dress ourselves in toilet paper veils and make bouquets out of plastic flowers and whisper about the handsome men we'd marry. Roxanne found her Prince Charming and they had four beautiful children together. But fairy tales don't always have happy endings, and a few years ago, Roxanne was forced to wake up and recognize that the man she married had turned from a prince to a big, fat, warty toad.

Though her husband walked away from their marriage and their family, Roxanne ignored her own pain and did everything in her power to help her children adjust. It was hard at first, but she's always maintained a positive attitude. Every day, she wakes up with a smile on her face, her only thought for her children's happiness. She's brave and resilient, patient and loving, and the best sister a girl could ever have. But beyond that, she's the best mother I know. And if I could be half the mother she is, then I know my children would grow up happy and healthy.

If Roxanne knew I was nominating her for this contest, she would be embarrassed. She believes that simply loving her children is its own reward. But I want her to know that the difficult path she's walking in life is important and it does count for something. I want everyone to know that Roxanne Perry is the very best mother I know.

CHAPTER ONE

CARL LAWRENCE reread the copy of the letter once more, then glanced at the photo of Roxanne Perry and her family. The publicity department at *Family Voyager* magazine had contacted WBAM, hoping that Carl's radio station would provide some additional media coverage for their contest, possibly an interview with Roxanne on Carl's afternoon show, *Baltimore At Home*. At first, Carl hadn't been interested. But then his promotions manager had called Roxanne's sister, Renee, and she'd provided more background, including the photo.

Roxanne Perry was a beautiful young woman, Carl mused. Dark-haired and slender, with a pretty smile and lively eyes. He tossed the picture on his desk and leaned back in his chair. She was exactly the kind of girl he'd always hoped his son, Kit, might one day marry, a woman who could make Kit happy for a lifetime. A woman who would provide Carl with a gaggle of grandchildren to occupy his retirement years. Instead, he spent his days as general manager of Baltimore's WBAM, Talk Ra-

dio 1010, a job he'd returned to after his wife
had died.

Grandchildren wouldn't be out of the realm of
possibility if Kit would just start to take his relationships with women a bit more seriously, Carl
thought. But, the women he chose to date were icy
beauties who had no interest in a future raising
children and keeping a house. In truth, Kit paid
more attention to Carl's sporadic social life than
he did to his own, determined to keep Carl's wid-
ower status and family stock portfolio intact.

Carl reached across his desk and picked up a
framed photo of his wife. She'd died ten years ago,
but there were times when it seemed as if it were
just yesterday. "I want him to be happy," he murmured. "I want him to have a real life. And damn
it, I want grandchildren."

Kit had been such a sweet and caring kid, a boy
who used to bring home hurt birds and stray cats,
who used to cry inconsolably when his goldfish
died. A boy with a soft heart and a big smile. Now,
all he cared about was his next deal. Kit measured
his success in terms of dollars and cents.

"You would have made a much better match-
maker, Louise," Carl said, setting the picture back
in its spot. He grabbed the photo of Roxanne Perry
and shoved it back into the file folder. And in that
instant, an idea hit him. More than an idea, a plan!
If Kit wasn't going to find a wife for himself, then

Carl would have to take on the responsibility. But he'd have to go about it in a very careful way. If Kit suspected he was being set up, the plan would be doomed to failure.

Carl smiled. "Grandchildren," he murmured. "If I'm going to get grandchildren, I've got to find the right daughter-in-law." And he knew exactly where to start.

He grabbed a pad of paper and scribbled Kit's name on the left side and Roxanne Perry's on the right. First, he'd have to find a way to put them together, a way for them to meet on neutral ground. He glanced at the photo. She was an attractive woman and Kit would see that immediately. But Kit knew a lot of beautiful women. What would spark an interest in Roxanne Perry?

"She has to be a challenge," Carl muttered, writing the word down between their two names. Most women fell all over themselves to date Kit. He was handsome and charming and rich, all the qualities that a good catch needed. But if a woman didn't show any interest at all, then Kit was usually intrigued and began a single-minded pursuit.

"This is more complicated than I thought." Carl rubbed his chin. If there was another man in Roxanne's life, that might create some interest. Maybe he could introduce her to Bill Mayer, the station's financial manager. He was single and considered cute by most of the girls at the station. And Carl knew Bill made a decent living, since he signed his paycheck. But what if Roxanne fell for Bill and wasn't attracted to Kit at all?

Carl grabbed the piece of paper and crumpled it up in his hands, then tossed it in the wastebasket beneath his desk. Maybe it would be best to just wing it and see what happened. He'd get Roxanne and Kit in the same place at the same time and if sparks flew, he'd be there to fan the flames. And if there were no sparks at all, he'd find another woman…and another and another, until he found the perfect mate for his bachelor son.

"I'll get us some grandchildren, Louise. Or I'll go down trying."

ROXANNE HEARD IT from the kitchen, the sound of the mail slot creaking open and the stack of bills dropping onto the hardwood floor of the foyer. She slowly turned away from the sinkful of dirty dishes, the familiar sick feeling growing in her stomach. Grabbing a dish towel, she wiped her hands dry then started for the front door.

On the way, she made a detour. Instead of picking up the stack of bills, she opened the hall closet door and stepped inside. When the door was shut, blackness surrounded her. Only then could she allow the tears to come.

Her daily afternoon cries had been a two-year habit. At first, she'd cried out of sorrow and then out of anger. But now the tears had become a way of coping, of focusing all her emotions into a few minutes so she could get on with the business of life—the kids, the bills, the house that seemed to be crumbling around her.

Roxanne drew a deep breath and thought about all those things that usually started the tears—her husband's infidelity, her deteriorating bank account, her loneliness. "And I'm never going to have sex again in my entire life," she murmured.

Usually that was enough, but today the tears just wouldn't start. Maybe she was dehydrated. She sat down on a box of mittens and scarves, listening to the sound of the television drifting out from the living room. Danny, Rachel, Michael and Jenna were watching Saturday afternoon cartoons and eating Jell-O cubes, their regular routine.

After she finished her cry, she'd pick up the mail and sit down at the kitchen table, the way *she* did every afternoon. And once she juggled the family finances and put off the bill collectors for a few more days, she's start supper…. Roxanne moaned, squeezing her eyes shut. "Just like I do every afternoon."

This was ridiculous! She was living a cliché, the abandoned wife with the dismal future. She'd become a bad Jerry Springer guest, filled with resentment and hidden anger and a list of grievances against her ex-husband that seemed to be unending. He couldn't just have decided that marriage wasn't for him. No, he had to completely humiliate her in the process.

She'd had such a perfect marriage—or at least that's what she'd thought. On the surface, John Perry seemed like the model husband, a good father and a generous provider. He'd wanted a big family and Roxanne had been thrilled to be a stay-at-home mother. They'd bought a beautiful old Victorian row house in the historic Mount Vernon neighborhood in Baltimore and had begun to restore it. His job as a lawyer gave them extra money for vacations and a nice car and dinners out twice a week. Though he spent long hours at the office she'd assumed it was all part of building a career.

But now she'd realized how naive she'd seen. John had run off to Barbados not with a pretty secretary or an aspiring supermodel, which she might have understood. He had thrown her over for a muscle-bound Amazon, a client with a career in professional wrestling and a complicated lawsuit brought by her greedy family. Roxanne had lost her man to "The Velvet Hammer," a woman she'd seen only once when she secretly taped *Wednesday Night SlamFest* and watched after the children when to bed.

"My children's stepmother has biceps bigger than my head," she said, hoping that might start the tears. But all it brought was a little giggle.

It was all so embarrassing. She'd always thought her husband was a rational, intelligent man, a man who loved his family and his position in the community. But then Roxanne had discovered the savings account empty and the stock portfolio gone. Luckily, she'd still had a small trust fund from her grandfather to pay the day-to-day expenses. Even after the divorce settlement was final, the child support had been slow in coming.

"This is my life," she muttered. "A dark, musty closet filled with mismatched mittens and moth-eaten scarves." She thought a silent recitation of all she'd lost would open the floodgates, but she couldn't seem to muster even a tiny sob. What did this mean?

"Mommy?"

Roxanne saw the light beneath the closet door flicker and she knew Danny, her six-year-old, was outside, his face pressed to the floor, trying to see if she was inside. Sometimes, when she came out of the closet, he was lying on the rug, waiting for her, always the little man ready to come to her rescue. Such a big burden for such a tiny boy, to be the man of the family.

"What is it, sweetie?"

"Rachel wants juice," he said. "When are you coming out?"

"Mommy's just dusting," Roxanne said. "I'll be out in a few minutes."

"I can dust the closet for you," Danny offered.

Roxanne sighed softly. For some reason, she just couldn't work up a good case of tears today. All the anger she'd kept so well hidden had slowly dissolved until there was nothing left. Two years ago, her husband had walked out. A year ago, the divorce was finalized. And her future began today. The revelation stunned her. She was finally over John. Six years of marriage and that was it.

"Mommy?"

She bent down and looked at her son beneath the door. "Yeah, sweetie."

"There's a man on the porch. Should I let him in?"

"It's probably just the mailman. Maybe he forgot something."

"He has flowers and balloons. Can I let him in?"

Frowning, Roxanne struggled to her feet and opened the door carefully, waiting for Danny to scoot back. But her son wasn't on the floor, he was standing at the front door, smiling up at a stranger who waited on the front porch. With a soft cry, Roxanne hurtled past him and slammed the door shut. Then she bent down in front of Danny and put on a stern expression. "Do you remember what Mommy told you? You never, ever open the door to a stranger."

"But he has balloons," Danny said.

"I don't care if he has a million cute puppies and ten tons of candy. You never, ever open the door to a stranger. Do you understand?"

Danny nodded, then glanced over at the door. "Can I let him in?"

"No," Roxanne said. "But you can ask me to let him in."

"Let him in, Mommy, let him in. He has balloons."

Roxanne patted her son on the head, then opened the front door a crack. A distinguished-looking gentleman in a rumpled overcoat stood in the chilly March wind, a huge bouquet of roses in one hand and a cluster of balloons in the other. "Can I help you?" she asked.

"Are you Roxanne Perry?"

"I am." She opened the door a bit wider. A bizarre thought raced through her mind. Publishers Clearing House! She'd filled out the entry forms a few months ago on a lark. Sure, she could use five or ten million dollars, she had thought. But she also had known the odds were against her. Maybe her luck had finally changed!

"Congratulations," he said, holding the roses out. "I'm happy to inform you that you've—"

"Oh, my God," Roxanne cried, throwing the door open and dragging him inside. "How much have I won? Where is Ed McMahon? Am I on television?"

The gentleman glanced over his shoulder, then back at Roxanne. "I'm sorry. I'm not from Publishers Clearing House. I'm Carl Lawrence, general manager of WBAM Talk Radio 1010."

"A radio station? Are you giving away money?"

He shook his head. "I'm here to congratulate you, Mrs. Perry. You've been named a finalist in the Mother of the Year contest, sponsored by *Family Voyager* magazine. My radio station is promoting the contest and I've come to congratulate you."

The kids gathered around his feet and he handed them each a pair of balloons. They ran off, the colorful balloons trailing after them.

"But I never entered a contest," Roxanne said. "Except for Publishers Clearing House."

"I entered you." Roxanne's sister, Renee, stepped up onto the porch. She held up her camera and snapped a photo. "I wanted to get here in time, but I got caught in traffic. Are you surprised?"

White spots danced in front of Roxanne's eyes. "I don't understand. Why would you enter me in a contest?"

"Because you're the best mother I know," Renee said. "And you deserve to be recognized for how well you've managed to keep your family together after that jackass scumbag loser you called a husband walked out on you." She turned to Carl Lawrence. "Pardon my French."

Carl Lawrence cleared his throat, clearly uneasy m̶ Renee's acidic commentary. "Mrs. Perry, if I you. Our̶e̶ to discuss some publicity ideas with promotion wi̶ station has agreed to do a cross-like to do several *ily Voyager* magazine. We'd public appearances with ̶ views and possibly some ̶dio remotes. As you probably know, we have a big listener base of mothers, ages 25 to 36."

"You announce the public school lunch menus," Renee said. "My kids and I listen every morning."

"Well, that's not all we do at WBAM," Carl said. "We're family-oriented talk radio. Have you listened to our *Baltimore At Home* show?"

"No, we just listen to the menus. Then the kids turn on cartoons and I make their lunches," Renee said.

"Can we get back to this contest?" Roxanne asked. "I really don't want to be on the radio. I mean, that's like giving me a dental exam for a prize."

"Oh, that's not the prize," Renee said. She pulled a glossy magazine out of her bag and held it in front of Roxanne, flipping through it until she found a page with a picture of the Eiffel Tower. "See? If you win the national contest, you'll win a romantic getaway trip to Paris for you and a guest. And since you don't have a husband, th guest would have to be me, since I entered w th the contest. Can you imagine it? You Paris?"

"So *you* want to win the cont yself. And you

"Well, I couldn't nomi an I do. I still have a make a much sorrier ca jackass scumbag lose ving at my house."

Roxanne laughed out loud when she saw the expression on Carl Lawrence's face. "Don't mind my sister. She has a very bizarre sense of humor. Her husband is a wonderful man." She turned back to Renee. "What else are you going to win if I win?"

"Besides the trip to Paris, you get a $5000 shopping spree."

"And Bob Compton Ford has decided to give you the use of a brand-new luxury minivan for a year if you win the national contest," Carl added. "He advertises with the station so we worked out a deal. And Food King will give you a year's worth of groceries. I've also worked out promos with Toy Emporium and a kids' clothing store. All of us at WBAM want you to win this contest. I'd like to take you out to dinner so we can discuss this in greater detail. How about Monday night?"

"I—I can't," Roxanne said. "I'd have to get a sitter and—"

"I'll watch the kids," Renee offered.

Roxanne shot her sister a frustrated look. "And my minivan hasn't been working very well—"

"That's no problem," Carl said. "I'll send a car for you."

"Go ahead," Renee urged. "It's about time you did something for yourself."

"All right," Roxanne said, realizing that it was better to give in than to face her sister's badgering. She could always cancel at the last minute if something came up. She groaned inwardly. What would come up? Her life had been pretty much the same day after day since her husband had walked out, the routine punctuated only by the occasional emergency.

Carl Lawrence handed her his business card. "Then I'll see you Monday night. Do you like crab?"

"What?"

"Crab. I know a great place for crab. I'll give the driver directions."

He stepped back through the front door and Renee closed it behind him, shutting out the damp wind. When she turned back to Roxanne, Renee's eyes were bright with excitement and her smile wide. "Isn't this wonderful?" she asked. "You're a finalist. I got the letter a couple days ago and I was almost tempted to tell you, but then the guy from the radio station called and insisted that we make a big deal of the whole thing."

"What would ever possess you to enter me in a contest like this?" Roxanne demanded.

"I thought it would be fun. And you deserve it. You're the best mother I know."

A surge of guilt washed over Roxanne as she remembered her son talking to her beneath the closet door. What kind of mother hid from her kids in a hallway closet?

"A trip to Paris?" Renee reminded her. "A shopping spree? You're going to turn that down?"

"Why would they pick me?"

"Because I wrote an incredible essay about your positive attitude and the love you have for your kids and the new life you're making for yourself. You forget, I was an English major in college. I gave them my best stuff." Renee reached out and gave Roxanne a hug. "Just think, you could meet a rich and handsome French man when you're in Paris, he could sweep you off your feet and take you away from all your troubles."

"You are living in a fantasy world if you think that's how it works. Men don't want an almost-thirty woman with four kids and a mountain of debt. John has been gone for nearly two years and I've been officially divorced for a year. And I haven't had a date in all that time. They're not beating down my doors."

"That's because you don't put yourself out there. You've been hiding out in this house. You're a beautiful woman, Roxy. And I'm sorry that your husband dumped a truckload of crap in your lap, but it's time to move on."

The tears that wouldn't come earlier, now flowed down her cheeks. "It is time to move on," Roxanne said. "I didn't believe that until today, but my life as a married woman is over. I'm on my own now and I've got to be strong for my kids."

"And you never know. That Lawrence guy has a radio station. You majored in mass communications in college. This might be good for you."

"I don't have the time to think about myself right now."

"You need to make the time," Renee said. "Why don't you put on a pot of coffee and we'll get started? I'll give you a pedicure. And we'll decide what you should wear to your dinner. What do you think of that Mr. Lawrence? He's kind of cute."

Roxanne started toward the kitchen. "He's old enough to be my father."

"Yeah, but a guy that age wouldn't run off with a professional wrestler. A guy like that would appreciate a woman like you."

Roxanne sighed inwardly. Was this what she'd be faced with out in the dating world? Finding a man whose only redeeming quality was that he wouldn't be attracted to professional wrestlers? Suddenly, she had the overwhelming urge to crawl back in the hall closet and never come out again.

KIT LAWRENCE pulled his car into the restaurant parking lot, steering the BMW into an empty stall. He stepped out and set the alarm, wondering why his father always had to choose some strange, out-of-the way restaurant for their regular Monday night dinners.

Since Kit's mother had died ten years ago, Carl Lawrence had become more and more eccentric. He'd gradually turned his business interests over to Kit, who had transformed a string of east coast radio stations into what *Fortune* magazine had recently called a "new media empire." Lawrence Media Enterprises now owned twelve radio stations, three newspapers, a television station, seven magazines and eight Internet providers up and down the Atlantic coast.

Kit had wanted to share his success with his father. He'd even tried to interest Carl in serving on the board of directors, but Carl had brushed him off, choosing instead to go back to managing the very first radio station he'd purchased, WBAM.

He and Kit's mother had started there, Carl working as an on-air newscaster and Louise working as a secretary. When the failing station went up for sale, his parents had invested every penny they had to buy it. Now, Kit suspected that his father only worked there for sentimental reasons, hoping to recapture something he'd lost, searching for some memory of his dead wife.

Kit strode to the front door of Fred's House of Crabs, the restaurant located on the outskirts of the city, near the waterfront. The inside was dark and noisy, the kind of mom-and-pop place that Carl loved, a place where the bartenders were generous, the food was great and the check small. He approached the hostess stand.

"I'm here to meet Carl Lawrence," Kit said to the harried woman carrying the stack of menus.

She checked her book. "He's already inside," she said, cocking her head in the direction of the dining room. "He and the lady arrived about fifteen minutes ago."

"The lady?"

"Real pretty," the hostess said. "Is she your sister?"

Kit frowned and shook his head, then walked to the dining room entrance. He paused and scanned the crowd, searching for his father's distinctive gray hair. He caught sight of Carl Lawrence sitting at a small table in a dark corner. Seated across from him was a woman, maybe thirty-five or forty tops, with shoulder-length dark hair and attractive features. Kit knew everyone who worked at the station and he'd never seen this woman before.

The two of them were involved in an animated conversation, their heads bent close so they could hear each other over the din in the dining room. He said something to her and she laughed. And when she replied, he reached across the table and patted her hand.

Making his way through the dining room, Kit considered all the possibilities. She could be an acquaintance, or maybe a new employee. But another more disturbing possibility pushed its way into his thoughts. She could also be his father's date.

Since Kit's mother had died, Carl had stumbled through a few relationships, all with grasping divorcées who were interested in finding a man to provide. Kit had warned him that a multimillionaire of his age would be easy pickings for the wrong kind of woman. Luckily, Carl had broken off the relationships before he had become legally entangled. But this woman was something new— she was prettier and younger, an irresistible combination for a man approaching the age of sixty.

"Aw, hell," Kit muttered. "I should have stayed home." He wove through the tables and stopped next to his father's. "Hi, Dad."

They both looked up from their conversation and Carl immediately rose and clapped Kit on the shoulder. "Kit, my boy. I was wondering if you'd make it." Kit glanced over at the woman and his breath caught in his throat. She wasn't thirty-five at all, probably not even thirty.

Her skin was flawless, luminous in the low light of the candle that sat in the center of the table. Her hair brushed against her jawline and he fought the impulse to reach out and touch it, to see if it was as soft as it looked. She smiled at him hesitantly. He watched in fascination as her lips parted slightly and he found himself wondering what it would be like to kiss a mouth like that. Good Lord, she was pretty.

"Kit, this is Roxanne Perry. Roxanne, my son, Kit."

Startled out of his fantasy, he took the hand she offered, folding her delicate fingers inside his.

"Your father has told me so much about you," she said. "It's so nice to meet you, Kit."

"Sit," Carl said. "I've ordered another bottle of champagne. Would you like a glass or do you want your usual scotch?"

Kit glanced back and forth between his father and Roxanne Perry. By the flushed look on his father's face, the guy didn't need any more champagne. "No." Kit turned and flagged down a waitress. "Chivas on the rocks," he said. When his attention returned to his dinner companions, he couldn't contain his curiosity any longer. "So, how long have you two known each other."

"Oh, just a few days," Roxanne said. "We met Saturday morning."

"Roxanne is a finalist in a contest that WBAM is promoting. I was the one who gave her the good news."

"A contest?" Kit asked. "What kind of contest?"

"I've been nominated by *Family Voyager* magazine for their 'Mother of the Year' contest," Roxanne said.

"And the prize includes dinner at Fred's House of Crabs?" Kit asked, trying to cover his embarrassment. She was married and a mother and this was nothing more than a simple business meeting.

"No. A trip to Paris. Your father invited me to dinner and I accepted."

A long silence fell over the table. "So, are you involved in radio?" Roxanne asked, glancing at Kit from over the rim of her champagne flute.

Kit chuckled softly. "Yeah, I guess you could say that." He dragged his gaze from her face, reminding himself that Roxanne, though attractive, wasn't available. "Why don't you tell me something about yourself?"

She gave him a shy smile. "Well, I'm divorced and I have four children."

Kit cursed silently. This did not bode well. His

father was already gazing at Roxanne as if she'd hung the moon and the stars. "And what do you do for a living?"

"Actually, I don't work. I have a little money from my father's family. It's hard to work with young children. But I hope to go back to work soon."

"I was just trying to convince Roxanne to take a job at the station," Carl said. "We need to increase our demographic with young mothers and I think she could help us. Every talk radio station in the world is chasing the conservative male demographic, but I'm thinking that we've found a niche with stay-at-home moms like Roxanne. That's what we were just talking about."

"I told Carl it makes sense," she said.

"I'm sure you did," Kit replied.

"When I'm taking care of the kids, it's impossible to watch television. But I would listen to the radio if the programming were interesting. And appropriate for little ears."

"You're already starting to think like a radio programmer," Carl teased.

A blush stained her cheeks. "I'm just telling you what I know about being a mother, that's all." She took another sip of her champagne, then smiled at Kit.

The conversation continued without Kit's participation. Though she tried to draw him in, he pre-

ferred to sit back and watch her in action, to eval-
uate her motives and to find the best way to
counteract her beauty. His father seemed completely captivated, hanging on every word she said,
lavishing her with compliments.

When she finished her champagne, she set her
napkin on the table and pushed back in her chair.
"If you'll excuse me. I need to call home and
check on the kids."

They both watched her walk out of the dining
room. "She's beautiful, isn't she?" Carl said.

"What the hell are you thinking? She's got to
be thirty years younger than you."

"At least," Carl said. "But what does that have
to do with anything?"

"Are you really that blinded by her beauty?
She's out to snare you, Dad. She knows you have
money and she's moving in for the kill."

"What?" Carl laughed, clearly taken aback by
Kit's comments.

"Come on, Dad. I see what's going on here,
even if you don't."

"You think you do," he said. "But you're
wrong."

"You can't date her."

He straightened as if suddenly insulted. "I suppose I could do whatever I want. I'm old enough
to make my own decisions."

Kit threw his napkin down on the table. "If you

expect me to approve, then you're crazy. I'm not going to condone a relationship with a woman who's young enough to be your daughter.''

"Are you leaving? We haven't even ordered yet," Carl said. "The crab here is fantastic. Sit down and stop acting like a spoiled child.''

"I have to go," Kit said. He strode out of the dining room and turned the corner to the front door. But he wasn't watching where he was going and ran, full tilt, into Roxanne Perry. She cried out in surprise and Kit grabbed her to keep her from falling backwards.

For a long moment, they stood in the foyer of the restaurant, his hands gripping her bare arms, their gazes locked. God, she was beautiful...and soft. And she smelled really good. No wonder his father found her irresistible.

"Did you need to make a phone call?" she asked. "The pay phones are just out there.''

"I know what you're up to," he said, his eyes fixing on her lush mouth.

"Up to? I just needed to check on my kids.''

"Don't think you're fooling me. Both you and I know what's going on here and if you hurt my father, you'll have me to deal with.''

"Hurt your father? Why would I hurt him?''

Hell, she was good. He actually found himself fooled by that wide-eyed innocent look. So why did he want to yank her into his arms and find out exactly how that pretty mouth tasted. With a soft curse, Kit released her, then stalked toward the door. But an image of her stayed with him, swirling in his head, imprinting on his brain. When he reached his car, he sat down inside, gripping the steering wheel.

This was a great move. A lot of good he could do out here in the parking lot. Kit cursed again. There'd be plenty of time to convince his father against a relationship with Roxanne Perry. And while he was at it, he might take the time to convince himself that Roxanne Perry wasn't the most beautiful and intriguing woman he'd ever met.

But until then, Kit was going to keep a close eye on her. Sooner or later, she'd show her true colors. And then he'd find a way to get her out of his father's life for good.

CHAPTER TWO

"COMING UP NEXT, we have Roxanne Perry. Roxanne was recently chosen as a finalist for the 'Mother of the Year' contest, sponsored by *Family Voyager* magazine. We'll be talking about the struggles of raising children alone and we'll be giving away free subscriptions to *Family Voyager*. So join us after these messages."

Roxanne wriggled nervously in her seat, the blinking lights and endless dials of the radio studio adding to her apprehension. She plucked the headphones off her head, ignoring the commercial for Big Bob Martin's Used Cars. "I don't know if I can do this," she whispered. "Just because I was nominated, doesn't mean I'm some shining example."

Carl sent her a reassuring smile. "You'll be fine. Just be yourself."

"I *was* myself last night and your son wasn't too thrilled that I'd be on the radio."

"That was all just a misunderstanding." Carl glanced up from his notes, a slow and satisfied grin sending a twinkle to his eyes. He leaned over and pressed a button on the board. "See? He's come here just to listen."

Roxanne spun around in her chair to find Kit Lawrence standing in the next room, staring at her through a plate glass window, his arms crossed over his chest, his expression unreadable. Her breath froze and, for a moment, she felt like slipping beneath the console and crawling out of the room. After her dinner with Carl, she'd gone home to a sleepless night, filled with images of a handsome, dark-haired man in a tailored business suit and silk tie—a man who looked a lot like Kit Lawrence.

She wilted under his stare, feeling as if he could read her thoughts. From the moment he'd walked up to their table last night, she'd had trouble keeping her eyes off of him. He had a dangerous air so magnetic and compelling that he made her heart flutter. He'd been the first man since her husband that she'd really looked at. And then, when she had, her pulse began to race and her mind spun.

Her cheeks warmed as she recalled the vivid dream she'd had last night. All morning, she'd tried to convince herself that it was only normal to have sexual fantasies about a man as attractive as Kit. After all, she hadn't had sex in over two years, and then, it hadn't been that great in the end anyway. The kids had pretty much exhausted her, so passion usually took a back seat to sleep.

But here was Kit Lawrence, gorgeous, successful and unmarried, the kind of man every woman
found attractive. Was it any wonder he'd invaded
her fantasies? Yes, he was rude and arrogant and
he obviously didn't think much of her, but in her
dreams, he didn't do a whole lot of talking. Just
whispering…and moaning…and— She swallowed
hard. "He looks angry. Maybe this isn't a good
idea."

"This is *my* radio station," Carl said, "and *my*
radio show. I can do what I want."

"But who would want to listen to me?"

"I would. I think your story will resonate with
lots of single mothers out there."

"What story? That I ran over my husband's designer suits with the lawn mower? Or that I
blacked out his face on every wedding photo I had?
One night, I even sewed a little voodoo doll and
stuck pins in the…well, in the groin area. Those
really aren't very positive messages to send out to
the public. And I don't think that's going to win
me any points in this contest." She looked over at
Kit Lawrence and saw a flicker of amusement cross
his face. "Could you ask him to leave? Why is he
staring at me like that?"

"He can hear you," Carl said. "The intercom
is picking up our conversation."

"He can—"

"And he thinks you're a gold digger," Carl added, before pushing another button.

Roxanne gasped. "What?" She looked over at Kit and noticed that the smile had faded from his face.

"And we're back," Carl said smoothly.

"He thinks I'm a—"

"And on the air," Carl interrupted. "Joining me in the studio is single mom Roxanne Perry, and today we're going to discuss the challenges that face single mothers. The phone lines are open. Give us a call."

The next eight minutes passed in a blur. Roxanne listened to the callers and bumbled through her responses, trying to keep the mood light and positive. To her surprise, she shared many of the same experiences and emotions as the listeners. She'd always felt so alone, but now it was clear that there were a lot of women, young and old, who were dealing with the same problems.

When Carl finally announced a commercial break, she sat back in her chair and drew her first decent breath since the On Air light blinked on. To her relief, Kit no longer stood in the control room. She covered the mike with her hand. "What did you mean, gold digger?"

Carl chuckled. "He's got some crazy idea that you and I are dating and that I'm about to drag you off to Vegas for a quickie wedding."

Roxanne blinked. "Dating? A wedding?"

"I guess it's not that far beyond possibility. A lot of guys my age find younger women attractive. I could never understand it, but now I do. I saw the way the men were looking at me in the restaurant last night. They were thinking what a lucky guy I was to be with someone as pretty as you."

"But—but it wasn't a date," Roxanne said.

"I know that. But my son doesn't. It's a nice little ego boost that he thinks I could get a lady like you to go out with an old guy like me. So I let him believe what he wanted."

"You're not old," Roxanne said.

"I'm old enough to know when you're humoring me. And though you're a very intelligent and captivating young lady, I'm not sure I could date anyone who doesn't remember when there was no television, only radio."

"All right, you're not *that* old," Roxanne said. "But you're not really interested in dating me, are—"

Carl held up his finger. "We're back with Roxanne Perry. Let's take another call."

The rest of the hour flew by. Roxanne wasn't sure when it happened, but sometime during the show she found herself having fun. She relaxed and began to play off the comments Carl was interjecting into the conversations. He tried to defend the male point of view, and Roxanne and the callers neatly countered his defense. When Carl finally signed off, she wasn't tired or stressed, she was giddy with exhilaration.

"Congratulations," Carl said. He reached out and took her hand and gave it a gallant kiss. "You did very well."

"It felt good," Roxanne said. "At first, I was so nervous and then I forgot what I was doing and just started talking. It was like talking to my sister on the phone."

"You're a natural." He picked up his papers and straightened them. "I'd like you to do another show. How about next week?"

"Oh, I don't know," Roxanne said. "I'd have to get a sitter again and I'm not sure—"

"I'll pay you," Carl said. "The money won't be great, but it's more than enough to pay for a sitter. And who knows where this might lead?" He scribbled an address on a scrap of paper. "Why don't we get together tomorrow night and toss around some ideas. Bring the kids along. I've got an indoor pool and I'm sure they'd enjoy swimming. We'll send out for pizza."

"Oh, they would enjoy swimming. We don't get out much."

"Around five?" he asked. "That will give the kids time to swim before dinner."

Roxanne nodded. "All right. Five tomorrow afternoon. We'll be there." She stood up and grabbed her jacket from the back of the chair. "I'll see you then."

She quietly slipped out of the studio and started down the hall. When she reached the end, she turned to the right, then found herself in unfamiliar territory. The station's programming played softly over the office P.A. system, and she listened distractedly to a cooking show, thinking how odd it was to have a cooking show on the radio.

When she reached another dead end, Roxanne realized she was lost. She glanced inside a well-appointed office and cleared her throat. "Excuse me. Could you tell me how to get out of here?"

The occupant in the high-backed leather chair slowly turned to face her and her stomach dropped.

"Hello, Mrs. Perry."

"Mr. Lawrence."

"Come in. Sit down. I was hoping we'd get a chance to talk."

"I really have to be going," she said, uneasy with the predatory look in his eyes.

"I heard the show. Not bad."

"Thank you," Roxanne said, twisting her hands in front of her. "I was a little nervous. I've never done anything like this before."

He leaned back in his chair and steepled his fingers in front of him, fixing his gaze on her. "I'd expect not. It's not often you run across a man who owns his own radio station."

His words were said so coldly it sent a shiver down her spine. "What is that supposed to mean?"

"I think we both know. My father is a wealthy man and you're a woman looking for someone to provide. It doesn't take a rocket scientist to put two and two together."

"How dare you!" Roxanne said, taking a few steps toward him. "You don't know anything—"

"I do dare. Carl Lawrence is my father and I won't see him hurt by a woman like you."

"A woman like me? You mean a gold digger? That's what you think, isn't it? Well, you're wrong. We're not romantically involved and don't intend to be. Your father has been very kind and encouraging to me."

"I'm sure he has," Kit said. "And if you stick around long enough, he may start giving you expensive gifts or taking you on luxury vacations. He's done that before. But sooner or later, he'll realize what you're after. He always does." He slowly stood, pressing his palms flat on his desk. "Don't waste your time with Carl Lawrence. Stay away from my father, Mrs. Perry."

Her temper flared. "Go to hell, Mr. Lawrence." With that, she turned on her heel and stalked out of his office. Let him think what he wanted. Let him believe that she and Carl were having a torrid affair. He obviously didn't want to listen to her. It served him right for acting so arrogant.

When she reached the lobby she stopped and pressed her hand to her chest. Her heart hammered inside. She tried to rationalize the anger she felt at his outrageous assumptions, but then realized that it wasn't anger making her heart beat faster. It was excitement and exhilaration. She moaned softly. And, if she were totally honest with herself, it was desire.

"Don't be an idiot," she muttered to herself as she walked outside into the cold. "How can you possibly want a man who thinks you're nothing more than a greedy little hussy?"

As she strode to her car, she considered calling Carl and telling him that she wasn't interested in a job at the station. The prospect of another encounter with Kit Lawrence was enough to smother any interest in a radio career. But she wasn't about to go back to crying in the closet. This was her life and she was going to start living it. And if that meant shoving Kit Lawrence aside to do something she enjoyed, then that's what she'd have to do.

KIT BRACED HIS PALMS on the edge of the pool and pulled himself up out of the water. His hair dripped as he grabbed a towel from a nearby lounge chair and toweled his chest dry. An hour-long swim, some Chinese food delivered and a hockey game on ESPN were exactly what the doctor ordered after a stress-filled day.

It wasn't that work had been so bad. He wasn't even bothered that a deal to buy a station in Newark, New Jersey, was about to go south for no good reason. He'd occupied most of his day trying to figure out what to do about his father and Roxanne Perry. What was it that he really objected to? That she was so young? That she was incredibly beautiful? That if his father married her he'd have stepsiblings young enough to be his own children?

Or was it that he was incredibly attracted to Roxanne himself? There was no use denying it. Every time he thought about her, he didn't think "stepmommy." He thought about yanking her into his arms and kissing her. Or pulling her down onto his bed to explore her perfect body. Hadn't Shakespeare written a play about this very problem? His thoughts were turning a bit too Oedipal for his liking.

The doorbell rang and Kit looked up at the clock. The housekeeper had left at four and he wasn't expecting visitors. The only person who came over to the house on a regular basis was his father and he had a key. But considering what was going on in Carl Lawrence's life lately, Kit wouldn't be surprised if he'd forgotten it—or lost it.

He cursed softly and wrapped a towel around his waist. It was obvious, even to himself, that he was making a mess of this whole affair. Maybe he just ought to let it run its natural course and stay out of the way. Though his father seemed fond of Roxanne Perry, he didn't seem so besotted that he'd become completely irrational. But it wasn't his father he was worried about. Women like Roxanne Perry were always hovering around men like Carl. Young, pretty, avaricious women who saw the bank account behind the man.

He shook his head. Surely his father would have to see Roxanne Perry for who she really was. Women her age didn't date men nearing sixty. Hell, she had four young kids. If he took her on, the kids would be part of the package and he'd be coaching soccer when he was seventy. At least Kit would have the whole evening to try to convince him to cut her loose.

The bell rang again and Kit jogged through the spacious foyer, his bare feet silent against the marble floor. He grabbed the door and yanked it open, ready to chide his father for his forgetfulness. But it wasn't Carl Lawrence who greeted him on the other side. Instead, he came face-to-face with Roxanne Perry. To make matters worse, her four children were with her.

"Hello," she murmured, her gaze dropping to his naked chest and back again.

"What are you doing here?" Kit asked.

"I—I was invited." She drew her children

nearer, as if he were about to snatch them up and eat them.

"Invited by whom?"

She tilted her chin stubbornly and his attention was once again drawn to her lush mouth. "Your father. He invited us all for dinner and a swim."

"That's funny," Kit said with a laugh that sounded a little too forced.

"And why is that?"

"Because this is my house."

She blinked in surprise, a blush staining her cheeks. "Why would your father invite me to dinner at *your* house?"

"I don't know. He does have a perverse sense of humor at times. And this house did belong to him. Technically, it still does, except that now I live here and he lives in a condo closer to the station." Kit opened the door wide and motioned her inside. "Come in. I'm sure he'll be along any second."

She shook her head, her mahogany hair tumbling around her face. "I'm going to go. There must have been some misunderstanding. Or maybe he got caught at work."

"No," Kit insisted. "I'm sure my father is on his way. Follow me. The pool house is through the kitchen."

He grabbed the bag she'd brought along, then turned and started through the foyer, trying to ignore the reaction he felt when he first looked into her pretty hazel eyes. The sound of little footsteps followed him and he smiled to himself, glad that she hadn't left. The opportunity to spend a little time with her was an unexpected treat.

A tiny sliver of guilt shot through him and he made a silent vow to be civil. There was something about her that seemed to bring out the worst in him. All his charm virtually disappeared when he got within five feet of Roxanne.

Usually, he was a pretty smooth guy around the ladies. Though work didn't allow for much time to date, he'd had his share of relationships over the years. But he'd always limited his scope of interest to single, unencumbered women, women who could meet him for dinner at a moment's notice, women who didn't have children sleeping in the next room.

He wanted to believe he was protecting his father. But now that she was here and he could smell her perfume and look into her eyes, Kit was forced to admit that maybe he was the one who was at risk. He ignored the tiny sliver of guilt he felt. After all, she'd insisted she wasn't interested in a romantic relationship with Carl. Who was he to argue?

"Four kids," he muttered as the little monsters ran ahead of him toward the pool.

"Wait!" Roxanne shouted. "Don't you go near that water without me."

In a few short steps, Kit caught up with the smallest child and scooped her up into his arms. She screamed in delight, giggling with glee. "Listen to your mother," he whispered.

"Hi," she cooed, sending him the sweetest smile.

Kit couldn't help but chuckle. The little girl would be a heartbreaker when she grew up. "Taking after your mother, I see." He held her out to Roxanne, who took her with a grateful smile. "What's her name?"

"Jenna," she said. "She's two. Danny is six, Rachel is four and a half, and Michael is three."

"Four children," he said. "Under the age of six. That's…brave?"

She shrugged. "We wanted four and they just came along one after the other. It didn't seem like such a large family at the time. But then I always thought I'd be raising them with a partner." Her expression shifted and for a moment, Kit could see the vulnerability in her eyes.

He opened the French doors into the pool room. The warm, damp air smelled of chlorine, and he was tempted to walk inside with her and the children. "Go ahead," he said. "Enjoy yourself. I'll give my father a call and find out when he plans to arrive."

"Wait, I can't do this myself," Roxanne said. "Four children around a swimming pool wouldn't be a problem if I were an octopus. I really could use your help. Danny is a good swimmer and Rachel will be fine if she stays in the shallow end." She hesitated. "Would you mind?"

He was about to blurt out a sarcastic answer, but to his surprise he found himself smiling. "No. I just got out of the pool. I wouldn't mind going back in."

"This is incredible," Roxanne said, glancing around the spacious glass house. "So nice on a cold night."

"My parents bought the house when I was a kid. The pool house was all old and moldy, but I was a competitive swimmer. So this seemed like the perfect place."

"Your father told me about your swimming. He said you have a room full of trophies."

"What else did he tell you?"

"He doesn't talk much about his personal life to me. He talks about you, though. He's very proud of you." She paused and drew a deep breath. "You have the wrong idea about me—about us. Your father has been very kind, but there's nothing going on."

"Are you sure?"

She frowned. "I don't understand."

"You know how you feel. Do you know how he feels?"

She opened her mouth as if to reply, then snapped it shut. Then she glanced over at the kids who were standing near the edge of the pool. "Come on, kids. Let's get your jackets and clothes off before you fall in."

He watched as her children gathered around her. Moments later, jackets were flying everywhere, shoes tumbled off and clothes fell in heaps on the tile floor. The children already wore their suits, so as soon as they shed their clothes, they were ready to go. But Roxanne spoke to them softly about their behavior and warned them that they were not to go into the water until she was there with them. She grabbed two tiny life vests from the bag she'd brought and put them on Michael and Jenna.

Then she slowly began to remove her own clothes. Kit tried not to stare, but she was completely oblivious to the effect that her little striptease was having on him. With each item she shed, Kit felt the anticipation growing. And when she was finished and stood in a sleek, black tank suit, he realized that he hadn't drawn a breath since she started.

"This is going to be so fun," Danny said, bouncing up and down with excitement.

Kit forced a smile as his gaze drifted over her slender body. "Yeah," he murmured. "This is going to be so fun."

ROXANNE SNUGGLED beneath a thick terry cloth towel, Jenna curled up in her lap, sound asleep. Michael sat beside her on the tile floor, playing with a toy boat she'd brought along in her bag. Her gaze drifted over to the pool, to Danny and Rachel, who were tossing a ball around in the shallow end with Kit.

Her gaze fixed on his naked back, on the play of muscle as he held the ball over his head. When he'd first opened the door earlier that evening, she'd had to keep herself from staring at his body, at the smooth chest and wide shoulders, at the flat belly and narrow hips. Though her ex-husband had been in shape, he hadn't had the raw material to work with that Kit did. The tall, slender body, the long limbs and the athletic grace that made him impossible to ignore.

When she realized it was his house, she'd nearly turned around and gotten back in the car. Kit Lawrence had made his feelings for her quite clear. He didn't approve of his father's job offer or her presence at the station. But for some strange reason, he'd invited her inside. Then he'd tried to make the evening as comfortable as possible, ordering pizza for the kids and playing with them in the pool.

Carl had phoned just before the pizza arrived to apologize. He'd been detained at the station with some technical problem. She'd almost been happy to hear that he wouldn't be joining them.

She glanced at the clock on the wall and noticed the late hour. "Come on, you little waterbugs," Roxanne called. "Time to get out of the pool or you'll start to look like prunes."

Kit grabbed Rachel by the waist and swung her up on the edge of the pool, then did the same with Danny. They both ran over to the table and grabbed a piece of cold pizza, then sat down to munch on the leftovers. Kit strolled over to Roxanne and flopped down onto the chair next to her.

He snatched up a towel and dried his face, then glanced over at her. "I'm exhausted."

"They take a lot of energy, don't they?"

"I don't know a lot about kids," Kit admitted as he pulled a T-shirt over his head. "But they're not so bad. In fact, they're pretty much fun."

"Right. Until they all have the flu at one time. Or until you're stuck in the middle of traffic without a snack. Or until they all decide to flush their shoes down the toilet. Then call me and tell me how much fun they are," Roxanne teased.

"You're a good mother," Kit said. "I can see that."

"It feels a little strange to be competing in a contest against other mothers." She grabbed a towel and began to dry Michael's hair. "But the trip to Paris would be nice. And I could use the shopping spree to buy clothes for the kids."

"I'd vote for you," Kit murmured, his gaze locking with hers.

A tiny shiver skittered down her spine. "Well, this mother better get her kids home. Danny has school tomorrow morning and Rachel has a dentist appointment. And I've got to take the van in and get the muffler fixed. It's dragging." Roxanne tried to struggle to her feet with Jenna in her arms, but Kit reached out and gently took the little girl. "Thanks," she said.

Roxanne quickly grabbed her jeans and tugged them over her wet suit. Then she pulled her sweater over her head and slipped her bare feet into her boots.

"There's a changing room over there," Kit said. "You don't have to go away wet."

"No, this is better. The quicker the better," Roxanne said. "I have precisely two minutes to get my children into their clothes and shoes and jackets before they start to complain about leaving. After four minutes, the whining starts and after five there are going to be temper tantrums. So unless you want a major meltdown on your hands, I'd help me get them ready to go."

"Tell me what to do."

She handed him a tiny pair of blue jeans and

pointed at Jenna. "I'm glad we can be friends," she said softly.

"Is that what we are?" Kit asked.

"Well, maybe not. But at least we're not enemies."

"No, we aren't," he agreed. "And to that end, I suppose I'd better apologize for being such a jerk when we met. I'm a little overprotective when it comes to my father."

She smiled. "Apology accepted."

Between the two of them, they got the children dressed and packed up in about three minutes, Kit keeping them distracted with entertaining riddles so that they didn't even realize that they were leaving. When the last boot was on and the last jacket zipped, he picked up Jenna and led them all back through the house to the front door.

They were almost out the door when Danny realized what was happening. "Why do we have to leave?" he asked. "I want to swim some more."

"Honey, we have to get home. It's almost bedtime."

"It's not my bedtime," he said. "Why do I have to leave?"

"Because I said so," Roxanne replied.

"Good answer," Kit murmured. "I always liked that one."

"But why?" Danny whined.

Roxanne grabbed her son's hand and pulled him

out to the van parked in the drive. Rachel skipped along behind her and Michael raced around to the other side, waiting for Roxanne to open the door. She got them all inside and strapped in, then took Jenna from Kit and put her in her car seat.

When she'd pulled the sliding door shut, Kit followed her around to the driver's side. She reached for the door, but he covered her hand with his. The contact sent a flood of warmth through her body. He slowly turned her around until their eyes met. She could barely read the expression on his face beneath the feeble light from above the front door. "You—you don't have any shoes on," she murmured. "Aren't your feet cold?"

He shook his head, his gaze drifting down to her mouth. When he leaned forward, she knew what was about to happen, but she couldn't do anything to stop it. His lips met hers in a gentle kiss. At first, her impulse was to pull away, but the warmth of his mouth was so tantalizing, so surprisingly wonderful, that she stood perfectly still and allowed him to kiss her. When he drew back, she sighed softly, then opened her eyes.

A gentle snow had begun to fall and she felt the flakes melt on her cheeks. He stared down into her gaze, then reached up and smoothed his finger along her jawline. Then he touched her damp hair. "You better go," he murmured. "You'll catch your death out here."

She rubbed her arms. "You're the one without a jacket."

"I'm not the one shivering," he said.

A blush warmed her cheeks. "Thanks again. For dinner and for helping with the kids. You didn't have to—"

He placed his finger on her lips and smiled. "I had fun." He pulled the door open and helped her inside, then closed it softly behind her. As he stepped away, Roxanne turned the key in the ignition, praying that the van would start and she could drive off with him staring after her. The engine rumbled to life and she threw it into gear and steered the minivan around the circular drive.

When she reached the street, she glanced in her rearview mirror and watched him walk inside the house. Then she released a tightly held breath. A tiny smile curved her lips, still warm from his kiss.

"Mommy?"

She shifted in her seat until she could see Danny's reflection. "Yeah, honey."

"You kissed that man," he said.

"Yes, I did," she said.

"Why?"

Roxanne wasn't sure of the answer herself. "I was just thanking him for letting us swim in his pool."

"Why?"

"Because it was the polite thing to do."

"Do you think if you kiss him again, he'll invite us over again? 'Cause I really had a fun time and the pizza was good. And Mr. Lawrence is nice."

"He is a nice man," Roxanne said. "Mommy didn't think so at first, but now I kind of like him."

"Me, too."

CHAPTER THREE

"YOU COULD HAVE at least told me you'd invited her. After all, I do live there." Kit leaned back in his leather chair, kicked his feet up on the desk, and clasped his hands behind his head.

His father looked unapologetic. "I knew you'd be home. And she'd already told her kids they were going swimming. I didn't want to disappoint them. Hey, I remember when you were a kid and I broke a promise. I'd hear about it for days."

"You could have told me," Kit repeated. "And what was so important that you had to stay at the station?"

"We had problems with the transmitter. We had dead air for seventeen seconds. It was an emergency. By the time everything got fixed, it was ten. I figured she'd be home by then anyway. I sent her a dozen roses this morning."

Kit slid his feet off the desk and leaned forward. "Roses?"

"Yeah." Carl grinned, as if he'd suddenly discovered the secret path to a woman's heart. "She forgave me."

"How do you know?"

"I spoke to her on the phone a few minutes ago. She called to thank me for the roses. And she said she'd be in this afternoon to talk about next week's show."

Kit ground his teeth. Hell, he should have sent her roses! He had every reason—they'd had a wonderful time last night. Then maybe she would have called him. He couldn't think of anything he wanted more than to hear her voice. Well, maybe he wanted to see her a little more than hear her. Touching her might be nice. Hell, kissing her again would be the best.

Though he ought to feel guilty about kissing Roxanne, he couldn't. At first, he'd rationalized it as part of a plan to protect his father, to keep Roxanne away from the family fortune. But in truth, he'd kissed her because he couldn't go another minute without tasting her mouth. "Only a dozen?" Kit asked. "Don't you think that's a little...cheap?"

"Cheap? Roses are three dollars apiece," Carl said.

"But these days, a guy usually sends two dozen. Or even three dozen. It's more impressive," Kit said, hoping to test the depth of his father's feelings for Roxanne.

"I figured you'd have something to say about the roses, but it wasn't that."

"Roxanne insists that there's nothing going on between you two." Kit watched his father's reaction, but to his surprise, Carl seemed unfazed by the comment. "I figure it's none of my business," he added, trying to draw a comment. "The more I protest, the more determined you seem to be. But how do you feel about her?"

"A dozen roses was always good for my generation," Carl said. He pointed to a chair and Kit nodded, a silent invitation to sit down. "You know, I can't figure why someone hasn't married her," Carl continued. "She's a beautiful woman. Don't you think she's beautiful?"

"Yeah, sure. She's great."

"She's smart and funny and she needs someone to take care of her. I can't understand why her husband would have walked out on her."

Kit fiddled with some papers on his desk, trying to appear only mildly interested. "What do you know about that? Her divorce, I mean."

"He ran off with some…" His father searched for the word.

"Bimbo?"

"No, professional wrestler. Female professional wrestler. She calls herself the Velvet Hammer. He cleaned out their savings and stock accounts and headed for Bermuda or Barbados. From what I understand, she and the family had a pretty cushy life before he left. Now she's struggling to keep a roof over her kids' heads.''

"So, is that why you want her to work at the station?''

Carl ignored Kit's question. "I'd imagine she's going to make someone a great wife.'' He sighed wistfully and reached for a framed photo on Kit's desk. "She reminds me a lot of your mom,'' he said, pointing to the picture. "When we met, she was working three jobs and going to college at night. She was determined to have a career. That was when women's lib was in full gear and your mom was right in the middle of it. Roxy has that same kind of tenacity.''

"You call her Roxy? So you two must be getting close.''

"It's a nickname for Roxanne. It fits her, don't you think?''

"She comes with four kids, Dad.''

"What difference does that make?''

"I'm just saying that if you take her on, you're taking on her kids, too.''

"You don't think I'd be a good father? Wasn't I a good father to you?''

"You were thirty years younger at the time.''

"I suppose it would be like riding a bike. You never really forget how.'' With that, Carl stood and set the photo back on Kit's desk. "That's a nice one of your mom. I remember when I took that.''

He slowly walked out of the office, his mood suddenly pensive.

Kit groaned softly, then rubbed his temples with his fingers. "This is just great." It was clear how his father felt about Roxanne Perry. He'd gone from interested to besotted in a matter of a few days. Though Kit could relate. Hell, he'd changed his own tune pretty drastically.

But Carl Lawrence had been out of the dating pool for nearly forty years. The pretty little goldfish Carl was used to had been replaced by sharks. Kit knew what it was like. He'd been out there and it was brutal, not exactly the kind of world his father was prepared to handle.

Back when his parents were courting, women were willing to wait for a relationship to develop slowly. Marriage was serious business. But these days, if a man wasn't sure after a few months of dating, the relationship would end and the woman would move on, not willing to waste another day in the quest for the perfect husband.

If his father was in love with Roxanne Perry and she wasn't in love with him, then Kit would be the one to pick up the pieces. He pressed his intercom button, buzzing the secretary that he and his father shared. "Linda, will you call the receptionist and ask her to send Roxanne Perry up to my office as soon as she arrives? And then I'd like to send her some flowers. A big bouquet. Really big."

"Roses?" Linda asked.

"No. Spring flowers. Tulips, daffodils, those really nice-smelling ones."

"Hyacinths?"

"Yeah. Real colorful. Cheerful flowers. Not... serious flowers." He could imagine the smile on his secretary's face. "You know what I mean."

"No frowning or depressive flowers. Got it," she said.

Kit stood up and paced the width of his office, trying to decide how to approach Roxanne. After last night, he had a serious conflict of interest. He'd kissed his father's girlfriend. Now was the time to remain objective, to separate his feelings from his father's feelings. Sure, he liked Roxanne, but he wasn't in love with her. If he had to give her up to protect his father, then that was a sacrifice he was prepared to make.

The phone rang and Kit leaned over the desk to snatch it up. "Kit Lawrence."

"Mr. Lawrence, Mrs. Perry arrived a few moments ago. I've sent her to your office."

"Thanks, Melanie."

Kit stood, nervously fiddling with his tie. A minute later, Roxanne appeared at his door, her coat thrown over her arm.

"Hi," she murmured.

Kit's breath caught and he wondered why she

looked more beautiful every time he saw her. Was she doing something different with her hair or her makeup? Or was the anticipation of seeing her again simply causing him to imagine it? "Come in," he said.

She glanced around, as if stepping into his office was dangerous. She was right. If he closed the door behind her, there wouldn't be much to keep him from sweeping her into his arms and kissing her again. But before he did that, he had to get a few things clear between them. "I wanted to talk to you about my father."

Roxanne smiled. "Oh, don't worry. He apologized for last night. He also sent roses." She sent him a shy smile. "And I wanted to thank you for the swimming and the pizza. We had a lot of fun."

Her gaze met his and Kit knew she was thinking about the kiss they'd shared. He wondered how she'd react if he stepped out from behind his desk and repeated the experience. Would she melt into his arms or would she push him away? But kissing Roxanne would not solve the problems standing between them. "Please, sit down."

She did as she was told, folding her hands on her lap and watching him expectantly.

"What are your intentions regarding my father?" he blurted out.

"My intentions?"

Kit paused, trying to frame his words as delicately as he could. "Though he won't admit his feelings to me, I think it's time you made your feelings clear to him. I don't want to see him hurt. I want to know what it would take for you to walk away."

She frowned. "I don't understand. Walk away from what? I'm not in love with your father! He's a nice man and he's been very kind to me. How many times do I have to say that?"

"Don't say it to me. Say it to my father."

"He's never given any indication that he has serious feelings for me. As far as I can tell, he's still in love with your mother."

Kit drew a deep breath, knowing that he should end the conversation. But he couldn't help but push it. He needed to know how she really felt, and not just for his father's sake but for his own. "I know how difficult things are for you now, financially. And this job that he's offered you does have a small salary. I'd like to help you out if you'd agree to walk away before you hurt him."

"Wait." Roxanne stood up. "I don't need to listen to any more of this. Your father offered me a chance. And I'm going to take it."

"My father owns thirty-three percent of my company. If you think I'm going to let you—"

"Don't even say it," she warned, holding out her finger to silence him. "If you really cared about your father, then you'd want him to be happy. And if he had the good fortune to find happiness with me or any other woman, then you should be jumping for joy. Because real happiness...real love...is very hard to find.''

She turned on her heel and strode out of his office, slamming the door behind her. He stared after her, suddenly wondering what had possessed him to take such a tack with her. Maybe his first instinct had been right—to let his father's infatuation run its course. But he didn't want to watch his father fall more deeply under her spell. And he didn't want to learn that Roxanne Perry was the kind of woman to take advantage of a vulnerable man. But even worse, he didn't want to believe that she'd choose his father over him.

He punched at his intercom button and when Linda answered, he schooled his voice into relative calm. "Cancel those flowers," he said. Hell, he didn't care whether Roxanne Perry kidnapped his father and turned him into a sixty-year-old sex slave. From now on, he was staying out of it!

"AND THAT'S OUR SHOW FOR TODAY. Join us next Tuesday when we'll be talking about the perils of dating for a single mom. This is Carl Lawrence, for Roxanne Perry. Thanks for listening to *Baltimore At Home.*"

Carl flipped a switch and turned to face Roxanne. "Great show. I enjoyed our conversation about discipline. I didn't realize how different things were in a single parent household. No good cop, bad cop."

"Carl, I need to talk to you about something," Roxanne murmured.

"And I need to talk to you. Let's go to my office."

Roxanne followed him out of the studio and when they reached his office right next door to Kit's, he closed the door behind her. She nervously took a seat across the desk from him and tried to put order to her thoughts. She needed to tell him how she felt. Though she respected him and cared about him, there was no romantic spark. He was old enough to be her father.

"Carl, before we talk about next week's show, I need to clear the air."

"You can clear the air after you look at this," Carl said. He slid a sheaf of papers across the desk and she picked them up.

"What is this?"

"It's a contract. I'm offering you a permanent job here at the station. Twenty-five thousand a year with benefits. I know it's not a lot, but there's a clause in there that allows you to renegotiate after six months if the ratings increase the way I think they will."

She stared at the paper, the words a blur. "A job? You're offering me a real job?"

"Radio is a strange gig," he said. "Either you're good at it or you're not. You're a natural, Roxy. People listen to you. You're compassionate and outspoken and funny and that's a rare combination."

"But I don't have any professional training."

"I didn't either. Before I got into radio, I was selling used cars. I came into the studio to do some commercial work for my boss and they liked my voice. I did more voice-overs and they offered me a job reading the news. That's how I got my start."

"I don't know what to say," she murmured, clutching the contract in her hands as if it might suddenly disappear. She thought finding a job would be difficult, that she'd have to suffer months of rejection before someone would hire her. And now, he was handing her a career on a silver platter.

"Say yes," Carl urged. "It would be a great job for you. You'd need to be here from about nine until three on Tuesdays and Thursdays and that's it. You can do research for the show from home. We'll get you a computer with Internet access. You know how to use a computer, don't you?"

"Sure. I used to help my ex-husband with his research when he was just starting up his law practice."

"We'll go over the show in the morning before we go on the air. And then we'll spend an hour afterwards brainstorming for the next week. We should—''

"Why are you doing this?" Roxanne interrupted.

"I told you," Carl said. "Because you're good."

"There isn't another reason?"

He shrugged. "Well, maybe I'd like to help you out."

She drew a slow, even breath. "Your son says that you're falling in love with me. Is that true?"

Carl chuckled. "That's what he thinks?"

"He offered me money to stay out of your life."

He didn't seem to be surprised. "How much?" Carl asked.

Roxanne gasped. "He didn't offer me a specific amount." She paused. "You don't seem surprised."

"I'd hold out for a hundred thousand," Carl advised in a serious voice.

"Dollars?"

"Ever since I turned the business over to Kit, we've switched roles. He's been treating me like the kid and I'm supposed to treat him like the parent. He's the one who suggested I move into the condo so I wouldn't have to make the drive home when I worked late at the station. He's the one who insisted on the car service after I had a few little accidents on the freeway. And now he's trying to control who I spend my time with. Yes, Kit has this notion that I'm in love with you. And maybe I haven't disabused him of it quite yet. I'm trying to teach him a lesson.''

''And what's that?'' Roxanne asked.

''That it's time for him to stop running my life and start living his.'' He paused. ''Now do you want the job?''

''Can I have a few days to think about it?'' Roxanne asked.

''Sure,'' he replied. ''As long as you promise to say yes, you can take as long as you want.''

Roxanne stood, pressing the contract to her chest, then started toward the door. When she got into the hallway, she searched for a quiet spot, a place to absorb everything that had happened. She opened the door to the janitor's closet and stepped into the dark interior, needing just a moment to reflect.

She had a job, a way to provide at least some measure of security for her family. Though it wasn't much, if she worked hard, she could make the show a success. After all, she'd wanted to go into television work after she'd gotten her degree. But then she'd married John and they'd started their family and she'd put all thoughts of a career behind her.

Now she had a second chance and a job offer that would leave her plenty of time to be a mother.

It was like a dream come true. And on top of it, she'd get to see Kit Lawrence every now and then. Though until Carl set things straight with Kit, Roxanne wasn't sure she wanted to come within a hundred feet of him. If Carl was determined to prove some point, why did he have to use Roxanne to do it? And why did Kit find it so easy to believe that she had ulterior motives?

In reality, there were probably a lot of divorced mothers who might jump at the chance to find a man like Carl. He was emotionally stable and financially secure. And he wasn't exactly the type to go running off with a woman wrestler. The prospect of weeding through a world full of frogs in order to find a prince was daunting for any single mom.

And if she were looking for security maybe she might consider the possibility. She had her children to think about and if the radio show didn't pan out, she'd be back in the same position she was in a few days ago.

But Roxanne wanted more from marriage the second time around. She wanted security, but she also wanted passion and excitement and overwhelming, everlasting desire.

Those fantasies had gotten her through some tough times. After John had walked out, she'd tried to convince herself that divorce was a good thing, that there was another, more perfect husband waiting for her. She had dreamed about meeting a man who would drive her wild with his touch and calm her fears with his smile. A man like—Roxanne cursed softly. A man like Kit Lawrence. One little kiss was all it had taken to wonder about transforming her fantasy into reality.

She turned and pressed her forehead against the door, squeezing her eyes shut. She knew she could make a success of this job, with or without Kit Lawrence's approval or support. She could take advantage of this opportunity. But what she didn't know was how she'd continue seeing Kit without falling into vivid speculation about what they might have shared.

She stepped back from the door, confident that she would handle whatever Carl or Kit threw her way. But at that very moment, the door swung open and hit her in the face, the impact with her nose causing stars to dance in front of her eyes. Roxanne cried out and stumbled around in the dark, nearly falling over a mop bucket.

The bare bulb hanging from the ceiling went on and for a moment, she had to cover her eyes, waiting for them to adjust. When she pulled her hands away, she found herself squinting at Kit Lawrence.

"In the closet? Are you waiting for my father or has he already left?"

She sent him a withering glare, even though the effort caused her nose to throb. "You have a very dirty mind.'' Roxanne pushed past him and walked out the door.

"Rox, wait a second.''

"No! I don't need to listen to you anymore.''

He grabbed her arm and spun her around to face him. Then he gently pulled her fingers away from her nose, examining it carefully. "Does it hurt?''

"Like hell,'' she said, trying to keep her eyes from watering.

"I'm sorry. I didn't expect you to be inside the closet. I needed a lightbulb. What were you doing in there?''

"I could tell you, but you wouldn't believe me. You prefer to think the worst of me.''

"Give me a reason not to.''

"I needed a quiet place to think. A moment alone.''

"In the closet?''

She pushed his hands away. "I have to go.'' She hurried down the hall, this time finding her way out without a problem. When she reached her mini-van, she quickly climbed in. Roxanne rubbed her nose, trying to ease the ache along with the humiliation. Her professional life might be coming together and her family life was getting on track, but her romantic life was a complete shambles.

Carl pretended to lust after Roxanne. Roxanne secretly lusted after his son, Kit. Kit hated Roxanne, even though he'd kissed her once. "My life has turned into a soap opera," she murmured. "And I can't find the damn remote to turn it off."

ROXANNE GRABBED the box of cereal and poured a bowl of Frosted Flakes for Danny. Car pool was due to arrive in fifteen minutes and her son still wasn't dressed. "Danny," she shouted. "Come down right now. You'll be late for school."

"I can't find my basketball shoes," he shouted from the top of the stairs.

"Wear your hiking boots."

"No, I have to wear my basketball shoes."

Roxanne put Jenna in her high chair, then spread some graham crackers onto the tray. "Good morning, my little sweetie."

"Mama," she said. She stuck her finger out and touched Roxanne's nose. "Dirty."

Roxanne giggled and captured her daughter's finger in her mouth. "Mmm, tastes good."

Danny came racing into the kitchen followed by Rachel and Michael, who were still dressed in their pajamas. "Tell them to quit following me," he shouted.

"Quit following your brother," Roxanne said.

"When can I go to school?" Rachel asked.

"Next year."

Danny slid into his spot at the kitchen table, then glanced up at his mother. His spoon froze halfway to his mouth. "What happened to you?" he asked.

"What do you mean?"

"You have a black eye," Danny said. "Cool."

Roxanne turned to look at her reflection in the stainless steel refrigerator. When she didn't like what she saw, she ran to the powder room tucked beneath the stairs and flipped on the light. "Oh, no!" she cried.

The thunder of running feet on the hardwood floors followed her to the bathroom and Michael crawled up on the toilet and peered at her reflection in the mirror. "Wow," he said, clearly in awe of the swirl of color around her right eye.

"It's purple," Rachel said. "Purple is my favorite color."

The doorbell rang, but the kids were so fascinated by her black eye that none of them ran to answer it. When it rang again, Roxanne cursed silently and told Danny to get his shoes and coat. Before she opened the door, she peeked through the curtains, expecting to find Janelle Verrick, one of the car pool mothers. Another moan slipped from her throat. Kit Lawrence stood on her front porch, holding a huge bouquet of flowers.

Danny ran up with his school bag and his jacket. "Why don't you let Mrs. Verrick in?"

"It's not Mrs. Verrick," she said. "I want you to wait a few seconds while Mommy hides in the bathroom, then I want you to open the door."

"But you said I should never open the door."

"You know who is on the other side. Mr. Lawrence is out there."

"Does he have some puppies and candy?"

"No. Just tell Mr. Lawrence that I'm in the bathroom and I can't be disturbed. Then close the door and come back and tell me when he goes away. Got that?"

"Does he have balloons?"

"Not that Mr. Lawrence. The other Mr. Lawrence."

"With the swimming pool?" Danny asked.

"Honey, just answer the door and tell him what I said."

Roxanne rushed to the powder room then left the door open a crack. Rachel, Michael and Jenna were still inside, playing with the toilet paper. She shushed them, then she tried to hear what was going on at the front door. She heard the familiar squeak of the hinges, then held her breath.

"Hi, Danny."

"Hi, Mr. Lawrence. My mom says she can't see you because she's disturbed. And she has to go to the bathroom. You're supposed to go away."

"Is she sick?" Kit asked.

"No. When can we come swimming again?"

"Whenever you want. Would you like to come tonight?"

"Sure. What time?"

Roxanne groaned. This was not going well. She

raked her fingers through her tangled hair, then tightened the belt on her tattered chenille robe. The robe made her look like a pink sausage tied in the middle and there was a huge coffee stain on the lapel. Maybe if she stayed far enough away, he wouldn't notice the black eye.

She stepped out of the bathroom and the kids scooted out around her, running to the door. Rachel leapt into Kit's arms and gave him a hug, then stuck her face into the flowers he held. Michael clung to his leg.

"Are those flowers for me?" Rachel asked.

"They're for your mom," Kit replied. "But reach in my jacket pocket. There's something in there for you."

Rachel did as she was told and came back with big red lollipop. She found three more and passed them out to the other kids, then wriggled out of Kit's arms. "Mommy, look what Mr. Lawrence brought!"

"Sugar," Roxanne said. "And artificial coloring. And a sharp stick. Very nice."

"My ride's here, Mom," Danny called.

"Leave the lollie. You can save it until after school." He set the sucker down on the hall table and ran out. Then Michael grabbed it and raced out of the room, the girls hot on his heels. "Don't you dare eat that," she shouted. "That's Danny's."

Kit took a step into the house. "Sorry. I probably should have brought them something a little more healthy, like alfalfa sprouts or yogurt." He took another step closer, then frowned. "What happened to your eye?"

"A closet door," she said. "And you looking for a lightbulb."

Kit tossed the flowers aside, crossed the hall in a few long strides, then gently took her face in his hands. He carefully examined her eye, probing at it with his thumb. "Does that hurt?"

Roxanne shook her head. "I put ice on it last night. I don't think anything is broken. Just a little bruised."

"Maybe you should see a doctor."

"That wouldn't be a great idea. I don't have health insurance. The kids are covered by a policy I bought, but since the divorce, I let my coverage lapse."

"You were hurt in the workplace. The station's insurance would probably cover it."

"I'm fine," she said, touched by his concern and warmed by his touch. "What are you doing here?"

He picked up the flowers from the floor and handed them to her. "I wanted to say I was sorry. About the argument we had. About the black eye. And I wanted to take you and the kids out to breakfast."

Her first impulse was to accept. But then she shook her head. She had vowed not to get caught in the middle again. Carl and Kit were going to have to work out this misunderstanding first. "Have you ever been out to eat with three children under the age of five? I'm telling you, you'll never be the same again. The jelly, the juice, the syrup. It's not for amateurs."

Kit laughed. "I've put together multimillion dollar deals. I've run a few triathlons. I've sailed across the ocean in a forty-foot sailboat. I think I can handle breakfast. Why don't you and the kids get dressed? I'll put these flowers in water."

She nodded. Breakfast with Kit did sound intriguing. And maybe it would give her a chance to improve his opinion of her. "All right. I'll just be a minute."

She ran into the living room and retrieved the lollipops from the kids, then herded them upstairs. When she got to Rachel's room, she pulled out a shirt and pants and laid them on her daughter's bed. "I want you to go find something for Michael and Jenna to wear and then get them dressed. Then I want you to get dressed. Can you do that for Mommy?"

"I don't like these," she said, pointing to the outfit. "I hate that shirt. It makes me scratch. And those pants are green. I hate green."

"Just pick out anything and get dressed. When

I get out of the bathroom, I want to see all of you ready to go. Mr. Lawrence is going to take us out for breakfast.''

Rachel sighed dramatically, then began to rummage through her closet. Satisfied that her daughter could handle the task, Roxanne hurried into the bedroom. She quickly brushed her hair and pulled it back, tying it with a pale blue scarf. Then she found a sweater set that matched and wasn't stained with spaghetti sauce or colored marker. Corduroy pants and boots finished off the look, along with a quick bit of makeup to cover the black eye.

By the time she got out into the hall, her three children were waiting. Rachel had dressed them in a wild assortment of patterns and colors. ''You look—'' Like little clowns, she wanted to say. But Rachel was smiling up at her with such pride in her accomplishment. ''Fantastic. Good job, Rachel.''

''Thanks, Mommy.''

''Now, I want everyone to be on their best behavior. No crying, no whining and no crawling underneath the table. And if you drop food on the floor, it stays there.'' She reached down and picked up Jenna. ''Let's go.''

CHAPTER FOUR

"I FEEL AS IF I've been through a war," Kit said.

They slowly strolled through one of the small garden squares that surrounded the Washington Monument, a tall white column that served as one of Baltimore's more impressive landmarks. Kit carried Jenna on his shoulders while Roxanne held on to Michael and Rachel.

Kit playfully placed his hand on Jenna's knee, then didn't pull it away. "Jelly," he said. "I'm stuck."

"I warned you." Roxanne laughed. "And they were really well behaved. They didn't spill anything, which has to be some kind of record."

Pedestrians passed, greeting them with smiles, and Kit wondered at the impression they created. Did the five of them look like a happy family, a father, a mother and three children? A few weeks ago, he would have cringed at the notion. He'd barely given marriage a thought and children hadn't even crossed his mind. He'd been happily single and determined to stay that way.

But now, he wanted people to assume that this

was his family, that the woman at his side had chosen to spend her life with him, that the children loved him and depended on him. It was a life he suddenly wanted to experience.

Kit turned to stare at the fountain, now drained for the winter. This was crazy. He wasn't supposed to fall in love with Roxanne Perry. Hell, he wasn't supposed to fall in love with anyone.

He had always taken a pragmatic approach to passion. Work came first and women, though an enjoyable part of his life, ranked a little further down the list. But today, he'd cancelled four meetings and a trip to New York in the hopes that she'd accept the flowers and an invitation to spend the day with him.

When they reached an open area, Kit set Jenna down and Roxanne let the kids go, allowing them to scamper ahead. "Stay on the sidewalk," she called. "And no climbing on the fountain. Rachel, you watch Jenna. Don't let her get all muddy."

Kit was tempted to return his hands to his jacket pockets, but instead he let his palm slide down her arm until he wove her cold fingers into his. Winters in Baltimore were pretty mild, but the cold was damp and seemed to cut right to the bone. The children didn't seem to be bothered, but Roxanne's nose and cheeks were a pretty shade of pink.

They watched as Rachel and Michael jumped across a small puddle, Jenna screaming in delight when the water splashed. From what he could tell, Roxanne was the best of mothers. She was patient and firm, yet she let her kids experience the world. She rarely scolded and when she did, it was with a gentle voice.

"It smells like spring," Kit commented.

"The weather is supposed to warm up later this week." She glanced around the park. "It feels good to get out. Sometimes that house just presses down on me."

"It looks like you're in the middle of a renovation," he commented.

"We've been stalled at that stage for two years, ever since my husband walked out. John was determined to live in that neighborhood. Mount Vernon was close to downtown, it had the proper mix of culture and social life for him. I wanted to look in Roland Park or Guilford and find something a little more practical for children. But that's the house we bought. Looking back on it, I think that was the first sign of trouble."

"How is that?"

"John put his wants and needs above those of his family." She sighed. "I've been thinking of selling it, but who wants to buy it as it is now?"

"Where would you go?"

"Someplace cheaper. My parents live in upstate New York in a pretty little town near Saratoga Springs. It would be nice for the kids."

Kit forced a smile, but the notion that she could just move out of his life without a second thought bothered him. He groaned inwardly. They'd known each other for three days and suddenly he was certain he loved her. Either he was going crazy or— or— Kit paused. No, there was no other alternative. He *was* losing his mind.

He'd been forced to admit that perhaps her motives weren't what he'd first believed. In the time they'd spent together, he found no trace of greed or selfishness in her. Roxanne Perry wasn't a schemer or a gold digger or anything but a sweet, sexy woman.

She'd bewitched him the same way that she'd bewitched his father. His thoughts had been consumed with the way she moved, the sound of her voice, the color of her eyes. And now, when presented with the possibility that she might walk away from them both, he suddenly didn't want her to leave.

Hell, he should feel guilty about kissing her, but he didn't. She'd insisted there was nothing between her and Carl. And Carl refused to admit his feelings for her. For now, that left the door open for Kit, a door he planned to open even wider. "My dad told me he offered you a job. It's a long commute from upstate New York to Baltimore."

"Can we not talk about your father?" Roxanne asked. "Every time we do, we get in an argument.

You two have some issues you need to discuss. Let's just enjoy the morning.''

''All right,'' he said. Without thinking, he lifted her hand to his lips, pressing a kiss below her wrist. ''So what would you like to do today? We can go anywhere. How about the zoo? Or the aquarium? At least it would be warm there. When does Danny get off school?''

''He's done at three.''

''That will give us plenty of time.''

''Why are you being so nice to us?'' Roxanne asked, her tone suspicious.

''Because it's so easy,'' he replied.

''Are you sure *you* don't have any ulterior motives?''

''Just one,'' he said.

''And what's that?''

Kit glanced around, then grabbed her and pulled her behind a tree, pressing her back against the trunk. He bent close and kissed her. But this time the kiss wasn't soft and fleeting and tentative. She opened beneath his assault and the taste of her went right to his head.

Slowly, he explored her mouth, instantly addicted to the sweet warmth. A flood of desire raced through his veins and suddenly he wished they were alone, all alone, in some quiet, dark spot— like the janitor's closet.

He wrapped his arms around her waist, knowing

that he only had a short time to enjoy the experience. Then, certain that he'd satisfied his craving for the moment, he let her go. He grabbed her hand and pulled her out from behind the tree and they continued their walk.

"Sorry," he murmured. "I just had to do that." He glanced at her and watched as a tiny smile curled her damp lips.

"The aquarium would be nice," she said, acting as if nothing had happened. "And after that, maybe I can make you dinner? I promise, no jelly on the menu."

Kit didn't even bother to hide his delight. "It's a deal."

He jogged up to the puddle that Rachel and Michael had found, grabbed Jenna and jumped into the middle of the water. The kids laughed and screamed and before long, Roxanne had joined them. Kit reached out to her and pulled her against him. She looked up into his eyes and smiled, as if there were no other place in the world she'd rather be.

And Kit had to admit he felt the same way.

"I LIKED THE BABY SEAHORSES," Danny said. "Did you ever think there would be horses that swim?"

"Seahorses aren't really horses," Kit said, reaching for the milk to refill Michael's cup.

"They're *syngnathids*. That means 'bony fish.' They just look like horses. Did you see how they swim? They have two dorsal fins that they flap together."

"Like butterfly wings," Danny said.

"Yeah, like butterfly wings." Kit looked over the table at Roxanne. She felt her heart skip a beat, as it had so many times over the course of their day together.

There was a time when she wondered if she'd ever completely forget her troubles, or if she'd feel normal again. But today had been a good day—a great day. She was ready to move on, to make a life for herself and her children. And maybe, if she was lucky, Kit would be a part of that life.

"How about you, Mommy?" Kit asked. "What was your favorite thing at the aquarium?"

"Mommy?" she asked, raising an eyebrow.

"Sorry. What was your favorite thing, Roxanne?"

"The parrot fish," she said. "I thought they were the prettiest."

"I liked the birds," Rachel said. "The puffies."

"Puffins," Kit corrected. "What about you, Michael?"

"Frogs," he replied.

This is what Roxanne had always dreamed family life would be—sitting around the dinner table, talking to the children, enjoying one another's company. John had never wanted to eat with the kids. He'd always insisted that Roxanne feed them first, then put them to bed so he could have a "quiet" dinner with his wife. In truth, John rarely spent any time with the children.

"Yeah, that poison frog. He was cool," Danny said.

"You know there's a difference between poison and venom," Kit said.

"How do you know so much?" Danny asked, staring up at him in awe. "You're really smart."

"I used to spend a lot of time at the aquarium when I was younger," he said. "I was there on the day it opened up and after that, I used to visit whenever I could."

"What was your favorite?"

"I always liked the stingrays."

"Danny, why don't you take your brother and sisters into the living room," Roxanne suggested, "and clean up your toys. I'll wash the dishes and then maybe we'll watch a movie together."

"What movie do you want?" Danny asked, turning to Kit.

"Oh, honey, I don't know if Mr. Lawrence wants to stay for—"

"I do," Kit interrupted. "I'd love to stay for a movie."

Danny jumped up from the table, then helped Jenna down from her high chair. They raced off to the living room, Danny insisting that they choose *Aladdin* and Rachel countering with *Beauty and the Beast.*

Kit pushed away from the table and picked up his plate and glass. When Roxanne made a move to do the same, he gently pushed her back into her chair. "I'll clean up. You made dinner. It's the least I can do." He glanced around. "Where is the dishwasher?"

"It's in a box in the basement," Roxanne said, her face warming with embarrassment. "That's one of the renovations we never got around to. Actually, it goes pretty fast if one person washes and the other one dries. Rachel and Danny often help me. That's why we usually use plastic." She slowly stood and joined him at the sink. "I'm glad you stayed for dinner."

"So am I. You're a good cook."

Roxanne looked up at him, then let her impulses take control. She pushed up on her toes and kissed him, their lips meeting for an instant before she pulled away. But when she did, he moaned softly and caught her mouth again.

The kiss was slow and lazy, warm and deep. Roxanne's knees went weak, but she didn't need to worry about falling, since Kit had slipped his hands around her hips and held her tight. But they didn't stay there. As they kissed, he smoothed his palms along her waist, pushing her sweater up until he met bare skin.

Her breath caught in her throat, then came out in a sigh. It had been so long since she'd been touched, since a man had made her feel this much desire. His hands were gentle, sliding around to the small of her back, then up to the nape of her neck.

She'd never experienced such intense longing, for every sensation. The taste of his tongue and the heat of his hand and just the smell of his cologne was enough to send every rational thought from her head. She wasn't a mother of four kids or John's ex-wife anymore. She was the woman Kit Lawrence desired, the woman he couldn't keep from kissing.

Roxanne liked to believe that she held some kind of power over him, but she knew the opposite was true. With anyone else, she might have been more hesitant, more circumspect. But since that first time he'd kissed her, all Kit had to do was turn his gaze in her direction and a rush of unbidden thoughts would fill her mind, wild, crazy, sexual images. Roxanne had already fantasized about how it would be between them. And now she wanted those fantasies to come to life.

Kit grabbed her waist, then gently lifted her up onto the edge of the counter, setting her down next to the sink. He stepped between her legs and gave her one long kiss, then pressed his forehead to hers. "I'd better get to work."

"Yes," she said, breathlessly.

He finished clearing the table, then filled the sink with soapy water. Every few minutes, he'd steal another kiss and Roxanne would oblige. With the kids in the house, she knew it could go no further, but she didn't care. For now, kissing him was enough.

"So, what's going on with the contest?" he asked. "Have you heard anything?"

Roxanne shrugged and took a wet plate from his hand. "My sister entered me. She wrote an essay and I guess they judge me on the essay. I don't know if I have to do anything else, except be a good mother."

"You'd love Paris," he murmured.

"Have you been there?"

Kit nodded.

"John always promised we'd go, but we never did. It sounds wonderful, though when it comes right down to it, I'd miss the children. I've never been away from them. Your dad has some other prizes set up with the radio station. Those would be nice to win." She took another plate from him. "But I'm not counting on winning. I'm not even sure why I'm a finalist. Renee must be a better writer than I thought."

"You're a great mother," Kit said. "And this is

coming from a guy who grew up with the greatest mother in the world.''

''My mom was great, too. If it weren't for her, I'm not sure I would have made it through all this. After John left, she lived with us for a couple of months. And my parents are always here for the holidays, so that makes things easier.'' She sent him a sideways glance. ''You'd make a good father,'' she said.

''You think so?''

''You're really good with my kids. I mean, not that I expect you to be *their* father.'' She fumbled to cover her mistake. ''I don't expect anyone to be their father. I—I don't know if I'll ever get married again.''

He seemed surprised by her revelation. ''Don't you think your kids will need a father someday?''

Roxanne frowned. ''No father is better than a bad father. One that might walk out on them again. Marriage is a risky proposition as it is. But if I fail at it a second time, it's not just me who gets hurt.''

''You didn't fail at your marriage,'' Kit said. ''Any guy who would walk away from a family like this would have to be crazy.''

Roxanne giggled. ''I think he did go a little crazy. He ran away with this huge, muscle-bound woman who throws other muscle-bound women and men around a wrestling ring for a living. She's got all these tattoos and she wears this tiny little outfit. I don't know what he sees in her."

"I don't know, either," Kit said. He leaned over and kissed her, gently drawing his tongue along the crease of her lips, then drawing away. "But, for very selfish reasons of my own, I'm glad he saw something."

KIT SLOWLY OPENED HIS EYES. Daylight filtered through the living room windows. He glanced over at the television and noticed that the morning news shows had started. The weather forecast promised a sunny day with temperatures in the mid-fifties.

With a soft sigh, he turned into the warm body stretched alongside of him on the sofa. He wasn't sure when they'd fallen asleep, sometime after they'd put the kids to bed and before the late news came on. He usually didn't sleep so soundly, especially when he was fully dressed and lying next to a beautiful woman. But a day spent chasing Roxanne's kids around gave him a better workout than the average marathon.

Kit nuzzled his face into her hair, breathing deeply of the scent. He couldn't think of a better way to start the day than with Roxanne in his arms. Oddly, he'd usually preferred to leave a woman's bed before dawn, but Kit pulled her closer and closed his eyes. The house was silent and it would probably be a few hours before the kids were up. He'd just catch a little more shut-eye.

But as he pulled her closer, she stirred. Her eyes fluttered open and she looked up at him with a sleepy expression. "Hi," she murmured.

He brushed a kiss across her mouth. "Morning."

She snuggled closer and pressed her face into his chest. "What time is it?"

"Six-thirty."

She stiffened, then pushed herself up, instantly wide awake. "You can't be here," she said, crawling over top of him and tumbling to the floor.

Kit reached over, concerned that she'd hurt herself, but she brushed his hand away and frantically began to straighten her rumpled clothes. He watched her rake her fingers through her hair then he reached out to pull her back down on top of him, but she deftly avoided his reach.

"Get up," she said.

"Why?"

"Because the kids will be up in a few seconds."

"It's quiet up there."

"You don't understand. They have radar. The minute I get up in the morning, whether it's at 5:00 a.m. or 7:00, their little bodies automatically kick into gear. I never have a moment to myself in the morning. I barely have time to brush my teeth before they descend on me."

"She's not going to say anything. She can barely talk."

"That's not the point."

Kit slipped his arms around her waist. "So, now that you're here, what are we going to do?" He kissed her neck. "They'll never find us, you know."

"Mommy?"

Roxanne stiffened, then reached up to cover his mouth with her hand. "Don't make a sound."

"Mommy, are you in there? Who are you talking to?"

The doorknob jiggled and before Kit could reach for it, the door swung open. Danny looked up at them both, a quizzical expression on his face. "Hi, Mr. Lawrence. Did you find my basketball shoes, Mom?"

Roxanne forced a smile. "I haven't had a chance, honey. Mr. Lawrence just stopped by and he was helping me clean the closet. But we'll find them, won't we, Mr. Lawrence?"

"Yeah," Kit said.

A scream reverberated through the house, a scream that Kit recognized as Jenna. Roxanne moaned softly, then slipped out of the closet, leaving him to make the explanations to Danny. "Well, should we look for your basketball shoes?"

"Was my mom crying?" Danny asked.

Kit frowned. "Why would she be crying?"

"She goes in the closet every morning and cries," he explained. "She says she's cleaning the closet, but I don't think she is, 'cause she never takes the vacuum cleaner in."

"What does she cry about?"

Danny shrugged. "Don't know. Last week she didn't go in there. I sure hope she's not sad again."

"I hope not, either." He ruffled the boy's hair. "Find your shoes. Your ride will be here soon."

"My mom has to drive me today. There's no car pool on Fridays. But she has to get everyone ready first, 'cause they all have to go along."

"How about if I drive you to school?" Kit suggested.

Danny's eyes lit up and he nodded enthusiastically. "Yeah. That would be cool. I have show-and-tell today. Can I take you? You can tell everyone about your swimming pool."

"Why don't we try to come up with something a little better?" Kit stepped to the bottom of the stairs and called out for Roxanne. A few seconds later, she appeared, a sobbing Jenna in her arms. "If it's all right, I can drop Danny at school."

She stared at him for a long moment. "You don't have to do that."

"I want to. And I'll call you tonight. Maybe the kids can come over to swim again?"

"Maybe," she said softly.

He winked at her, then turned to Danny. "Come

on. If we get there a little early, you can show me your classroom.''

They walked out to Kit's car, which was parked on the street just down from Roxanne's house. He unlocked the door for Danny and then made sure he buckled his seat belt. When Kit got inside, he looked over at the boy. ''You'll have to show me how to get there.''

''It's not too far. I could walk, but my mom doesn't like me crossing the streets alone. But when I'm bigger, I'm going to walk.''

Kit pulled out into traffic, then steered the car around the block and followed Danny's directions.

''I'm glad you're driving me to school.''

''And why is that?''

''When Mom drives me, she always makes me kiss her goodbye and everyone watches.''

Kit smiled. Funny how he had a completely different attitude about Roxanne's kisses. As far as he was concerned, she could kiss him whenever and wherever. ''She loves you. I'd say you were a pretty lucky guy to have such a great mom. She takes very good care of you.''

Danny shrugged. ''I guess. But she's gotta stop kissing me all the time.''

''Would you like me to have a little talk with her? I could suggest that she saves the kisses for when no one else is around.''

A smile brightened his face. ''Would you? That

would be really, really good,'' Danny said. ''I'm afraid if I say something she might cry.''

''Does she cry a lot?''

''She used to. She said it's because my dad went away.''

''And how do you feel about that?''

Danny considered his answer for a long moment. ''I don't remember him much. He left when I was four. And now I'm six.''

''You handle things pretty well around the house. You take good care of your brother and sisters.''

''They're a big pain,'' Danny said.

''Yeah, but they're your brother and sisters and that counts for something.''

''I guess.'' Danny looked over at Kit, a frown on his face. ''Do you like my mom?''

The question was asked as if it was the most logical course of conversation and it took Kit by surprise. ''Yeah. I guess I do. No, I do. I really like her a lot.''

''There's a girl in my class who likes me,'' he said. ''She keeps saying we're gonna get married, but I tell her that I don't like her. I'm never gonna like girls.''

''You say that now, but I think you'll change your mind. Girls can be pretty neat. I mean, hanging out with the guys is all right. But girls are different. They're really nice.''

Danny made a face. "They always wanna kiss me. Yuck."

"Well, that's not so bad, either—when you're older."

"You kissed my mom," he said. "I saw you."

Kit chuckled. "You did."

"My mom likes you, too. I can tell. She's always smiling at you."

"I like it when she smiles," Kit said.

"Yeah," Danny said. "Me, too."

CHAPTER FIVE

"AND AFTER THE KIDS went to bed we sat on the couch, with all the lights off, and we just kissed...and kissed...and kissed. It made me feel so young. As if he was my first boyfriend." Roxanne pressed her hands to her warm cheeks, trying to hide the blush that she knew was there. "We do everything, but...you know. It's so hard not to go any further."

"Yeah," Renee said. "Because he's too embarrassed to buy condoms from the drugstore and you're afraid that all your high school friends will think you're easy. Geez, Rox, you're grown-ups. You can have sex if you want."

"No, we can't. The kids are always upstairs. I couldn't possibly let things get out of control. Besides, it's only been a month." Roxanne sighed, still remembering the feel of his hands on her skin, the sensation of his palm cupping her breast. With each evening they spent together, they took another step toward the inevitable.

Her life was a routine again, but this was a routine that Roxanne had come to crave. Over the past month, she'd settled into her job at the station, working Tuesdays and Thursdays. While she was gone for the day, an elderly lady from the neighborhood watched the children. Most evenings, Kit would come over for dinner or she'd take the kids to his house and they'd swim. On the occasional night he was out of town on business, she found herself at a loss, reaching for the phone to call him for the silliest little things and unable to sleep until he called her to say good-night.

"Why don't you ask that sitter you hired to stay late some day? You and Kit could go out on a real date."

"I'm not sure I'm ready for that," Roxanne murmured. "You know what really scares me?"

"That when he's got you in the bedroom, he'll recoil in horror at your stretch marks? God, that's what I'd be afraid of."

"No!" Roxanne cried, the sudden image searing into her brain. "I—I never even thought about that—until now. Oh God, I've had four children. He's probably only ever slept with single, svelte, non-mothers." Roxanne pulled up her shirt. "I wonder if I could cover them with makeup."

"Yeah, and when he's running his tongue along your belly he gets a mouthful of Cover Girl. *That's* romantic." Renee shrugged. "So what are you afraid of?"

"Everything now," Roxanne said.

"No, tell me. I promise I won't open my big mouth again."

Roxanne paused, hesitant to voice her apprehension. It would sound so stupid. "I'm afraid of it being too good."

"How can it possibly be *too* good? Unless, of course, you die of cardiac arrest midorgasm."

"With John, I was so in love, I didn't see who he really was. I thought I had found the man of my dreams. The sex was so good. Then we got married and had kids and the passion just seemed to fade away. Then he found someone else."

"You had sex with John before you got married? You told me you were a virgin until your wedding night."

"You were my younger sister," Roxanne said. "What was I supposed to tell you?"

"Does Mom know?"

"Can we stay on subject here? I'm afraid that the same thing is going to happen with Kit. We'll be intimate and then I'll make the same mistake, thinking that he's the love of my life and I can't live without him."

"Then there's only one thing to do," Renee said. "Just use him for sex."

Roxanne gasped, then was forced to stifle a giggle. "I couldn't do that."

"Why not?"

"Because I think I'm in love with him," she

admitted. "I think maybe I've been in love with him since the very first time I looked at him. You should see him with the kids. He's so good with them, especially Danny. And he treats me like a queen. He's always bringing me flowers and doing special favors for me. A few days ago, he sent a workman over to install my dishwasher."

"Oh, dear. Well that messes up the use-him-for-sex plan. Maybe using him for home repairs is better."

"And then there's his father we have to deal with."

"He doesn't approve?"

"It's not that. I think Kit suspects that Carl's in love with me, which he isn't. Whenever Carl and I are together, all he talks about is Kit. I don't know. Maybe I should just forget men altogether."

"You're twenty-eight years old, Rox. That's too young to give up on men. You've still got lots of good years left. In fact, I'm going to take the kids tonight. I want you to call him up and invite him over to dinner. Wear a sexy dress, ply him with a few drinks and then get down to business." She paused. "And the minute he leaves, call me and tell me every detail."

"I can't," Roxanne said.

"You can. I'm not bringing your children back until you do. Don't waste the opportunity." Renee got up from the table and walked to the stairs. "Come on, kids, time to go. Your cousins are waiting for you. We're going to McDonald's for lunch."

Roxanne joined her sister in the foyer, then gave each of the kids a kiss as they reached the bottom of the stairs. "What about their pajamas?"

"I've got extras."

"What time are you going to bring them back tomorrow?"

"After you call me and tell me what a wonderful time you had."

"Where's Mommy going?" Danny asked.

"To a very happy place," Renee said, herding the kids to the front door. Before she walked out, she reached out and gave Roxanne a quick hug. "Have fun."

Roxanne slowly closed the door behind her sister, then peeked out the curtains, watching her children scamper down the sidewalk. With a sigh, she turned around and leaned back against the door. Could she really do this? Was she ready to risk it all for one night of passion?

"The longer I think about it, the more difficult it's going to be." She hurried to the kitchen and picked up the phone. She'd already memorized Kit's cell phone number. With trembling fingers she punched in the number, but before the call connected, she hung up.

"What am I going to say? Hi, Kit, we're having sex tonight, please bring condoms?" Maybe it was best to surprise him. He'd come over, thinking he'd be spending an evening with the kids and there she'd be, sexy dress, candlelit dinner, fire in the fireplace, fresh linens on the bed.

"Damn!" She didn't have anything to wear, she needed candles and firewood and the laundry was sitting in a big heap upstairs. And if she didn't tell Kit what she had planned, then she'd have to go buy the condoms herself. Roxanne glanced at her watch, calculating the time it would take for each task.

Sex was sure a lot harder than it was when she was married.

ROXANNE STARED at her reflection in the mirror with a critical eye. She smoothed her hands over her belly, drawing the fabric of her little black cocktail dress tight. She still had a good figure. She'd exercised during her pregnancies and watched her diet, but there was no denying she possessed the body of a mother.

Her stomach twisted and for a moment she thought the nerves might overwhelm her. She reached out and grabbed her jeans, prepared to toss aside the dress and forget everything she'd planned. But then the doorbell rang and the decision was made for her.

There would be no time to change, no time to unset the dining room table or throw water on the fire. Taking one last look in the mirror, she forced a smile and sucked in her stomach. "Just go for it."

When she pulled the door open, he was standing on the stoop, his arms filled with bags, his briefcase dangling from his hand. He was still dressed in his suit, but his tie was unknotted and Roxanne knew that he'd come right from the airport.

"Hi," she said, stepping back and letting him come inside.

He bent close and gave her a quick kiss on the cheek. "Hi. I thought I'd never get here. My flight was late and then traffic was terrible. Where are the kids?" Kit set the bags down and began to rummage through them. "You should see what I got them. There was this toy store just across the street from my meeting and I had some time to kill and a credit card."

He pulled out a remote-controlled police car. "This is great. It has speed control and direction control, plus the headlights flash and the siren works. And I got a steam shovel for Michael because I remember how fascinated he was by that one we saw over near Inner Harbor. Only, I'm not sure how good he'll be at the controls. And a teddy bear for Jenna. And look at this." He pulled out a pretty pink dress, covered with sequins. "Rachel is going to love this. The lady said it was a ballerina dress, but I think it's more like a princess dress, don't you?" He glanced up. "Where are the kids? Danny, come here and see what I got for you!"

Roxanne clutched her hands in the fabric of her skirt. He hadn't even noticed what she was wearing! She'd spent an hour on her hair and makeup and he'd barely looked at her. "The kids aren't here."

Kit slowly stood. "Where are they?"

"They're spending the night with Renee."

"Why?"

Roxanne's frustration grew. She'd imagined that he'd come in, see her and promptly begin ripping her clothes off. But it seemed that Kit was more interested in seeing her children than her cleavage. Was she really that bad at seduction? "I thought we could spend some time alone. We really haven't had any private time since we met, unless you count the few minutes we had in my hall closet."

"We're alone all the time after the kids go to bed. And we're alone at the radio station."

"No, we aren't. There are always people around. I wanted to be alone. Completely."

He stared at her, a frown furrowing his brow. "What is this about? Do you have something to tell me?"

"What would I have to tell you?"

"I don't know," he countered. "You tell me."

Roxanne moaned softly, then turned and stalked into the living room. He followed behind her, but stopped short when he saw the dimmed lights and the candles, the wine and the crackling fire. "I'm dressed in a sexy dress, I have makeup on, if you haven't noticed. And I've added all the romantic details. Right. I wanted to talk to you about tax shelters."

Kit's face relaxed into a smile. "I'm sorry. I'm just a little tired. This is really nice." He stepped over to her and wrapped his arms around her waist, pulling her close. He gave her a long, leisurely kiss. "Better?" he murmured.

"A little," she said.

He kissed her again, this time more deeply. "How about now?"

"Almost."

With a low growl, Kit swept her up in his arms and carried her to the sofa, kissing her as he stretched out on top of her. When he finally finished, she was flushed and breathless. "I could keep doing this all night."

Roxanne reached up and ran her fingers through his hair, then smoothed her palm over his cheek. "That's what I'm counting on."

"You know, I did bring a present for you. But maybe I shouldn't give it to you." He jumped off

of her and hurried back to where he'd dropped the
bags. When he sat back down on the edge of the
couch, he was holding a long, velvet-covered box.
"It isn't remote controlled and it doesn't sparkle.
I hope you like it."

"You didn't have to get me a gift," Roxanne
said.

With a grin, Kit pulled it away. "No, I didn't,"
he teased. "On second thought, maybe I should
take it back."

"No. I want to see it."

He handed her the box and she slowly opened
it. Inside was a perfect string of pearls. Kit reached
out and took them from her, then fastened them at
her nape. "They're beautiful." Roxanne wrapped
her arms around his neck and kissed him and he
pressed her back into the pillows until he was lying
on top of her.

"So how long have you been working on this?"
he asked.

"Almost all day. I got a new dress," she said.

Kit slipped his fingers beneath the spaghetti
strap and gently pulled it off her shoulder. Then he
pressed his mouth to the spot and bit softly. "I like
it."

"I bought new underwear, too."

His eyebrow arched and he shifted above her,
sliding his hand down her hip and slowly gathering
the hem of her skirt in his fist. He pushed up on

his elbow and watched as he revealed the lacy top of her black stocking. "Very sexy."

"I figured I needed all the help I could get."

"Rox, believe me. You don't need sexy underwear to make me want you. I don't care if you're wearing a little black dress or a baggy sweatshirt. It doesn't make any difference to me. I always want you." He pressed a kiss below her shoulder, then moved to the soft swell of her breast. Roxanne closed her eyes and arched her back, reveling in the feel of his tongue on her skin. This was going much better now. Although she hadn't removed any of her clothes yet.

Maybe it would be best to just get it over with, to take control. Gently pushing against his chest, she rolled him over and straddled his hips. Her skirt bunched around her waist and she reached around to unzip her dress. But Kit brushed her hands aside and did it himself. When her dress fell in the front, she grabbed it and held it up, unable to completely banish her fears.

"I think I should tell you something," she said. "Not so much tell you as warn you."

He reached up and grabbed her fingers. "You're shaking," he murmured, pressing his lips to her palm.

"I'm—"

"What? Tell me?"

"Scared. That—that you won't...like me. I'm

not perfect, Kit. I'm a mother. Of four children. Do you know what that does to a woman's body?''

With a soft sigh, he grabbed her waist and swung his feet to the floor. Then he slowly pulled her up to stand in front of him. "From the first moment I saw you, I thought you were the most beautiful woman in the world. Nothing is going to change that opinion.''

"You hated me the first time you saw me.''

"I was an idiot.''

Roxanne let her arms drop and her dress slid off her shoulders and over her hips. The straps caught on her wrists, but she twisted her hands and, a moment later, the dress fell to the floor. Holding her breath and trying to gauge his reaction, she watched as his gaze raked her body. It had taken her nearly an hour to choose the underwear and from the low moan that slipped from his throat, she could tell it had been an hour well spent. "Now you," she said, sliding her hand over his chest.

He shrugged out of his suit jacket and tossed it aside, then added his silk tie to the pile. A few moments later, he pulled his shirt over his head rather than unbutton it. Roxanne took it from him and dropped it with the rest of his clothes. After he kicked off his shoes and socks, he stopped, choosing to leave the rest for later.

The beauty of his body took her breath away—

the wide shoulders, the muscular arms, the flat belly. With deliberate ease, she ran her hands over his chest, exploring the hard sinew and smooth skin. A soft line of hair traced a path from his collarbone to a spot beneath his belt. Suddenly, she wanted to know where it led. She reached down for his belt, but he drew her hands away.

"When are the kids coming back?"

"Tomorrow," Roxanne murmured.

"Then we have all the time in the world."

The fire crackled and Roxanne felt her skin flush with warmth. His fingers moved to the clasp of her bra and her pulse quickened. And when he'd discarded it and covered her nipple with his mouth, her knees went weak. Every caress of his tongue sent a wave of sensation racing through Roxanne's body. She forgot all her apprehensions and focused on the feel of his hands and his lips on her flesh.

He wasn't satisfied to linger in one spot. Where hands went, his mouth followed, as if he felt compelled to taste as well as touch. Roxanne had never really experienced foreplay, but Kit seemed to relish it. He was at times playful, then intense, his only aim to make her moan with pleasure.

They ended up on the floor in front of the fireplace, lying amidst the pillows she'd tossed there. He stretched out on top of her, their bodies pressed together. The ridge of his erection pressed into her belly, hot and hard through the fabric of his trousers, and Roxanne arched against him. Kit reached down and grabbed her legs, drawing them up alongside his hips, making the contact even more erotic and enticing.

"Touch me," he murmured, his voice ragged, his lips pressed against her neck.

Roxanne reached between them and tried to unbuckle his belt, but when she couldn't, Kit moved to lie beside her. A tiny squeak sounded from beneath his hip. Frowning, he reached beneath him and pulled out one of Jenna's stuffed toys, a little penguin. He chuckled softly as he stared at it. But then his smile faded.

"What is it?" Roxanne asked.

Kit cursed softly. "What the hell am I doing?" he muttered. "What the hell are we doing? I can't do this."

"What do you mean?"

"Oh, I can, believe me. The body is quite willing. I just…can't."

"I bought condoms," Roxanne said. "Five different kinds."

He shook his head. "That's not it. This isn't right, Rox."

"Why? We both want each other. We're both adults. And the kids are gone."

"But what happens after this?"

"After?"

"Tomorrow. The next day. A month from now. Where is this leading?"

"Does it have to mean something? Can't it just be about sex?"

His jaw went tight. "What do you want from me, Rox?"

"I don't know," she said, tears pressing at the corners of her eyes. Right now, she didn't know anything at all! Except that he wasn't touching her and he wasn't kissing her and it had something to do with a stuffed penguin.

He got up and began gathering his clothes. "And that's exactly why I shouldn't be here." As he walked to the door, he pulled his shirt over his head and stuffed the tails in his pants. He didn't bother with his socks, just shoved them into his pants pocket and slipped his bare feet into his shoes.

"Don't leave," she said, grabbing her dress and clutching it to her chest. She scrambled to her feet, humiliated and confused.

"I have to," Kit replied. "I've got to straighten out a few things." He paused, then strode back across the room. In one quick movement, he furrowed his hand through her hair and pulled her into a deep, mind-numbing kiss. "I love you," he murmured.

With that, Kit walked out, leaving Roxanne to stand amid the flickering candles, completely baffled by his behavior. And dumbstruck by his words. "He loves me," she repeated as she fingered the string of pearls.

The problem was, she didn't know if that was good news or bad.

KIT STOOD AT THE DOOR of his father's condo, trying to figure out what he was going to say to Carl Lawrence once he knocked on the door. It was nearly ten o'clock, late for Carl who usually was in bed by nine and back at the station by 5:00 a.m. But this couldn't wait. This was about Kit's future and he wanted that future to begin tonight.

How had this all happened? A little more than a month ago, Kit had been a confirmed bachelor, enjoying all the perks that came along with a string of beautiful women—including sex without guilt. But the minute he met Roxanne, his life completely changed.

At first, he'd told himself that he sought her out so he could discern her motives. He'd rationalized his interest as an attempt to protect his father. But all along, he'd spent time with her because he couldn't help himself. He was in love with Roxanne Perry.

He used to look upon "family men" with pity. They were always forced to divide their energy, between work and family. And what could be more tedious than coming home to the same woman every night, dealing with the same problems, listening to the same conversations. He'd just assumed that life wasn't for him.

But it wasn't like that at all. There was a real pleasure in coming home to Roxanne and her kids. He enjoyed the noisy dinners at the kitchen table and the quiet evenings snuggled up with her on the sofa. And the kids. He liked helping them put on their shoes and watching them brush their teeth. It balanced him, making him forget the stress of his business day. And it gave him perspective. Acquiring the next radio station or newspaper didn't seem so important compared to the problems Danny was having with a bully at school.

Kit raked his fingers through his hair and tried to settle the chaos in his head. Loving Roxanne was a big responsibility. It wasn't just the two of them. He would become a part of five lives. Was he really prepared to be a full-time father? Could he make Roxanne happy for the rest of her life?

Deep in his heart, he knew he could. But that didn't stop the doubts from bubbling to the surface. And then there was the problem of his father. If Carl still had any feelings for Roxanne, he hadn't made them obvious of late. But Kit needed to be absolutely sure before he and Roxanne went any further.

He reached out and knocked at the door. He wouldn't know until he asked. A few moments later, the door swung open. "Hey, there. What are you doing here?" Carl asked.

Kit walked past him, then turned. "We have to talk."

"Sit down. Do you want a drink? I think I have some scotch."

Kit shook his head, ignoring the sofa for a space on the rug to pace. He thought better when he was moving. "Just tell me one thing. Do you love her?"

"Love who?" Carl asked.

"Are you in love with Roxanne Perry?"

"Are you still worried about that?"

"Answer the damn question. Do you have any romantic feelings for her at all?"

His father chuckled and shook his head slowly. "No. But I'd expect you do or you wouldn't be here. You've been spending nearly every night with Roxanne for the past month. Even if some poor sap did have romantic feelings for her, you've been monopolizing her time. When she's at the station, you're always hanging around. Ernie the janitor saw you two coming out of his closet, and ever since then, it's been pretty obvious."

"How does that make you feel?" Kit asked.

"As if I was right all along. I knew she'd make a great wife...for you. So, have you asked her to marry you yet?"

Kit held out his hand. "Wait a second." He

paused, trying to read his father's expression. "Oh, no. Don't tell me you set this all up. You pretended to have a thing for her so I'd throw myself in between you two."

"It got you off your ass and moving in the right direction, didn't it? Protecting the family fortune from a greedy little gold digger. Well, you certainly changed your tune."

"I thought you were in love with her!" Kit said.

"Did I ever say that?"

"Well...no, not directly. But you implied it. You were always talking about how wonderful she is."

"I wasn't trying to convince myself, I was trying to convince you." Carl paused. "Kit, I loved your mother very much. And that feeling doesn't go away. Not in a year, not in ten. I've been lucky in my life to have just one good woman to love me. That's enough. I wanted that for you. And I thought maybe Roxanne might be able to provide it."

"You set me up," Kit repeated, unable to believe he'd been so gullible.

"I greased the gears a little," Carl said. "I want grandchildren. Can you blame me?"

Kit slowly lowered himself to the sofa. "This is serious." He groaned softly then buried his face in his hands. "Oh, hell. I walked out on her because I had to square things with you. She had this sexy dress on and all the candles lit. And now I find out, there's nothing to square. We could have…''

"I don't need to hear the details," Carl said. "I assume you're in love with her?"

"Yeah, I am."

"And she loves you?"

"I don't know. It's all happened so fast. We've only known each other a month, but it doesn't seem to matter. We just fit together. When I'm with her, I don't need anything else. But I've never been in love before. How am I supposed to know if this is real? Or more to the point, if it will last?"

"You have to make it real," Carl said. "Falling in love is the easy part. Keeping the relationship interesting takes a lot of work." His father paused. "The moment I met your mother, I knew she was the one for me. She hadn't even said word. I just saw her across the room and I told myself she was the one I was going to marry."

"I can't make a mistake on this, Dad. She has kids and they need a father. I can't step into their lives and then step out again if it doesn't work."

Carl reached down and clapped Kit on the shoulder. "Well, you're an adult now. You'll need to make that decision for yourself." He paused. "You know, this is going to mess everything up."

"I just told you I'm in love with Roxanne. How will that mess everything up?"

"We've done all this promotion, positioning

Roxanne Perry as a single mom and she's captured the audience's attention. Our afternoon ratings for the show have increased. If you decide to marry her and she accepts, her blossoming radio career might go right down the tubes.''

''Are you saying you're more concerned about ratings than about your son's happiness?''

Carl shook his head and smiled. ''I know she makes you happy. And you certainly make her happy. I suppose I can deal with the ratings.''

''This job you gave her was part of the plan, too?''

''It was the only way to keep you two in the general vicinity of each other. And you have to admit, she's good.''

''She is,'' Kit admitted.

''So what are you going to do, Kit?''

''I don't know. I've got to think about this for a while.''

''Well, don't take too long,'' Carl said. ''I might just decide to steal her away from you.''

Kit glanced over at his father and smiled ruefully. ''And I might decide to break both your arms.''

CHAPTER SIX

"COME ON, ROX. You have to put this behind you and move on. Aren't you glad you found out before it was too late?" Renee gave Roxanne's hands a sympathetic squeeze.

"Found out what? I'm not sure what happened. One minute we were rolling around on the floor half-naked and the next he was running out the door." Roxanne swallowed hard. "And I don't know if this means anything, but before he left, he told me that he loved me."

"What?" Renee shouted.

"He said he loved me. At least, I think he did. I could have imagined it. Or maybe he said something else and I misunderstood." Roxanne rubbed her temples, trying to calm her confusion.

"What could he have said that sounded like 'I love you'?"

"I don't know. Isle of doom? Eye glob do? I've been trying to come up with something all morning. If he really loved me, then why did he run out on the only chance we had to…you know."

''You can say the words, Rox. Have sex. Do the deed. Get nasty.''

''Shh! The kids are upstairs.''

''So what are you going to do?'' Renee whispered.

Roxanne sighed. ''I don't know if there's anything I can do. He walked out on me. He said he couldn't make love to me.''

''You have a man who loves you, but who can't *make* love to you. That's a real bummer.''

Roxanne sighed. ''I guess that's better than a man who makes love to other women. At least I'd know he wasn't cheating on me.''

Renee nodded her head. ''He's not going to run off with the Velvet Hammer.''

''I suppose I'm going to have to talk to him,'' Roxanne said, getting up to pour herself another cup of coffee.

Renee stood and slipped her arm around Roxanne's shoulders. ''Talk to him. Maybe he just got scared off.''

''I'm going to wait until he calls me.''

Roxanne walked her sister to the front door, then waved at her as she walked down the front steps. She turned around and went back inside, drawing a deep breath as she closed the door behind her. It was odd not having something to look forward to. For the past month, she'd lived her life in anticipation of the next time she'd see Kit. Was that all over now?

She glanced up as footsteps sounded on the stairs overhead. Danny raced down, his new remote-controlled car tucked under his arm. "Mom, can we go over to Kit's tonight to swim?"

Roxanne forced a smile. "Honey, we weren't invited."

"Sure we were. I asked Kit and he said I had to ask you."

"When did you ask Kit?"

"I called him to thank him for the car. Rachel talked to him, too."

"You called Kit?"

Danny nodded. "He gave me his number and he said I could call anytime. So can we?"

Roxanne bit her bottom lip. She had to straighten this mess up. Their lives had become so tangled with Kit's it was impossible to know what to say. "I'll think about it," she said.

Danny started back up the stairs, then stopped and came back down again. "Are you going to marry Kit?"

She laughed, a high-pitched, slightly hysterical giggle. "I don't know, Danny. We haven't known each other very long."

"But he makes you happy, right?"

Roxanne climbed up the stairs and gave him a long, hard hug. "Why don't you go upstairs and get your brother and sisters? It's a nice day. We'll drive over to the park. And after we play, we'll go out for some dinner.''

"And then we'll go swimming?''

"No, sweetie, not tonight.'' Maybe not ever, she mused. She climbed the stairs and walked into her bedroom, then flopped down on the bed. The remnants of the night before lay scattered on the floor—her little black dress, the sexy underwear. She reached up and skimmed her fingers over the pearls.

With a soft oath, she rolled over on the bed and grabbed the phone. Renee answered her car phone after just one ring. From the background noise, it was clear she was still in her car. "Hi, it's me,'' Roxanne said. "Can you come back and get the kids? I've got to find Kit and talk to him.''

"Four and a half minutes,'' Renee said.

"What?''

"That's how much time it took. Four and a half minutes. I was giving you five before I went home. I'm still parked out front.''

"OUR FIRST QUARTER ad revenue was up five percent from last year. And we've had a nice ratings bump in our early-afternoon programming. Some of Roxanne's listeners are tuning in on Mondays, Wednesdays and Fridays.''

Kit took the report from his father and set it on

the kitchen table, then went over to the refrigerator and pulled out a bottle of water. He took a long drink, then leaned back against the edge of the counter. "So what is this leading up to?"

"I want to offer her a contract for five afternoons a week."

"She has kids," Kit warned. "She probably won't take it."

"We won't know until I offer," Carl said. "With the increased ad revenue, we'll more than pay for her salary. And it's building our core demographic."

"And what if I ask her to marry me?"

"I've been thinking about that since we talked last night. And I don't think it will make a difference. She's still a mother of four and she's still a solid on-air talent. And if I make the offer attractive enough, she'll take it."

"That means I'll be seeing a lot more of her around WBAM," Kit murmured.

"And that's a bad thing?"

"Only if she refuses my proposal of marriage."

"Do you want me to wait?" Carl asked.

Kit shook his head. "No. I'm going to go over there this afternoon to talk to her. I don't like living in limbo."

"Good," Carl said.

The doorbell rang and Kit started toward the

door. "That's the messenger with the bids for the studio renovations in Raleigh."

Carl held up his hand. "I'll get them," he said. "I've got to get back to the station. Thanks for breakfast."

"Just leave the envelope on the hall table," Kit said. "I'm going for a swim. It'll give me time to think."

Kit watched his father walk out, then took another long sip of his water before starting toward the pool house. He didn't bother going upstairs for his trunks. He was alone in the house so he stripped off his clothes, walked around to the deep end and dove in.

Swimming always gave him a good opportunity to think. The repetitive movement, the sound of the water rushing past his ears, the feel of his body skimming over the surface.

He came to the end of the pool and flipped, but caught sight of something out of the corner of his eye. Kit kicked his feet beneath him to tread water, then shook his head. Roxanne stood at the shallow end of the pool, watching him. A surge of desire raced through his body as he thought about what had happened last night. It was quickly followed by guilt. He never should have walked out.

"Hi."

"Hi," she said. "Your dad let me in. He said you'd be back here."

"I was just taking a swim," Kit said.

"I can see that," Roxanne replied, her gaze fixed below the surface of the water.

He smiled. "I was planning to call you when I finished. We need to talk."

"I want you to know that I understand about last night," Roxanne said, her words coming out in a rush.

"I shouldn't have walked out," Kit said. "Fear of commitment might scare a lot of men, but it doesn't scare me. At least, not anymore."

"I was putting too much pressure on you. I know."

"No, it wasn't your fault," Kit said. "It's just that I wasn't really sure that we should be making love. I left because I didn't want you to regret what we were about to do." Kit raked his hand through his wet hair. "I left because I had to find out how my father felt about you. I left because you deserve more from me than one night of lust and passion."

She pressed her palms to her cheeks. "I'm sorry."

Kit swam over to the side of the pool, then pulled himself up and out of the water. He stood in front of her, naked and dripping wet. Then he took her face in his hands and kissed her, slowly and deeply. "I meant what I said last night. I love you. And I'm not afraid of what that means."

"And I love you," Roxanne said. "And I *am* afraid of what that means."

"You never have to be scared of me," he murmured, covering her mouth with his. "I promise, I will never, ever hurt you."

When he drew away, she looked up into his eyes. Then with a tiny smile, she slipped out of her jacket and tossed it on a nearby chair along with her purse. "I could really go for a swim right now."

Kit watched as she took her clothes off in front of him. But this time, he knew there wouldn't be a swimsuit underneath. When she stood in just her bra and panties, he expected her to stop as they had the night before. But Roxanne just smiled and discarded them, as well.

With a giggle, she stepped around him. "I'll race you." She dove into the shallow end, just skimming the surface. He watched her stroke through the water, her naked body slick and smooth. When she reached the other end of the pool she stopped. Stretching her arms out on the edge and kicking her legs, she smiled at him, daring him to come and get her.

He drew a deep breath and slipped beneath the surface, swimming underwater the entire length of the pool. He came up right in front of her, allowing his body to slide along hers. The contact was electric, the water amplifying the sensations, her breasts against his chest, his hips against hers. Kit grabbed her around her waist and held on, bobbing in front of her.

"Now that I have you, what am I going to do with you?"

She smiled, then pushed his head underwater. Caught by surprise, Kit let go of her and when he came up again, she was swimming for the other end of the pool. He caught up with her halfway to the end, grabbing her foot and pulling her down. But she was slippery and wriggled through his arms, a reluctant mermaid.

By the time he reached her, she was waiting. Tired of chasing her around the pool, he grabbed her and pulled her legs around his waist. Then, holding her tightly, he carried her over to the steps at the far corner of the pool. Though she weighed nothing in the water, she weighed next to nothing out. Kit carried her over to a chaise and laid her down, bracing his arms on either side of her head.

He wanted to take his time, to enjoy her the way he had last night, to make her moan with pleasure. But they'd waited long enough.

She grabbed her purse and pulled out a box of condoms.

"You came prepared," Kit murmured with a smile.

"I was optimistic." She tore open the foil package and gently sheathed him, then leaned back and drew him down with her. When she arched against him, he slipped inside of her.

Desire raced through him, heating his blood and

making his pulse pound in his head. As they made love, Kit knew that this time, for the first time, it meant something. The physical pleasure was intense, but with every stroke, he felt the emotional connection to her grow stronger.

He loved Roxanne. He loved the color of her eyes and the scent of her hair, the feel of her flesh beneath his hands and the sound of her voice urging him on. He loved her laugh and her smile and the way she blushed after he kissed her. And he loved her children, as if they were his own.

And as he brought her to her release, then joined her there, Kit knew that no matter how many years they had, it would always be like this, so sweet and so perfect and so simple.

That's what it was to love Roxanne.

"COME ON, KIDS!" Roxanne shouted. "Get down here. Kit is going to pick us up for the zoo soon. You need to find your shoes. And it's windy, so everyone has to wear a hat."

She smiled to herself. Shoes. How much of her day was spent searching for shoes? Like socks, they always seemed to separate themselves. She walked over to the living room sofa where Jenna was sitting. The toddler held out a sock and as Roxanne took it from her, she realized it didn't belong to one of the children. It belonged to Kit.

Roxanne fingered the soft wool and smiled. Such a simple domestic chore, picking up his socks. But there was a time when she thought she'd never have that responsibility again, that she'd spend the rest of her life as a single parent. Now she had a partner. Although they hadn't discussed marriage, Roxanne knew that their relationship was serious. Kit had become part of the family. They hadn't spent a day apart in an entire month. She and the kids had all come to depend upon him.

Still, he didn't spend the night. Roxanne had been adamant about that, unwilling to confuse the children with questions about the relationship. So they found the occasional afternoon or evening when Renee offered to take the children or they'd lock themselves in Kit's office at the station. Once a week, the baby-sitter Roxanne had hired to take care of the kids while she worked at the station would stay late and they'd go out for dinner.

Though having a sex life was complicated, that made it all the more exciting and passionate. She was in love with a wonderful man and Roxanne wasn't about to ask for anything more.

The doorbell rang and she walked over and pulled it open. Kit stood on the porch, a huge box in his arms.

"What have you bought them now?" Roxanne said.

"Just a little present. Come on, Mommy, don't be such a stick in the mud."

"A little present? You spoil them. You have to stop this."

"This is the last present for a while, I promise."

"Wow! What's in the box?"

Kit grinned as Danny, Rachel and Michael came thundering down the stairs. "It's a present." He set the box down and Danny pulled off the huge bow. Then Rachel opened the top.

"A puppy!" she screamed.

Roxanne gasped. "A what?"

"Look, Mommy, it's a puppy. Kit brought us a puppy." Danny reached into the box and withdrew a wiggling cocker spaniel pup. He gave it a kiss then set the little dog on the floor and Roxanne knew the puppy wasn't ever going to leave the house.

"May I speak to you?" she said, sending Kit a look that made her feelings perfectly clear. "In the kitchen, please?"

When he joined her there, she turned on him. "How could you do this without talking to me? We can't have a dog. We live in a busy neighborhood in a house that has a yard the size of a postage stamp."

"Dogs are easy," Kit said.

"Do you know how much work a dog takes? You have to feed it and walk it and the vet bills can be horrible."

"The kids can help take care of the dog. It will teach them responsibility."

"They had a goldfish once. It went belly-up."

He reached into his jacket pocket and pulled out a small box, then placed it on the counter next to her. "I gave the kids a dog. I figured I'd better bring you a present, too."

Roxanne snatched up the box. "A present for me is not going to make up for the dog."

"Just open the box," Kit said.

Roxanne did as she was told, fishing through the tissue paper. She pulled out a key ring with two keys dangling from it. "What's this? You didn't buy me a car, did you?"

"Those are keys to my house," he said. "I want you and kids to move in. That way the dog will have a yard. So will the kids. I live in a nice neighborhood with good schools. And parks."

She stared at the gift for a long moment, knowing she'd have to refuse. But as she put the keys back into the box, the light caught something on the ring and she froze. Slowly, she held the key ring up. A diamond ring hung between the two keys. With a soft sigh, Roxanne looked over at Kit.

"Marry me?" he asked.

She bit her bottom lip to keep it from trembling as she tried to get the diamond off the key ring. But her hands were shaking and Kit finally had to take it from her. When he had the diamond in his fingers, he took her hand.

"Say yes," he said, "and I'll spend the rest of my life loving you and taking care of your children."

"Yes," she said, her voice barely a whisper. He slid the ring onto her finger. "Yes, yes, yes." With a tiny cry, she wrapped her arms around his neck and hugged him hard. "I love you, Kit."

"And I love you, Rox."

Danny appeared in the doorway and Roxanne smiled at him through her tears. "Are you crying, Mommy? Do you need to go in the closet?"

Roxanne laughed. "No, sweetie, I don't need to go in the closet. I'm crying because I'm happy."

Her son smiled weakly. "You're not gonna be happy anymore. The puppy just pooped on the floor."

Kit groaned, then picked Roxanne up off her feet and spun her around. "I'll clean it up," he said.

"No, we'll clean it up."

He set her back on her feet then bent close and brushed a kiss on her lips. "There is some other bad news, besides the puppy poop," he said.

"What? You have a pet elephant waiting out in the car?"

He cupped her cheek with his hand and grinned down at her. "No, my dad signed on to the *Family Voyager* Web site. You didn't win the contest. There won't be any trip to Paris or any shopping spree." He reached into his pocket and pulled out a stack of airline tickets. "So here's the plan. I figured we'd fly everyone to Disney World for a vacation. I've got tickets for your parents. I think it's about time they met the man who's in love with their daughter. And there are tickets for Renee and her family, too. And sometime during the vacation, we can get married.''

Roxanne gasped, amazed at all he'd done. "The kids would love that." She paused. "But where are the tickets for us?"

"I thought we'd drive," Kit said. "I'd like to spend some time with my new family."

Roxanne sent him a dubious look. "Have you ever spent twelve hours in a car with four children? They all have to go to the bathroom at different times. Every time you pass a place to eat, they start whining about how hungry they are, and I can't tell you how many times I've had to stop and retrieve a shoe or a book or a hat that mysteriously found its way out the window and into the middle of the highway."

"I guess you've got a lot to teach me about kids," he teased.

"I guess I do," Roxanne replied.

Kit pulled her into his embrace and hugged her. "I've got plenty of time, too," he said. "We've got the rest of our lives."

DADDY COME LATELY

Jacqueline Diamond

PROLOGUE

Remember back in high school when you read *The Odyssey*? Remember Penelope, the woman who got stuck at home while everyone else went off having adventures? Remember the suitors besieging her to get their hands on her property?

Well, that's kind of my situation.

Don't get me wrong. I love my ranch, the Wandering I. Since I inherited it last year, though, I've learned what a big job it is running a spread like this, even compared to teaching second grade, which is what I did before.

Then there are the guys. In high school, I was a wallflower, so it's nice to have admirers, if that's what they are. The problem is, none of them noticed me before I became a property owner. Now they keep popping up under my nose, telling me that my four-year-old twins need a daddy.

Sometimes I'm tempted to marry one of these guys just to get a break from the others. Then I read about *Family Voyager*'s wonderful contest, with the first prize a trip to Paris for me and my kids. It sounds like a dream come true!

My little guys, Benjamin and Jeremy, have never been outside Texas. The farthest I ever got was to Santa Fe for the Indian Days festival. I'd sell my freckles for a chance to inhale fresh bread from a bakery instead of smelling cattle all day and to dine at the Eiffel Tower instead of flipping hamburgers on the barbecue.

If anyone needs a trip to Paris, it's definitely me!

CHAPTER ONE

CALLUM FOX shoved back a rebellious hank of silver-blond hair and stared in disbelief at the e-mail on his computer screen. When had Jody Reilly had twin sons? How could her parents have died and left her the ranch without his hearing about it? And who said she'd been a wallflower in high school?

The publisher of *Family Voyager* stared into space, ignoring the manuscripts, galleys and photos scattered across his broad desk. The plush office and framed magazine covers on the walls faded from his mind.

He was back in high school, suffering from a crush on a laughing minx with flyaway reddish-brown hair. Even as a teenager, Callum had been in a hurry to set the world on fire. He hadn't expected to fall for a high-spirited, slightly chubby girl whose aims in life were to teach elementary school and have lots of kids.

Despite their incompatible goals, he and Jody had had a lot of fun. They'd performed together in the school band and hung out after school and during college before heading their separate ways.

Five years ago, when Callum returned to the small town of Everett Landing to settle his parents' estate after his father's death, they'd spent a night of lovemaking that still made his chest tighten and his hands grow damp whenever he thought about it. He'd invited Jody to move to L.A., but she'd turned him down. End of story.

Through the open door of his office marched the managing editor, Tisa Powell, her high heels soundless on the plush carpet. A tall, slender African-American woman with a sense of style as well honed as Callum's, she moved with energy and purpose. At twenty-eight, she was only a year younger than he was and equally ambitious.

"We've got a problem." Tisa stood with hands on hips. "Have you checked out our Web site today?"

"As a matter of fact, no." Usually that was the first thing Callum did each morning. He'd launched *Family Voyager* on the Internet half a dozen years earlier. Its runaway success, boosted by features on celebrity families and his knack for spotting new trends in travel, had enabled him to move into glossy print two years before. The magazine still maintained a dynamic presence online as well.

"I thought the senior staff was going to pick the finalists in the contest," Tisa said.

"That's right." The Mother of the Year contest,

sponsored by the magazine and several major advertisers, had been Callum's brainchild. The grand prize was a trip for two to Paris and a shopping spree for the most deserving woman.

"Then why…"

Too impatient to wait for her to finish the sentence, he said, "I asked Al to winnow the entries down to a manageable number for us to review." Al Johnson, the advertising director, had seemed like a suitable person to filter through the barrage of essays that had poured in through the Web site and the mail. "I sent them to his office last week. He's not actually picking the finalists, though. In fact, I was just reading some of the entries myself."

"Al's been out since Monday with a strained back," Tisa said. "Somebody winnowed them, all right. The names of ten finalists were posted on the site this morning."

"What?" A few clicks on the computer brought Callum to a page flashing the words: "Contest Finalists! One of These Ten Moms Will Win a Trip to Paris!"

He scanned the finalists' names and thumbnail descriptions with a sinking sensation. Some of the ladies were exactly the type of person he'd had in mind, including the mother of quadruplets. He had to admit, the choices looked interesting, including both married and single women.

But why, oh why, had someone selected Jody? There was an obvious conflict of interest for Callum, since the two shared the same hometown, although whoever had pulled this stunt couldn't have known that there was an even stronger bond between them.

Uh-oh. There was a second finalist from his hometown, as well, a restaurant owner whose children had grown up and moved away. According to her entry, she wanted to take her pet cat to Paris.

"This is inexcusable!" Mentally, Callum searched through the staff roster, trying to divine which of his employees might hate him, because the situation reeked of sabotage. Yet he hadn't fired or demoted anyone. In fact, he'd given them all a large bonus a few months ago at Christmas.

"You realize that we're stuck," Tisa said. "If we disfranchise any of these ladies, they could slap us with a lawsuit."

"Did I insult someone at a staff meeting?" Callum asked. "I know I speak without thinking sometimes."

"That's because you've got so many ideas, you can't keep them all inside." The editor smiled fondly. "Nobody's mad at you."

"Then who's behind this?"

"Let's go down to David's office and find out."

David Renault, the Web master, apologized profusely when he learned of the problem. "The advertising department e-mailed them to me,'' he said. "I thought they'd been approved.'' He uttered a string of colorful curses. "I had no idea. I feel terrible.''

After reassuring David that it wasn't his fault, he and Tisa trooped to Al's office, which was only slightly smaller than Callum's and had an even better view of the Los Angeles skyline. He'd been out all week, the secretary confirmed.

"I've been covering for him,'' chirped the young woman, whose nameplate read Sally Sinclair. Although she must be in her twenties, to Callum she seemed about eighteen. "Don't you just love the finalists? I tried to pick people our readers would identify with. I put my own stamp on the contest, don't you think? My mother says that's what I need to do to get ahead in publishing, to put my own stamp on things.''

"*You* picked the finalists?'' Tisa asked in disbelief.

"I was showing initiative.'' Sally's cheerful confidence began to crumble. "Wasn't I supposed to?''

"I asked Al to narrow down the entries, not choose the finalists and post them on the Web site,'' Callum said. "Do you have any idea what a disaster this is?''

The secretary's lips trembled and tears sparkled in her eyes. It was enough to melt a man's heart.

Not a woman's, though. "You are not the editor of this magazine. I am," Tisa growled. "And Callum is the publisher. If you ever again presume to 'put your stamp' on anything without our approval, you can haul your initiative right out that door and pound the pavement with it."

"I'm sorry." Sally's contrition might have been more impressive had she not added, "But aren't they wonderful? I especially like that woman with the cat! And I chose two finalists from your hometown, Mr. Fox! I thought you'd appreciate that."

The next thing Callum knew, Tisa had grabbed the collar of his designer jacket and tugged him into the corridor. "You had steam coming out of your ears," she told him. "We'll let Al deal with that twit when he gets back."

Callum spared another glance at the door to the advertising department before accepting her advice. "We've got to run damage control," he said.

"Maybe we could add a few more finalists," Tisa suggested. "So we have more to choose from."

"That might only complicate matters." They were pushing a tight deadline. The winner had to be posted on the site by the end of May, and it was already March. A write-up about her and her trip would provide a future cover story for the print edition of *Family Voyager*. "I'm sure we can find a suitable Mother of the Year from that list."

"*Not* the woman with the cat." Tisa accompanied him down the hallway. "Some people may consider pets part of the family, but I doubt our advertisers do."

"The readers will get a charge out of her, though." Already Callum's brain was making the best of things.

There was, however, one issue that he couldn't erase from his mind: Jody Reilly and her boys. One sentence about the suitors stuck with him: *They keep popping up under my nose, telling me that my four-year-old twins need a daddy.*

If Jody wasn't married, who was the father?

The timing looked suspicious. Five years ago, Callum and Jody had steamed up the windows of her bedroom. She'd amazed him with her unrestrained passion and he'd amazed himself with an all-night response that, he suspected, could have stretched much, much longer.

Was it possible she'd become pregnant from their encounter? Despite Jody's fiercely independent nature, Callum couldn't picture her keeping such a secret. Besides, he'd used protection when they made love. Well, the first time, anyway. After that, he didn't remember.

No doubt she'd had plenty of other boyfriends before and since. In fact, during the days after the funeral when she helped him prepare his family's old home for sale, he seemed to recall her mentioning that she'd recently broken up with someone. Perhaps they'd gotten back together later.

"Anyway, I'd make a lousy father," he said aloud.

"What?" Tisa stopped outside the traffic department, the organizational arm of the magazine.

"Something just started me thinking," he explained. "It's a good thing I'm not a father, because I'd be lousy at it."

"Oh, I don't know," she said. "I'll bet lots of ladies think you've got potential."

"You know what I'm like on Take Your Kid to Work Day," Callum said. "That's the only day of the year when I shut my door."

"You and me both."

"I have no patience. I don't even know how to talk to children." Seeing the managing editor frown in confusion, he said, "Never mind. The problem is, we've got to get the women from my hometown to withdraw their applications."

"I thought you said the readers would love the one with the cat," Tisa said.

"Yeah, I did. But the other one..." Callum decided to be frank, because he didn't know how to be anything else. "She's my ex-girlfriend."

"I see." A smile played around the corners of Tisa's mouth. "Around here, she'd have to stand in line."

"Appearances can be deceiving." Although

Callum's picture frequently appeared in print as he escorted models and actresses around L.A., mostly it was a mutually convenient setup in which the women landed a suitable escort while he made contacts for *Family Voyager*. It was true that some women had pursued him and a few times he'd pursued them, but there'd always been something missing. "Jody was the only one who counted."

"I can see why there's a conflict of interest," Tisa said.

"Even if I disqualify myself from the selection process, there'd be the appearance of unfairness," Callum said.

"You should call her and offer her an inducement to drop out," Tisa said. "She might prefer a guaranteed trip to a one-in-ten chance at the grand prize. How about a stay at the Paris hotel in Las Vegas?"

At the mention of Vegas, an imaginary slot machine whirred into Callum's head. A ticket pinged into place, followed by a second and then a third. They weren't tickets to Nevada, though. They were tickets to Texas, and they were for him.

"I'm going to have to do this in person," he said. Even though there was only the slightest chance that those boys belonged to him, it wasn't the sort of situation he wanted to discuss long-distance.

"Now? There's so much going on."

"I'll take my laptop and my modem," he said. "Trust me, I'll be completely plugged in."

"This isn't like you," Tisa said.

"I'm always jumping on planes," Callum corrected. "I'll fly into the airport at San Angelo, hook up with a rental car and maybe scout some stories along the way. You know how I hate to waste time."

"So it's a working vacation?" The editor shrugged. "You're the boss. Just don't stay away long."

"Do I ever?" It was a rhetorical question, but Tisa replied anyway.

"I hope not," she said. "I'm good at my job, but we all need you."

"Thanks." The vote of confidence buoyed Callum.

The trip might not be so bad. The boys' father would turn out to be lurking in the background, Jody was going to jump at the chance of a guaranteed trip to Vegas and Callum would be back in L.A. before he knew it.

"I KNOW ADOPTION CAN WORK. Give it a chance, Elsie." Jody called all her cows Elsie on those occasions when she addressed them directly.

Elsie stood glumly in her stall, trying to ignore the calf pulling at her udder. The baby, called Half-Pint like all calves on the Wandering I, had been one of a pair whose mother didn't have enough milk for two. Since Elsie had lost her own spring calf, Jody had decided to pair her off with Half-Pint.

Jody had a strong sympathy for babies and mothers. According to her forewoman, Gladys, it should take about two weeks for Elsie to bond.

"You'll thank me for this," Jody told the cow. "On the other hand, maybe you'll turn out to be as stubborn as I am. Lots of people gave me advice, but did I take it? No. And I'm glad I didn't."

The prevailing sentiment in town had been that Jody Reilly was out of her mind to keep the twins. It had been tough enough standing up to the censure of those people who wanted to fire her from her teaching job for having loose morals.

Complicating matters had been her refusal to name the father. Some people had suspected her ex-boyfriend, Jim, a fellow teacher who, after he and Jody drifted apart, had decided to join the Peace Corps. Others suspected a blond cowboy who'd visited the school when he was in town with a traveling rodeo. In fact, Jody had discreetly spread a rumor about him herself. As far as she was concerned, she had a right to keep her personal business private.

Despite the gossip, she'd slowly put her life in order. Her mother had volunteered to baby-sit while Jody worked. Restaurant owner Ella Mae

Nickerson had trumpeted the fact that many of the town's other children had been born less than nine months after their parents' weddings. Tongues had fallen silent after she threatened to post a list in her café window.

Four years later, the kids fit seamlessly among the youngsters at Sunday school. The same people who'd scowled at first now joked about the fact that she'd named the pair after their grandfathers without realizing that, together, Ben and Jerry could open their own ice-cream stand.

Leaving Elsie and Half-Pint in the stall, Jody strolled through the barn to a normally unused stall from which came the sound of barking. On this rainy Saturday, the boys were amusing themselves by playing with a mongrel puppy that had wandered onto the ranch a few days earlier, most likely abandoned on the highway. Jody always did her best to find homes for strays.

"Can we keep him, Mommy?" asked Benjamin. "We're going to call him Lassie."

"Lassie is a female name," Jody said. "Besides, we've already got enough dogs."

"They're always working," Jeremy piped up.

"If Lassie sticks around, he'll have to work, too." Animals, like people, had to earn their keep on a ranch.

"We'll take good care of him!" That was Benjamin.

"Children need pets," added his brother. "It says so on TV."

"Does it? Well, I'm not making any promises. Where's Louise?" Gladys's daughter had been baby-sitting the pair.

"She's getting us a drink." There was a refrigerator in the tack room for storing animal medicines and cold drinks.

"Well, great." Jody leaned down and ruffled the two blond heads. Despite being twins, the pair had distinct personalities. Jeremy was stubborn like her, and Ben a smooth talker like his father.

Oh, darn. She didn't want to think about Callum Fox. For a long time, she'd pushed him out of her thoughts, but entering the *Family Voyager* contest had reawakened memories and longings. Maybe it hadn't been such a good idea, although she doubted the publisher of such a fancy magazine would read the entries himself.

She'd been surprised yesterday when Ella Mae called to report that they were both finalists. That proved Callum hadn't done the picking, because Jody knew he never would have chosen two people from his hometown.

He probably didn't give his old friends a moment's thought. Judging by the photos she'd seen of him and his many girlfriends in *People* and *Us,* his social life rivaled that of a prize bull. No wonder he hadn't even bothered to show up for their tenth high school reunion last year.

Her heart was safe enough. Safe from everything except her daydreams of a man with a smile to die for and a lean body that drove her crazy, even in memory.

From outside the barn, Jody heard the swish of tires on the muddy driveway. She hoped it wasn't one of her would-be boyfriends, racing over after the morning's downpour to make sure her ranch hadn't washed away. Although she always needed help, sometimes she could hardly bear to look at eager men, none of whom were the one she wanted.

She'd loved Callum enough to let him go. Sure, she'd hoped he would come back, but she'd understood five years ago that having to take responsibility for a wife and children would destroy his dreams. He'd just been getting his magazine started and had been working a part-time job to make ends meet while he poured his energies into *Family Voyager*.

If he'd married her with two kids on the way, he'd have had to work full-time. The magazine would have lost its window of opportunity. By the time Callum came up for air, someone else would have seized the chance he'd let slip.

Although she sometimes wondered if she'd been a fool, Jody was glad she'd avoided a marriage that, under the circumstances, would have made them both miserable. She just hoped Callum would understand if he ever found out the truth.

Shrugging off her reflections, she stepped through the barn's double doors and blinked as a shaft of sunlight broke through the parting clouds. Who on earth could be driving that aging boat of a convertible with the top jammed half-open?

The light must have dazzled her, because she could have sworn the man parking in front of the big house had Callum's shaggy good looks. He bore little resemblance to his glitzy photographs, however, with his silver-blond hair hanging wetly and his clothes plastered to his body.

Jody's pulse speeded. This wasn't possible. Yet—being ruthlessly honest with herself—she'd known there was a chance he might read her essay and wonder about the twins. Was that why he'd come? Suddenly she wished she'd never entered the darned contest.

Feigning nonchalance, she strolled toward the car. Not yet aware of her, Callum got out and surveyed its sopping interior ruefully.

No other man could match him for broad shoulders and slim hips, or for the expressiveness of his sharply defined face. Jody remembered how he'd moved when he was on top of her, and beneath her, and most especially inside her. To her dismay, her body rippled with the memory.

"You forgot to put the top up!" she called.

"Jody!" Bright blue eyes fixed on her and she felt the connection crackle between them. "You look great!"

Self-consciously, she tucked her frizzy hair behind her ears. It was like trying to empty the *Titanic* with a teaspoon. "Oh, yeah? Says who?"

"Says me, and I should know." With a couple of long strides, Callum reached her. "Don't I get a hug?"

Jody nearly succumbed the moment she entered his arms. He smelled like expensive indulgences and honest maleness. No, no, no. She needed to keep a protective distance between them.

"So what brings you here?" she asked, extricating herself.

"A couple of things," he said. "Hey, did I get you wet? I'm sorry. I should have reserved a car farther in advance. This was all they had. The roof doesn't work, obviously. Would you look at me?"

Callum's grin carried her back to their teen years, when he'd swept her off her feet by the open way he laughed at her jokes. He'd been irresistible. He still was.

"Come inside and dry off. You look like you could use some coffee."

"Thanks. I'd appreciate it." If he had any curiosity about the children, he gave no sign of it. He didn't even look around for them.

Most likely, Callum was heading somewhere else, Jody mused as they walked. He would dry off, chitchat for a few minutes and be on his way quickly. She quashed a sharp pang of disappointment. It was what she wanted, wasn't it?

"Do you have some business in town?" she asked.

"You're my business," he said.

Taken aback by this statement, Jody hesitated with one foot on the front porch. "Are you visiting all the finalists personally?"

"No," Callum admitted. "It's kind of a complicated situation."

"Complicated how?"

"There was a mix-up."

"What kind of mix-up?"

"The finalists' names were posted without approval." He bounded onto the porch with a litheness she'd missed more than she wanted to admit. "In fact, they got picked by an overenthusiastic secretary."

In spite of her resolve not to let him get close, Jody's spirits took a dive. He hadn't come here for any personal reason. He'd been driven purely by pragmatism.

"So she picked your old pal as a finalist and it looks bad," she hazarded. "You want me to withdraw, right?"

"More or less." Quickly, he added, "Not without compensation, of course. We would guarantee you a trip to Las Vegas.''

From what she'd heard, Vegas could be a lot of fun, particularly if you scored tickets to the top shows. It wasn't Paris, though. Paris was a fantasy, a dream of shrugging off the little disappointments and obligations that sometimes weighed on her spirit. It meant one last, glorious chance to fly.

All her life, Jody had been a good sport and the sporting thing to do right now was to cooperate. But she didn't feel sporting. She felt determined.

Five years ago, Callum had made such tender, passionate love to her that he'd nearly spoiled Jody for any other man. Then, after she turned down his offhand suggestion that she pull up stakes and run away to California with him, he'd left without a backward glance.

The only reason he'd returned now was because she'd accidentally created an awkward situation for him. He expected her to give up the chance of a lifetime just as a favor? Not likely.

If she signed on the dotted line, he'd smile, thank her, slosh back to his pathetic rental car and drive out of her life forever. Although that was what she wanted, Jody refused to let him off the hook.

''Forget it,'' she said. ''I'm a finalist because I deserve to be one. I want that trip to Paris and that shopping spree. I'm going to enjoy buying some pretty dresses on my trip and, once I get home, I'll hang them on the walls and enjoy the sight of them forever.''

She caught her breath, taken aback by her own defiance. Surely Callum, whose jaw had dropped open at her tirade, would respond with the scorn she'd always secretly suspected he must feel toward the homespun, unglamorous woman who'd briefly been his lover.

''Well, if we can't come to an agreement,'' he said, ''I guess I'll have to bring my suitcases in and stay for a while.'' Before she could stop him, he retrieved two bags from his trunk and walked into the house ahead of her.

The sky had fallen, Jody thought. What was she going to do now?

CHAPTER TWO

CALLUM HADN'T HAD an easy trip. Airport security had searched him right down to his Italian leather shoes, his connecting flight in Dallas had been delayed and the sole vehicle available for rent in San Angelo might have served as a prop in the film *American Graffiti.*

The downpour had added injury to insult. Stymied by a truculent convertible roof, he'd plowed on for miles through rainswept ranchlands, certain that mildew was forming even as he drove and too uncomfortable to scout for potential magazine articles. Thank goodness his suitcase and laptop had been locked inside the trunk.

Callum knew he should have called Jody ahead. She had every reason to be grumpy with him. He didn't blame her for refusing to withdraw from the contest, although he hoped she would change her mind.

Besides, he was glad for the excuse to stick around and get reacquainted with his old friend. He decided not to mention the children yet. For one thing, she would probably laugh him out of the house when she learned he'd imagined even for a moment that he might be the father. Also, it might be a sore point about the real dad—whoever he was—not being her husband.

The guy must be crazy to give up a woman like Jody. Even in her overalls, she had more earthy appeal than most models and actresses, whose bones stuck out.

He and Jody entered the airy house through a sunken living room. Three steps led up to the kitchen and dining area, where she poured coffee from a half-full carafe. Callum set down his cases, tossed his jacket over the back of a chair and went to towel off in the bathroom. He returned a few minutes later, slightly less damp.

"I don't remember your house looking like this when we were in high school." He was certain it had been a conventional ranch-style structure.

"It was falling down. My parents decided to rebuild six years ago." Jody gestured him to a butcher-block table, where he took a seat.

"You said in your essay that you inherited the place last year." Although Callum disliked mentioning what must be a painful subject, he wanted to acknowledge her parents' passing. He'd been fond of the elder Reillys.

"They died in a car crash on their way to a stock show in San Antonio." She offered cream and sugar.

"I'm sorry." After helping himself, Callum savored the chicory-laced brew, although his usual taste ran to mocha lattes. "So you gave up teaching?"

"It was that or sell the ranch. I couldn't do both." Jody went on to tell him about her forewoman, Gladys, and how well they worked together.

As Jody talked, he cataloged the small changes since they'd last met. She'd acquired a rancher's tan even this early in the season, and she held herself with a new maturity.

Beneath it all, however, she was the same breezy girl who'd played trumpet alongside him in the high school band. She'd nearly blown his socks off, literally, when she stumbled while marching during their first rehearsal and sent a blast of air along his pant leg. They'd both laughed so hard they had to sit down on the football field. Although the coach wasn't amused, Callum had been smitten.

He'd loved her honesty and valued her advice. And he'd missed her keenly, more than he'd allowed himself to acknowledge until now.

"Where on earth did you get the idea that you were a wallflower?" he asked.

She stopped in midsentence and he realized he'd interrupted a description of how she was learning to clean and oil the farm machinery. "What?"

"In your essay, you said you were a wallflower in high school," he said. "That's not true. Lots of boys had crushes on you."

Jody let out a hoot. "Name three!"

"Me, me and me."

"You're kidding." She studied him as if seeking confirmation that this was a joke. "Come on, Callum, all the girls wanted you. I was your buddy."

"You were my girlfriend," he said.

"I was not! When did we ever go on a date?"

"We went to the prom," he reminded her.

"You took pity on me. I said I didn't have anyone to go with and you said, 'How about me?'" Jody's forehead puckered. "Besides, you couldn't wait to get out of town. You were just marking time, hanging around with me."

"That's not true. We went together all through college." They'd both graduated from the University of Texas at Austin. "We dated for four years."

"Study dates don't count," she said. "When did you ask me out for a romantic dinner?"

"You'd have laughed in my face." Callum's pride wouldn't let him mention that he'd lacked money for such luxuries. The son of a feed store owner, he'd had to work his way through college and pay off student loans afterward.

"You should have tried me."

"Okay, I'll try you now," he said. "May I take you out for fine dining and dancing, Madame?"

"Where? At the Downtown Café?" It was the fanciest restaurant in Everett Landing. That's because it was the only restaurant.

"Just a minute." Callum checked his watch. "It's nearly five. People eat early in the country, don't they?"

"Oh! That reminds me. I've got to start cooking."

"Don't move. Tonight you're dining at Il Ristorante Callum, the finest Italian trattoria in Everett County." Ignoring her halfhearted protest, he whirled into action.

As he'd expected, Jody kept her kitchen well stocked. In no time, he'd put a large pot of water on a burner, retrieved spaghetti and sauce ingredients from the pantry and set to whipping up dinner.

A man of the world knew how to cook and cook well, Callum had concluded long ago. With the food editor at *Family Voyager* contributing to his education, he'd honed his skills. Thanks to his interest, the magazine now included recipes with its feature stories on restaurants.

Jody watched with her chin resting on the heel of one hand. "I never thought of putting black olives in my spaghetti sauce."

"Wait'll you taste it." The tomato mixture simmered, filling the air with the scents of basil, thyme and oregano. The salad, into which he'd tossed artichoke hearts and diced cucumber, stood ready on the counter. Careful not to break the strands of spaghetti, Callum stirred some into the boiling water.

With dinner under control, he skimmed down the abbreviated staircase to the living room and flipped through Jody's CD collection. Once he bypassed the *Sesame Street* stuff and some old-time country classics that must have belonged to her parents, there wasn't much left.

One label caught Callum's eye and he extracted the jewel case. "Would you look at this! *Everett County Regional High School Marching Band's Greatest Hits.* What a long title. And since when did we have any hits?"

"It was a fund-raiser," she said. "Remember? It came out the summer we graduated."

"How were sales?" He hadn't kept track, but he suspected Jody had.

"We made enough to buy the band new uniforms."

"Outstanding!" Callum put the CD into play. "I wonder if we can dance to it."

"I'm not even going to ask if you're kidding, because you're crazy enough to mean it," Jody said. "So tell me. How does one dance to a march?"

"By doing what the band director accused us of doing all along." He pulled her to her feet. "Ignoring the rhythm and just going with our instincts."

Laughter bubbled out of Jody as Callum drew her close. Small but lushly built, she flung her arms around his neck the way she used to in high school.

As they swayed together, ignoring the occasional flat blat of a trombone and the rousing beat suitable for a football halftime, Callum felt her breasts press into his chest. Through his shirt, he noticed the tips harden. Just like in the old days, his body sprang to full attention.

He buried his face in her hair and relished the fresh scent of hay. Let the pasta turn to goo and the salad wilt. He only had an appetite for the woman in his arms.

JODY HAD ALMOST FORGOTTEN how much fun Callum could be. He filled her house with a sense of magical adventure.

"This is better than a trip to Paris." Quickly, she added, "Almost."

"How would you know?" he murmured into her ear. "You've never been farther than Santa Fe."

"You read my whole entry?"

"All two hundred and fifty words of it."

"Tell me about France," she said. "You've been there, haven't you?"

"Several times." Judging by the lilt in his voice, Callum had found something new and wonderful every time he'd visited. "The whole city comes alive from early morning until late at night. The streets smell like fresh-baked bread. In the sidewalk cafés, people debate issues as if they held the fate of the world in their hands."

"I can't wait!"

"After Paris, we should go to Rome," he murmured, as if they were really planning to travel together. "We could dine beside the Spanish Steps and dance at a smoky little club I know. What else would you like to see? Venice? Sorrento? Perhaps Granada. There's a beautiful city."

He'd visited all those places, Jody thought dazedly. She could have gone with him if she'd accepted his offer five years ago to accompany him back to L.A. And, of course, if she hadn't been pregnant. But even if he'd somehow managed to keep the magazine going while supporting a family, their relationship would never have lasted. Kids apparently didn't mean much to Callum. He hadn't even asked about hers.

Speaking of the boys, it was time they came in for dinner. Reluctantly, Jody separated from Callum. "I have to go get Ben and Jerry."

"Great! I love ice cream."

"No, my children." From beyond the kitchen, she heard the side door slam. The boys still hadn't learned to close a door quietly. "Oh, there they are."

She hurried through the kitchen. In the hall, she found her two little guys wriggling out of their jackets. Despite traces of dirt on their jeans and shirts, both had shining clean faces and hands.

"Louise made us wash at the pump," Ben said.

"There's someone I'd like you to meet." Jody took a deep breath. Her decision not to notify Callum about her pregnancy had seemed the best choice at the time for both of them. She'd had second thoughts, third thoughts and fourth thoughts as she watched the boys grow up without a father, but until last year their grandfather had done his best to fill that role.

She had no idea how Callum might react when he learned the truth. Had it even occurred to him on reading her essay that the boys might be his? If so, he'd given no indication of it since his arrival. But then, he hadn't seen Benjamin and Jeremy yet.

It was too late to turn back now. At some level, she'd been hoping for, and dreading, this moment ever since she entered the contest.

Gathering her courage, Jody shepherded her sons into the kitchen. Callum stood in profile, draining the pasta into a colander.

Although he'd stopped the music, he was humming to himself and his hips swiveled as if he were dancing. Like the twins, he was never completely still except when sleeping. And not always then, as Jody had reason to know.

"Wow," Ben said. "He looks like us."

The tall man glanced up, his gaze riveted on the boys' hair. Silver-blond, it was identical to his own.

A stubborn streak inside Jody urged her to deny the obvious. If she made up some plausible story about a long-vanished blond lover, she knew Callum would believe it because he trusted her. He would never discover how intrinsically his life had become interwoven with hers. Maybe, just maybe, she'd escape from this encounter with her self-control intact.

She couldn't do it. Fibbing to nosy townspeople was one thing. Lying to the man she loved would be intolerable.

"Mine?" He mouthed the word as if unable to speak aloud.

Jody nodded. "Callum, meet Benjamin and Jeremy." She pointed to each in turn. Since Ben preferred red shirts and Jerry's favorite color was blue, he should have no trouble keeping them straight.

Callum stood there staring at them. For once, he'd lost his aplomb.

"Who's he?" Jerry demanded. "Why is he wearing our hair?"

Approaching the newcomer, Ben reached up boldly. With a bemused smile, Callum bent so the boy could finger his stylish cut. "It feels soft," the boy said.

Tentatively, Callum rested one palm atop the boy's head. "So is yours." He turned to Jody, his expression that of a man lost in a wilderness. A bright and shining wilderness, perhaps, but one with no known pathways. "What do we do now?" he asked.

"I'd suggest we eat dinner." She waited tensely. Callum wasn't the sort of man to explode at her in front of the boys. In fact, she couldn't recall him ever losing his temper, although he did get a bit edgy sometimes. But he had every right to be angry.

Although four years ago she'd believed she was doing the right thing, she could see now that she'd been protecting herself as much as him. And it hadn't been fair to the boys. The older they grew, the plainer that had become.

Callum pulled himself together. "I hope you guys like spaghetti," he said.

"It's my favorite!" When Ben grinned, he looked like an exact miniature of his father. *His father.* A lump formed in Jody's throat.

"I like mine plain." Jerry planted himself firmly next to Jody.

"How plain?"

"No sauce," the boy said. "Just cheese."

Galvanized into action, Callum transferred the pasta to a glazed bowl and poured the tomato sauce into a separate container. "I'll tell you what. We'll serve the sauce on the side and you can suit yourselves. Do they eat salad?"

"Surprisingly, yes." Jody wasn't sure how she'd been lucky enough to get children who liked vegetables. "As long as it has ranch dressing."

They gathered around the table. Callum and the boys bowed their heads while Jody said a prayer, and she was pleased to see her sons minding their manners as they ate. That didn't prevent a fair amount of tomato sauce from spattering across Ben's shirt, but since it was already bound for the laundry, she didn't care.

As the twins chattered about the new puppy, Callum stared from one boy to the other, wearing a puzzled half smile. Jody admired the way he'd kept his poise after being hit with a revelation that would have sent many men into either a towering rage or a mad scramble for the exit.

"Freddy asked Gladys whose car was in front of the house," Ben said between mouthfuls of salad. "She told him Mommy had a handsome visitor."

"Who's Freddy?" Callum had mastered the art of twirling his pasta smoothly around his fork, while Jody's spaghetti kept slipping off her utensils. Finally she gave up and chopped it into pieces.

"Freddy Fallon is our full-time assistant," she answered. "He lives in the bunkhouse next to Gladys's place, past the machine shop." Because of the unpredictable hours and the distance from town, it was customary for full-time employees to live on the property. "He's one of those fellows I mentioned in my essay."

"One of your admirers?" Callum's jaw jutted forward.

"You could call him that. We went square dancing once." Jody had agreed in hopes of pacifying the man, who'd been tagging after her like a lovesick hound. It hadn't worked.

"He's got a brother," Jerry said. "Frank works on Mr. Widcomb's ranch."

"Frank likes Mommy, too." Ben helped himself to more spaghetti from the bowl, trailing a few strands across the table. When he reached for the sauce, Jody grabbed it first and ladled it onto his plate.

"Who else likes your mommy?" Callum asked.

"Everybody likes Mommy," Jeremy said.

"Mr. Landers from the newspaper brings her flowers," Ben said.

Callum's eyebrows shot up. "Old Mr. Landers? He must be nearly seventy."

"No, his son, Bo," Jody said. "Don't you remember him? He was a year behind us in high school."

"That's right, he worked on the school paper." Callum drummed his fingers on the table. "Skinny kid with braces, wasn't he?"

Bo had improved with age, Jody reflected. Although his gangly lope and gee-whiz style of talking were no match for Callum's smoothness, he was the most interesting single man in Everett Landing, and he clearly cared about her. Sometimes she'd wondered if that might be enough.

"He took over the newspaper after his dad retired," she said. "He's a good friend."

"Who else?" Callum asked.

"Who else what?"

"Who else is after you?" He'd stopped making any effort to eat.

"Mr. Lamont invited Mommy to one of his parties," Ben piped up.

Jody felt her cheeks grow hot. Andy Lamont, a pretentious newcomer from the East Coast who'd sold his high-tech stocks at the right moment, was known for strutting around his ranch in glitzy cowboy gear and throwing wild parties for out-of-town friends. "I didn't go."

"Gladys said it was going to be an or-gee," Jerry added. "What's an or-gee? She wouldn't tell us."

"Who is this guy?" Callum's tone took on a harder edge.

"He's nobody," Jody said. "Believe me."

"An or-gee is a party with lots of food," Jerry said.

"How do you figure that?" she asked, grateful for the distraction.

"People offer you two pies. You go, 'Oh, gee, I can't pick,'" her son explained.

Ben wrinkled his nose. "I'd say, 'Or, gee, I'll have both.'"

Callum's expression mellowed. "I like their style! Speaking of pie, what's for dessert?"

Jody was tempted to deny having any, just to tease, but she couldn't bear to crush the three hopeful looks beaming her way from around the table. "Cookies."

"What kind?" Callum asked.

"Chocolate chip with pecans."

"I've died and gone to heaven."

"This isn't heaven," Jerry said solemnly. "Heaven's where Grandma and Grandpa went." He pointed toward the ceiling.

"You're right." Callum didn't say much after that, letting the boys' chatter eddy around him as they finished dessert. He kept watching them, as if fascinated. Or shell-shocked, perhaps.

Once the pair began yawning, Jody excused herself to bathe them and put them to bed.

"Mommy?" Jeremy asked sleepily as she tucked him into the lower bunk. "Who's Callum?"

She stroked his hair and slipped her free arm around Ben, who nestled beside her. "Remember when you asked me if you had a father, and I said you did but he was far away?" Two tousled heads bobbed in accord. "You asked when he was coming home and I said some daddies don't ever come home."

"Like Joey's," Ben said. A Sunday school friend, Joey lived with his divorced mother and never saw his father.

"Kind of," she agreed. "Well, Callum's your father."

"Really?" Ben said. "That's why he looks like us?"

"That's why," she confirmed.

Both boys started shifting around, as if they couldn't find the words to express themselves and needed to move. Then they pelted her with questions. Why had their daddy been gone so long? Was he going to live here now?

She answered as best she could. "He's here for a visit. Then he's going back to Los Angeles. That's where he works and he has to live there. He's been really, really busy until now. I hope we'll see him more often now, but he can't move to the ranch."

Surely they'd stay in touch, now that Callum knew the truth. At least, she hoped so.

"I like him," Ben told her. "I always wanted a daddy."

"He's okay, I guess," Jerry said. "But we're your little men, aren't we, Mommy?"

"You sure are." She hugged them both. "Forever and ever."

When they were both under the covers, Jody turned out the lights and paced toward the living room. She wasn't looking forward to facing Callum's questions, not one little bit.

CHAPTER THREE

HE WAS A FATHER. It was amazing. Wonderful. Scary.

Alone on the couch, Callum tried to sort out how he felt. His first reaction had been an indescribable thrill as he gazed down at those two little fellows who could have posed for his own childhood photos.

Over the years, Callum had considered it irritating when a friend brought a child to dinner because he spent the meal getting interrupted, peppered with nonsensical questions and kicked in the shins. Yet tonight, he'd enjoyed the boys' liveliness and the twists and turns of their thinking. Was it because they belonged to him? Or were they simply, as he suspected, exceptional human beings?

He wished he'd seen them as babies. Leaning back, he tried in vain to picture the two of them as newborns. His mind just couldn't shoehorn all that alertness and those full-blown personalities into such tiny packages.

Imagining the future proved easier. He could see the three of them rollerblading at the beach, weaving in and out of pedestrian traffic on the promenade. They'd enjoy Disneyland, and when they were older he could take them to the Page Museum to see the prehistoric beasts from the La Brea Tar Pits.

The details of how he and Jody were going to arrange things remained fuzzy. As a father, he knew he ought to take charge of the situation, but he wasn't quite clear yet on what the situation was. Callum decided to play this one by ear.

Even with his eyes closed, he felt Jody's nearness the moment she entered the kitchen from the bedroom wing. When he opened his lids, the air shimmered as she eased into an upholstered chair across from him.

"So how angry are you that I kept them a secret?" she asked. "On a scale from one to ten?"

"I'm not angry." Callum realized it was true. He supposed he ought to feel cheated because he hadn't been here for the twins' infancy. He had no illusions about his own unreadiness for parenthood when he was twenty-four, however. He'd have done his best, but he was honest enough to acknowledge that he might not have been able to provide as much stability as the elder Reillys. "You've done a great job under difficult circumstances."

"Would you have preferred it if I'd gone on

keeping them a secret?'' She twisted her hands together.

''No, of course not.'' He wished she were sitting closer so he could take her hands to reassure her. They were cute hands, with plump fingers and short, clear nails.

She crossed her denim-clad legs. ''They asked about you just now. I explained that not all daddies live with their children and that we might see you occasionally. Was that all right?''

''Of course you'll see me.'' He had no hesitation on that point. ''I'll be paying my share of their expenses, too.''

''We don't need your money!'' She squared her shoulders.

Callum understood about pride. He'd grown up on a tight budget, helping out at his parents' store and earning extra money with odd jobs. ''Maybe not, but I'd like to provide them with extras. Kids grow fast, or so I hear, and there must be a lot they'll need once they start school. Don't forget about college, either.''

''I haven't given it any thought,'' Jody admitted. ''I've been taking life one day at a time since they were born.'' She waved one hand. ''That isn't a criticism.''

''You mean you're not complaining about the fact that I got you pregnant and hijacked the course of your life?''

"You didn't do it on purpose," Jody said. "Besides, I could have told you."

That brought them to the sticking point. "Why didn't you?" Callum asked.

"It would have killed you to come back here and give up your dreams."

He supposed she was right. It wouldn't have had to happen that way, though. "I invited you to California."

"We'd have ended up hating each other," Jody said. "Besides, I don't belong in California."

She belonged there as much as anyone he'd ever met! "Do you think there's a panel of judges that rates people who want to move to the Golden State?" Callum asked in amusement.

"Don't make fun of me!"

"I'm sorry. I didn't mean to." The hurt in her eyes filled him with remorse. "Please tell me why you don't think you'd fit in L.A."

"I'm not glamorous." A narrowing of her eyes warned him not to interrupt. "I neither know nor care what the latest styles are, and neither do my kids. They've got lots of learning opportunities here, and a lot of emotional ties. Besides, I have a responsibility to the ranch."

"Surely your parents never meant to chain you to it," Callum said. "If you want to come with me, you should."

"You're asking me to join you now?"

"Sure." He hadn't known he was going to say that or considered the consequences, but it made sense. Besides, he was a father now. He had responsibilities.

"What happens then?" Jody demanded. "If I go to California, what's our relationship going to be?"

"I haven't thought that far ahead." Flying by the seat of his pants had always been in Callum's nature. If he'd stopped to weigh every possible angle, he might never have launched *Family Voyager.* "We'll work it out. Trust me, Jody. I won't let you down."

Her long hair whipped through the air as she shook her head. "I took charge of my fate five years ago and I'm sticking with what I know. You're a great guy, Callum, but I need someone down to earth, more of a homebody. Like one of the guys I mentioned in my entry."

Wait a minute. She wasn't seriously considering marrying one of those fellows, was she? "I thought they were a pain in the neck."

"Sometimes," Jody admitted. "But people can grow on each other."

"I could be a pain in the neck if that's what appeals to you," he teased.

"You already are!" At least she smiled when she said it.

"You have to give me a chance," Callum said.

"Remember, I just learned I've got two sons. It may take me a while to formulate a plan."

"I don't want anybody making plans for me," Jody answered fiercely. "I'll make my own plans. Now if you don't mind, I've had a long day and I've got some paperwork to do. I'll show you where you can bunk."

He didn't like the sound of that. "You're not sticking me out in the machine shop with Gladys, are you?"

Her laughter flowed around him in a warm current. "Gladys doesn't sleep in the machine shop! She has her own house. And no, I meant you could use the spare bedroom."

After being shown to a small bedroom off the hallway, Callum unpacked his suitcase and set up his laptop. Jody had explained that he would share a bathroom with the boys, while the master bedroom and her office were located off the living room. Although that was too far away for Callum's taste, at least he got to be near his sons.

Fortunately, there was a phone line in the room, which meant he could read his e-mail and hook up with the Internet while talking on his cell phone. Eight o'clock in Texas was six in California. Tisa might still be in her office.

In a few minutes, Callum was immersed in work as if he'd never left.

"WOW. DO YOU HAVE any good games on your computer?" The little boy stood in the doorway, blond hair rumpled, blue eyes wide. His pajamas had cartoon robots printed on them.

Tearing himself away from his editing, Callum searched for a clue to the twin's identity. At dinner, the boys' different-colored shirts had made it easy to tell them apart, but which... Aha! The robots were red.

"There's a few games, Ben, but I use the computer mainly for working," he said. "Aren't you supposed to be sleeping?"

The four-year-old climbed onto Callum's lap as if it were the most natural thing in the world for him to do. "I'm not sleepy."

He closed his file. He'd been working for two hours and deserved a break, anyway. "Let's see what we can find." A few clicks later, a Roman centurion appeared on the screen. "My goodness. Where did he come from?" he joked.

His son felt warm and solid on Callum's lap as he snatched the mouse. "I want to play!"

"Do you know this game?"

"Yeah." The little boy worked the mouse eagerly. Although it soon became apparent that he had no idea of either the rules or the strategy, he had good aim. "Yay! I wiped him out!" he crowed as a hairy Visigoth bit the dust.

"You sure did." It occurred to Callum that Jody might not appreciate his encouraging Ben to commit mayhem. "I think that's enough for one night."

"Okay." His son gave him the mouse.

"Are you always this cooperative?"

"Mostly. Jerry's not." Ben nestled against Callum's chest. "He doesn't like you."

This was news. "Why not?" he asked. "I'm such a likable guy."

A sigh greeted this blatant play for sympathy. "He says he can take care of Mommy. I want a daddy."

Callum wrapped his arms around the boy. He didn't want to make promises, not yet. Having barged into his family's lives without warning, he had no right to try to change everything to suit himself.

Although he hadn't deliberately abandoned them, five years ago he'd been so absorbed in trying to make a go of his Web site that he'd only called Jody once after he got home, and hadn't pressed to make sure she felt all right about what had happened between them. Maybe if he had, she'd have told him the truth. At the very least, he didn't want to upset the delicate balance she'd achieved in his absence.

"You do have a daddy," he told Ben. "I'm him, and from now on I'm going to see you as often as

I can. But my magazine is based in Los Angeles, which is a long ways from here.''

"You can take a plane," said his son.

"You mean commute long-distance? It's a bit far," Callum said.

The child yawned and snuggled closer. "We need a daddy who lives around here."

Callum frowned. "Anyone in particular?"

Ben didn't answer. Apparently he'd fallen asleep between one breath and another.

As Callum carried his son across the hallway and tucked him into the top bunk, his mood darkened. He'd only just discovered that he had a family. He wasn't about to lose them to some Johnny-on-the-spot.

The key was to get rid of those other guys before Jody foolishly married one of them. All he lacked was a plan.

By morning, he intended to come up with one.

JODY AROSE EARLY, downed a bowlful of cereal and went about tending the animals with Freddy's help. Usually Louise came by to fix breakfast and watch the boys, but Jody had given the girl the day off, assuming Callum would want to fill that role.

In their stall, Elsie and Half-Pint had settled into wary mutual toleration, she was pleased to note. At least one relationship was on track around here.

It was several hours later before Jody returned

to the big house. In the play yard, Ben dug in the sandbox while Jerry swung as high as he could on the swing set.

Gladys, taking a break from her own chores, sat on the side patio sharing a cup of coffee with Callum. Designer jeans and a denim jacket highlighted his lithe body and, in the bright sunlight, he seemed to glow from within.

Usually, the forewoman treated male visitors the way she treated stray dogs, with casual tolerance punctuated by the occasional sharp command. It surprised Jody to hear her laughing freely.

Tall, with her light-brown hair pulled into a ponytail, Gladys looked like what she was: a woman who'd grown up on a ranch. The daughter of a foreman, she'd married a man who owned a small spread and treated her little better than a hired hand. When they split up, she'd taken their daughter and set out on her own.

Eight years ago, she'd persuaded Jody's father to hire her as forewoman, despite the scoffing of some neighbors. She'd more than proven them wrong.

Without her, the Wandering I would never have survived the past year. And without her daughter, Louise, who'd graduated from high school early and was taking a correspondence course in medical transcribing, Jody didn't know where she'd have found a baby-sitter for the twins.

She'd phoned Gladys this morning and explained about the boys' father. In her usual low-key manner, the forewoman had accepted the situation with only a few questions. She'd no doubt intended to decide for herself whether she approved of the man. Apparently, she did.

Callum waved when Jody came through the door. "I can heat up some pancakes if you're hungry."

"No, thanks." She poured herself coffee from an insulated pot and leaned against the railing. Even on a Saturday, there was too much work left for her to get comfortable.

"Gladys was telling me about the Curly Q," Callum said. The spread, dubbed a "non-dude ranch," took paying guests who pitched in with the chores. "I think I'll drive over there later and conduct an interview for the magazine, if the owners are willing. I'll take my digital camera."

"I want to get one of those." Turning to Jody, the forewoman explained, "Callum took some shots of the boys earlier and you could see the pictures right inside the camera. You can get rid of the bad ones, and e-mail the good ones to your friends."

"I thought you hated computers," Jody said. Although her friend used one occasionally for ranch business, she avoided them otherwise.

"That doesn't mean I have to act like a mule

about every kind of new technology that comes along,'' Gladys answered.

That was Callum's good influence, Jody thought. Still, she hoped Gladys wasn't going to get too cozy with him, because he'd be gone soon. ''We need to move those steers today. Freddy's going to be tied up seeding a field.''

''Darn right.'' Gladys uncoiled from her chair. ''Callum, I'd love to stay and chat, but duty calls.''

''For me, too,'' he said. ''Jody, if it's all right with you, I'll take the boys with me over to the Curly Q. Gladys gave me directions.''

Although she didn't want the boys getting too used to being around him, Louise needed to put in more hours on her studies. The young woman would always rather tend the livestock or play with the kids than do her assignments, to Gladys's dismay. ''Okay. You can get their booster seats out of the pickup.''

''Thanks for trusting me with them. I know it isn't easy under the circumstances.'' He gazed at her in a way that made Jody want to forget about moving the steers and corral him instead.

''No sweat,'' she managed to say, and turned to follow Gladys.

Callum should find it easy to persuade the Wiltons to grant an interview, since their enterprise would benefit from publicity. Too bad their six-year-old son had school today. He and the twins enjoyed playing together.

All morning as Jody worked, Callum made guest appearances in her thoughts. Whipping up dinner for the boys. Dancing with his arms looped around her. Burying his face in her hair.

She could so easily fall in love with the man again. Heck, she was halfway there already, but she refused to make a fool of herself by running after him to California and getting her heart squashed like a bug on a highway. Life in the fast lane was out of Jody's league and she knew it.

What she needed was that trip to Paris—a few weeks of enchantment, a chance to reawaken the devil-may-care attitude of her younger days. Then she could return to her familiar world and live contentedly without the things she'd loved and lost, like teaching and, above all, Callum.

At noon, when she rode back to the big house, Jody got an unpleasant surprise. She mopped her forehead with a sleeve as she stared at the battered sedan and *Everett Landing Weekly News* van parked in front. There was the tractor Freddy had been using this morning, too. What on earth were all these people doing here?

Not just people. Male friends.

Since she had no intention of greeting visitors in her mussed condition, Jody slipped around to the rear of the house, where she entered her office through its exterior door. The office connected to her bedroom, into which masculine voices drifted from the front. She recognized Bo's, then Freddy's and finally his brother, Frank's. They sounded polite and uncertain.

Callum had gathered her suitors together, omitting only Andy, who didn't count anyway. What colossal nerve! Jody was so steamed at his interference that she nearly stomped into the living room, smelly clothes and all. What steadied her was common sense plus the memory of her mother's admonitions to act like a lady.

Twenty minutes later, damp from the shower, she marched out wearing a long denim skirt and a ruffled blouse. The three men scrambled to their feet. Callum, who was fixing sandwiches in the kitchen, was already standing.

He'd swapped his jeans and jacket for a silky dark-blue suit that looked casual yet sleek. "Perfect timing," he said serenely. "Lunch is about to be served."

"What's going on?"

"I called a summit meeting." Callum set a pitcher of lemonade on the table. "We'll have to eat buffet style. It would be too cramped at the table with five of us. Louise is making macaroni and cheese for the boys at her place, by the way."

His gift for taking charge had impressed the

heck out of Jody in their early days. Now, she wanted to kick him for his arrogance.

"You had no right to invite my friends without asking me," she said in a low voice. The three guests shifted uncomfortably in their seats. She guessed that they all wished they could disappear, which was probably Callum's goal.

Bo, who had the advantage of already knowing their shameless host, wore an eager-to-please expression. It wasn't his fault that his brown slacks and tweed jacket appeared baggy compared to Callum's stylish outfit.

As for Freddy, his incomplete effort to clean the morning's mud from his boots and overalls had left him with a kind of sepia tone that did nothing to enhance his short, stocky build. His older brother, Frank, wore a nearly identical outfit, sans dirt and, while several inches taller, he was even stockier.

"I didn't mean to go behind your back, but you were busy and the idea just struck me," Callum said with feigned blandness. "I got their phone numbers out of your directory." He indicated a spiral address book on the counter.

"What do you mean by a summit meeting?" Jody demanded.

"We'll get to that in a minute." Callum set out plates of sandwiches on the counter. He'd also fixed celery stuffed with reddish cream cheese.

Following her gaze, he explained, "Pimientos. Guys, come and get it!"

Bo rubbed his hands together as he surveyed the spread. "This looks tasty."

"I did work up an appetite this morning," Freddy agreed, and took one of the paper plates.

"By the way," Bo said, "is there any chance I could interview you for my paper? You're the closest thing to a celebrity we've got around here."

"I'd be honored." Callum sounded as though he meant it. "Later, all right?"

"Sure thing."

Soon the men were arrayed around the living room, balancing paper plates and cups as if at a tea party. The only one not noticeably ill at ease, Callum had chosen to eat standing by the mantel. This saved him from having to juggle his food and gave him a commanding advantage over the others, Jody noted with grudging admiration.

When the men were on their second helpings and the sound of chomping had slowed, Callum spoke. "As you probably know, Jody is a finalist in the Mother of the Year contest presented by *Family Voyager* magazine, which I publish. She and I also were close friends for many years. After reading her entry, I wanted to meet the people who are important to her now."

"Are you interviewing all the finalists?" Bo asked.

"Well, no," Callum admitted.

"Then why fly all the way to Texas to see Jody?" In his own polite way, Bo was defending his territory, or what he wished was his territory, Jody surmised.

"I wasn't sure I should bring this up, and I hope Jody will forgive me, but the truth is, I'm the father of her children," Callum said.

Freddy choked on a piece of celery until his brother whacked him between the shoulder blades. Bo paled. Oh, great. Although Jody had realized she wouldn't be able to keep the secret much longer, she hadn't expected Callum to make a public announcement. Even though he'd begged her pardon, he sure had a lot of nerve!

"You?" Bo said. "I thought..." His voice trailed off. Guiltily, Jody remembered mentioning that nonsense to him about the alleged rodeo Romeo. That had been several years ago, before there was any suggestion of Bo's courting her.

It wasn't as if she'd owed anyone an explanation. Still, she wished he hadn't found out in such a blunt manner.

"Where've you been, huh?" Freddy demanded. "Where've you been all these years?"

"I should have come sooner. A lot sooner," Callum began.

"I didn't tell him he was a father." Jody knew

the fault was largely hers. "I didn't even mention that I'd had children."

She winced at Bo's expression of disappointment. "Didn't you think he had a right to know?"

"We've all made mistakes," Callum interjected. "Well, maybe not you personally, but Jody and I are working this out together."

"I knew you two used to date, but it always seemed kind of casual," Bo admitted. "I didn't know there was any more to it."

"There wasn't," Jody said. "Just that once."

"So you're not getting married?" Freddy persisted.

His brother fixed him with a quelling look. "That's none of our business."

"You like her, too! She ought to go to one of us." Realizing he'd overstepped his bounds, the hired hand said, "I mean, 'stead of some guy who hasn't been around since gosh knows when. We're the ones who understand about ranching. At least, Frank and I do. We're more her type."

"I guess you didn't read her contest entry on the Web site," Bo said. "I have to say, that was a clever literary reference to Penelope, although I hope you don't feel like I've been pressuring you, Jody."

She wished a herd of cattle would stampede through the living room and sweep her away. She'd never considered how her friends would react if they read what she'd written. "I was using poetic license," she said. "I just wanted to go to Paris with the kids. I'm sorry, Bo."

"From what Jody tells me, you've been a good friend," Callum said diplomatically.

"He stood up for me when some of the townspeople said the school ought to fire me because I was a single mother," she said.

To her relief, Bo smiled. "I understood what you were doing, Jody."

"Who's Penelope?" Freddy asked. "Don't tell me they've got a new waitress at the Downtown Café! I was just getting used to Evelyn. In fact, she's kind of pretty."

"She sure is." Frank looked at Callum. "Her folks moved to town a year or so ago." Already, Jody gathered, the brothers were turning their attentions elsewhere.

"Why did you really want to meet us?" Bo asked. "I don't mean any offense, but some people might say you were meddling in Jody's personal business."

"Those people would be right," Callum answered honestly. "I intend to interfere as much as I can because, no matter how things look, I really care about her and I'm hoping she'll forgive me. As for what else I'm hoping, I think I've shot my mouth off enough for one afternoon."

"You can say that again," Jody muttered.

"Fair enough," Bo said. "At least we know where we stand." The other two men nodded reluctantly.

"It strikes me that it's time for dessert. Does anybody like apple pie?" Callum said.

As it turned out, everybody did.

He fetched the dessert from a sideboard, doling out five pieces with enough left for the boys. It was delicious, of course. Jody had stocked her freezer with her favorite brand of pies from a sale two weeks earlier.

"Tell me about publishing a magazine," Bo said. "I'll get started researching my own article, if you don't mind."

"Sure." Callum stood at the mantel, radiating confidence. "I got the idea of starting *Family Voyager* six years ago. People said I'd never make any money at it, but I figured the key was to make it entertaining and adventuresome and original."

He regaled them with stories of how he'd stumbled and brazened his way to success. Callum made them all laugh, even the Fallon brothers, with anecdotes at his own expense. His sparkle eclipsed the modest living room.

Jody felt herself yielding to his charm. She wasn't sure what, if anything, he'd accomplished by confronting her friends, but he'd succeeded in a different way.

Until today, she had almost convinced herself

that liking could grow into love if she gave Bo a chance. After seeing him in Callum's company, however, she knew it was hopeless. Maybe she couldn't have the man she wanted, but she could never love anyone else, either.

Now she had to decide what to do about that.

CHAPTER FOUR

FOR THE SPACE of several minutes as he cleaned the kitchen, Callum allowed himself to wonder how he dared try to take over Jody's life. It was true, as Freddy had said, that he hadn't been here when she needed him. It was also true that he couldn't move back to Texas and she refused to consider California.

Nevertheless, if there was anything his experience with the magazine had taught Callum, it was to keep his eye on the goal and not worry too much about obstacles. They had a way of disappearing when he forged ahead. At the very least, he intended to play an active role in raising his sons and at best he intended to play an even more active role in Jody's future.

"Bo's a nice guy." In her denim skirt and a blouse that made no secret of her curves, Jody radiated appeal. "He's not as flashy as you but he lives nearby."

Her words reminded Callum uncomfortably of what Ben had said about needing a daddy who lived in the area. Since he didn't think Jody was in the mood for a serious discussion at the moment, he answered lightly, "I'll bet he can't play the trumpet. You and I used to be pretty good together. Do you still play?"

"Mostly I play piano these days." She indicated an upright in the living room. "How about you?"

"As a matter of fact, I joined a quartet. We jam at a jazz club once a month," he said.

Jody regarded him with interest. Callum doubted she had any idea how cute she looked. He nearly forgot what they'd been discussing until she said, "Want to jam with me?"

"Now? Sure!"

She left and returned with a trumpet case. "I give it a whirl every now and then, so it's in good condition."

Callum unsnapped the case and hefted the instrument, admiring its silvery sheen. "Didn't you used to play the clarinet, too?"

"I gave it up," she said.

"Why? The band needed clarinets." He recalled the bandleader complaining about the dearth.

Jody shot him a sideways glance. "You idiot."

"Excuse me?"

"I started in the marching band on clarinet and switched to trumpet so I could be in your section."

That was news to him. "You did? Why?"

"So you'd notice me." She bit her lip, apparently embarrassed by the admission.

"Wow, I'm flattered." Callum had figured it was just great luck when Jody started marching alongside him. "How did you happen to notice *me?*"

"How could I help it?" she said. "You were the golden boy of Everett County Regional High. I shouldn't tell you this since you've got a big enough ego already."

"Golden boy?" Callum refused to take offense at the comment about his ego. "I was simply one of the guys."

"That was your greatest asset," she said. "You weren't stuck on yourself."

"You just said I have an ego!"

"That isn't precisely right." She took a seat on the piano bench. "What you have is a self-assurance that I envy. I've always been more of a shrinking violet."

"Is that anything like a wallflower?" Callum deadpanned. "In any case, you're neither. You could teach assertiveness classes in your sleep." He stopped talking while adjusting the trumpet mouthpiece.

"Only when I'm defending someone or something I care about," Jody said. "Now are we going to jam or not?"

"You're calling the shots," he said.

After a couple of false starts, they launched into some old favorites. "Tijuana Taxi" and "The

Lonely Bull'' segued into "Hello, Dolly" and
"Mack the Knife." They were completely in
synch by the time they tackled, and more or less
conquered, "The Flight of the Bumblebee."

When they were finished, Callum set down the
trumpet. "My lips are going numb."

"We can't have that." Jody gazed up at him
from the piano bench, the angle of her face and
neck alluring. He cupped her chin with one hand.

"Care to help them heal?" Without waiting for
an answer, he brushed a kiss across her full mouth
and couldn't resist its sweetness. Sinking onto the
seat beside her, Callum caught Jody's shoulders.
She leaned toward him.

He kissed her again, lingeringly, his eyes drifting shut as the contact linked them in a hundred
ways.

It came as a shock when Jody drew away.
"What's wrong?" Callum asked.

"Nothing's wrong," she said. "I just got an
idea."

She knew that if she gave herself time to think,
she would change her mind or lose her courage. It
was an outrageous idea, worthy of some stunt Callum himself might pull. But she had to take action
before the kiss dissolved the last of her willpower.

As they jammed, Jody's spirits had soared with
every note. She could never return to the way

things had been before he arrived, she realized. He'd stirred up too many emotions.

Yet she had to cut off his courtship, or pseudo-courtship, or whatever it was. Callum was too mercurial to be the man she needed, and she was too much herself to fit into his high-flying existence in California. At the same time, she didn't want to deprive the boys of their father.

When he kissed her, Jody's soul had ignited in a pure blue flame. No other man would ever be enough for her. Any chance at the marriage she'd always dreamed of had been ruined.

That was when the solution had hit her. It solved almost everything, including the fact that, subconsciously, she'd been waiting five years to hear words Callum would never speak. So she decided to say them herself.

"Let's get married," she said.

He stared at her blankly. For once in his life, Callum Fox was speechless.

"I can be the respectable Mrs. Fox and you can give the boys your name," Jody went on. "When they start school, they'll be able to look any bully in the face and say, 'I do so have a father.'"

"Of course they do." He clearly had no quarrel with that point.

"You can fly home to L.A. and tell your friends anything you like," Jody went on. "I don't care how you act as long as you don't create a scandal that reaches Everett Landing. You can visit me every now and then. As far as anybody else is concerned, we'll have a long-distance marriage.''

''What about as far as we're concerned?'' Callum asked.

''If we try to act like a real man and wife, we'll end up hating each other.'' She'd resigned herself to that fact long ago. ''You'll try to argue me into giving up the ranch and I'll get jealous if you escort other women to movie premieres.''

''Why would I escort other women if I'm married?'' He was sitting so close, she could have buried her nose in his neck.

Jody held herself rigidly straight. ''Because it's going to be a marriage of convenience.''

Callum ran one hand through his hair. ''I thought those only existed in Victorian novels.''

''Not true,'' Jody said. ''You've heard of green card marriages, haven't you?''

''Neither of us is a foreign citizen.'' He appeared to be taking her seriously, at least, or maybe he was in shock.

''There's a rancher on the outskirts of town who married a widow because they were both lonely,'' Jody added, seeking ammunition. ''Of course, we'd be doing the opposite, getting married and living apart, but it will take care of our problems.''

''How's that?''

''I won't have to worry about men pursuing me.

No one will ask me out if I'm married," she said. "Of course, you can date if you want to." *I don't really mean that, do I?* "I mean, taking actresses to openings and things like that."

"I'd rather take my wife," Callum said.

"You don't have a wife."

"If memory serves, you just proposed to me," he said.

"I'd be your wife legally, but not in other ways." She figured she'd spelled that out plainly enough.

From his seat beside her, Callum ran one hand up her wrist and caressed the inside of her elbow. Jody gave a delicious shudder.

"It isn't going to work," he said.

"It has to work!" Irked at her own vulnerability, she slid away on the bench.

"Be reasonable," Callum said. "We can't have a platonic marriage when your scent alone gets me aroused."

"It does?" She could hardly breathe. She'd had no idea he felt that way.

"Come closer and I'll demonstrate."

Jody shook her head. "You react that way to lots of women! There's nothing special about me as far as you're concerned."

"That's not even remotely true," Callum said. "Nobody compares to you. No one ever has."

"It's taken you five years to figure that out?"

she demanded. "Let's not forget that, during that time, you failed to visit me or even call. If I hadn't entered your contest, you wouldn't be here now. I think it's safe to say that out of sight is out of mind as far as you're concerned. Right?"

Although she could tell by his expression that Callum wanted to argue, he didn't. "I'll admit, I've tended to live in the moment. Five years ago, I was barely scraping by running a Web site and writing ad copy part-time for a hotel chain. I asked you to move to L.A. because I knew we'd have fun together, but when you turned me down, I figured I had to move on."

"And I let you," Jody conceded. "I can't blame you for something that's partly my fault. Still, fundamentally, the only thing that's changed is that we have two sons."

"That's a pretty big change," he said. "Tell me why our getting married in name only would be good for them."

"It will placate the town gossips, for one thing." Jody's attachment to her idea grew as she spoke. "Also, it should make it easier for them to trust that you'll come back, if they know you care enough to marry their mother."

Callum considered. "Why couldn't we be a real husband and wife even though we live apart? Other couples do it."

"I told you, we'd be wretched. At least, I would

be," Jody said. "I'd miss you too much. I'd pester you and mope around and then I'd get mad. If I know up front that it's simply an arrangement for the boys' sake, I can get on with my life."

"It's important that we stay on good terms." He sounded thoughtful. "Let me mull this over, all right?"

"Sure." That was only fair, since she'd sprung this idea on him without warning. Besides, Jody was in no hurry, in case his answer happened to be no. If so, it would most likely be followed by "adios" and a quick exit in that ridiculous convertible. "If you'll excuse me, I've got a full afternoon ahead."

When she returned from throwing on her grubby clothes, Callum was dishing out leftover apple pie for the boys. "Hey, Mom, are we going to buy jeans?" Jeremy said.

"It's Saturday," Ben reminded her.

She'd promised to take the boys shopping at Banyon's Clothing Store. "Oh, darn, I forgot." Jody had gotten behind in her chores since Callum arrived. She had to prepare for next week, when she, Gladys and Freddy planned to vaccinate the spring calves.

"I'll take them," Callum volunteered.

"You don't need to." Her protest sounded weak.

"I want to." He made a shooing motion as if to

herd her toward the door. "It'll be fun to spend time with my sons. Besides, I'd like to talk to Ella Mae at the café. She's a finalist, too, you know."

Jody had been amused to hear about it. "All right. Have a good time."

"You bet."

As she turned to go, the sight of the three males standing close together, their silver-blond hair and supple bodies so much alike, tugged at Jody's heart. She hoped Callum would go along with her idea. She wanted this relationship tied up neatly with a bow so it wouldn't keep tearing at her heart.

RIDING IN AN OPEN CAR thrilled the boys, who whooped and chortled from their booster seats. Thank goodness they had no idea the decrepit vehicle was nothing short of a fashion felony, Callum thought wryly.

Everett Landing hadn't changed much since he'd last seen it. The grocery store had been repainted white with blue trim and the hardware store displayed computers and DVD players alongside tools in the window. Otherwise, there was a lazy 1950s feel to the sprawling main street that even the presence of a few late-model SUVs failed to dispel.

Although Callum knew that being stuck here after high school would have chafed him beyond endurance, he relished the small-town pleasure of walking into Banyon's and greeting the salesclerk and two customers by name. All welcomed him warmly, although there were startled looks as they saw him with the boys. From the way their glances trailed between him and his sons, he knew they were noting the similarities.

He forgot everything else as he helped the boys pick out clothes. Both wanted jeans, and they were delighted when Callum agreed to buy them new sneakers, as well. With a pang, he realized how tight money must be for Jody. Thank goodness he'd learned about the twins while they were little.

Ben's taste ran to T-shirts with pictures of teddy bears and puppies. Jerry fell in love with a black-and-tan short-sleeved shirt much too large for him and refused to give it up. "I want it! It's mine!"

"That's an adult small," the storekeeper, Al Banyon, commented. "It'll come down to his knees."

"I don't care." Jerry thrust out his lower lip.

What good was a father if he couldn't indulge his child? Callum reflected. "I'll tell you what," he said. "We'll buy this, but you have to pick out at least two other T-shirts that are the right size."

His son reflected and came to a decision. "Okay." He walked to the racks, grabbed two plain blue T-shirts, and returned with a triumphant smile.

"I'm hungry," Ben said after Callum finished paying.

He checked his watch. Three o'clock. Usually he sent his secretary out for a latte about now. "Let's stow these in the trunk and see what they've got at the Downtown Café."

They sauntered along the sidewalk to the corner of Main Street and Mesquite Avenue. The sight of children playing at the elementary school across the street unlocked happy memories of Callum's own school days.

Inside the gleaming eatery, a couple of cowboys were chowing down one of the café's famous round-the-clock breakfasts. The only other occupant was a pretty, dark-haired waitress mopping the tile floor.

Callum chose a table near the window. The waitress disappeared, exchanged her mop for an order pad, and returned.

"Hi, I'm Evelyn," she said. "Hello there, Ben and Jerry. What can I get for you folks?"

"Can we have a sundae, Daddy?" Ben asked.

When she heard the name "Daddy," the young woman dropped her pen. Apologizing, she scooped it up. "I didn't realize...I mean, you must be...I, uh, guess you're a good friend of Jody's." She smiled.

"That's a safe bet. I mean, yes, I am," he said. "Let's make that three sundaes. Is chocolate okay with everyone?'' Two small heads nodded. ''One coffee, too, please.''

''You bet!''

''I'd like to say hello to Ella Mae, if she isn't busy,'' he added.

''I'll tell her right away!'' The young woman gave an excited skip as she hurried to the kitchen.

''Do you guys eat here often?'' Callum asked.

''Grandpa and Grandma used to bring us,'' Jeremy said. ''Mommy says we can't 'ford it.''

''They make yummy burgers.'' Ben rested his chin on his palm.

''From now on, you and Mommy can eat here a lot more often.'' Callum hoped Jody wasn't going to argue about his paying her a generous monthly allotment. If they got married as she'd suggested, there would be no question about his helping to support them. That was one point in its favor.

While the boys amused themselves by identifying letters in their plastic-covered menus, Callum's mind remained fixed on Jody. Just thinking about their embrace this morning made him want her so much he ached. If she hadn't interrupted their kiss, history might have repeated itself.

She was right, though, that attempting to have a real long-distance marriage might blow up in their faces. Neither of them had any experience at maintaining intimacy even under ideal conditions. As for a marriage of convenience, however, he didn't see how they could be sure of resisting the temptation they hadn't been able to resist in the past.

In order to make a decision, Callum needed some criteria. What would the rules be, and did they have a chance at succeeding? If only there were some way to test their resolve....

"Oh, look!" Ben jumped up. "It's Abner!"

"Who's Abner?" Callum hoped this wasn't going to turn out to be another rival for Jody's affections.

Jeremy pelted past him. "Hi, Abner!" He squatted to stroke a large calico cat. Joining him, Ben ran both hands through the thick fur.

The cat rolled onto its back, purring so loudly the sound echoed from the restaurant walls. "He's certainly friendly," Callum observed.

"He's so outgoing, Ella Mae says he thinks he's a dog." Evelyn poured him a full mug.

A clap from the kitchen doorway announced the presence of a large-boned woman in her sixties. "Abner! Bad cat!" cried Ella Mae. "Go on, boy! Out!" Startled, the feline let out a disappointed sound halfway between a groan and a whine as it got to its feet and slouched away. "Sorry, folks," the owner announced. "He's not allowed in here, but he gets curious."

After shutting the door behind the cat, Ella Mae fetched a plate of homemade cookies and passed them out to her customers. "This is by way of an apology," she told Callum as she took a seat across from him. "It sure is good to see you. You've been gone far too long."

"It's good to be back," he said, and meant it. His mother had died not long after he graduated from college and his father, who liked to visit cousins in Arizona, used to drive there and on to California once a year in his motor home until his death five years ago. As a result, Callum had become almost a stranger around here.

Evelyn returned with three scrumptious sundaes. The kids dug in. He ate at a more leisurely pace while he and Ella Mae brought each other up to date on their lives. She nodded appreciatively when he admitted he was the boys' father.

"I always wondered about that," she said. "The older those boys get, the more they look like you. I figured maybe something had gone on between you and Jody, but she didn't like to let on and I'm not one to pry."

"How come other people didn't notice?" Callum asked. "Or did they?"

The café owner gave him a knowing smile. "People see what they want to see. Besides, Jody had another boyfriend before the kids were born. He moved away when he realized she could never really love him, or so I heard. I never did believe she had a fling with that rodeo rider, though, no matter what people said.''

''What rodeo rider?'' He glanced at the boys, but they were absorbed in making mush out of their ice cream.

''Nobody to be concerned about,'' Ella Mae said. ''Now, I wanted to talk to you about Abner.''

''The cat?'' Callum remembered about the contest. ''Oh, right. You want to take him to Paris.''

She folded her arms on the table. ''I entered the contest after I saw a picture on the Internet of some cats traveling with their owners. They looked real cute, but the more I think about it, the more I worry that Abner might get lost. I appreciate your making me a finalist, Callum, but I won't feel bad if I lose.''

He thanked his lucky stars that she'd smoothed over the situation. ''I'm sure our readers found the idea amusing.''

''Ever think about moving back here?'' Ella Mae asked abruptly. ''We've got a lot of nice things happening in central Texas. Maybe you could run your business from here.''

''I'd love to spend more time with my boys, but I don't know if that's feasible.'' Callum had a packed schedule: supervising weekly story meetings, mediating staff disputes, handling sudden emergencies. Sometimes his ability to crank out a last-minute cover story or charm a celebrity averted disaster. *Family Voyager* needed him at the helm, in person.

"Well, you'd better do something before we end up with our own soap opera." Ella Mae indicated the waitress, who was disappearing into the kitchen. "Evelyn's got it bad for Bo Landers, and he's got it bad for Jody. Or hadn't you noticed?"

"I noticed," Callum said between bites of ice cream. "The part about Bo and Jody, in any event."

"She doesn't look sick," Jerry said.

"Excuse me?" Ella Mae leaned over and ruffled the boy's hair. "Nobody's sick, sweetheart."

"You said Evelyn's got it bad."

She uttered a bark of laughter. "When somebody has it bad, that means they're in love. My point is, this whole tangle needs to get resolved and your father is the only person who can do it."

"Any suggestions?" Callum asked.

"Follow your heart," said the café owner.

He wasn't accustomed to following, he was accustomed to leading. Maybe that was part of the problem, he conceded. Maybe he talked too much and listened too little.

That was going to change. Callum intended to listen to Jody, even if it meant facing the possibility that a marriage of convenience was the right way to go.

CHAPTER FIVE

IF JODY had figured she could spread the word quietly that Callum was the boys' father, her hopes of discretion received a knockout punch on Sunday morning. As the four of them arrived for church, Ben greeted everyone he knew by announcing, "This is my daddy!"

"Mine, too," Jeremy said, a bit defensively.

Although a few people had already heard the news from Ella Mae and Bo, most were startled. Jody caught a disapproving frown from Melody Lee, a former PTA president who'd tried to get Jody fired from her teaching job when she became pregnant. Others shook Callum's hand, glad to see him again and willing to suspend judgment.

"The Prodigal Son has returned," he told the preacher ruefully.

"To stay, I hope," came the response.

"We're working on that," Callum said.

He'd certainly been working at being a father. Last night, he'd introduced the boys to the game of dominoes. Although they couldn't add their scores, they'd relished the challenge of counting and matching the dots on the tiles.

Jody's throat tightened as she recalled childhood evenings at the kitchen table playing with this same worn set in the company of her parents and friends. That was the way family life ought to be. If only she could have that kind of closeness with Callum for more than just a few days.

During the game, her gaze had fallen on his hands. Although they lacked the ranching scars her father had sported, they moved with strength and deftness. Between rounds, he'd built an elaborate domino structure and encouraged the boys to blow on the end tile until the array flattened itself amid an exhilarating series of clacks.

Later, Callum had directed the twins to sit beside their mother on the piano bench and sing while he stood behind them, providing bass. They'd harmonized until a muffed version of "Row Your Boat" dissolved into laughter.

If only Callum would stay. If only he belonged to her.

Jody was intensely aware of him sitting beside her through the service. The broad shoulders, the high planes of his face, the full, good-humored mouth all marked him as someone special.

For the rest of the service, she struggled to pay attention to the preacher. It was a good thing there wasn't a pop quiz at the end.

In the social hall afterwards, as people gathered

to talk before going their ways, the twins ran to play with friends. Old acquaintances surrounded Callum. Jody, hanging back in the crush, saw Bo approaching.

He seemed oblivious to the attention of the dark-haired waitress from the café, which had been riveted on him from the moment he arrived. Callum had mentioned yesterday, among various tidbits he brought back from town, that she had a crush on the guy.

"Have you two resolved anything?" Bo said quietly.

"Not yet," Jody admitted.

Spotting Bo, Callum disengaged from his group and came over. "The boys asked if it was okay to go home with the Wiltons and their son for the afternoon. I didn't think you'd mind. We're supposed to pick them up after dinner."

"It's fine." Already, Ben and Jerry were turning to their father as an authority figure, Jody mused.

"How long are you planning on staying?" Bo asked him. In case the question sounded rude, he added, "My interview comes out next Friday. I was hoping you'd get a chance to read it."

"I'm not sure how long the office can spare me," Callum admitted. "If I'm not here, maybe Jody will be kind enough to send me a copy."

"Of course," she said.

To her, Bo didn't look satisfied by the indefinite answer. Neither, for that matter, was she.

On the road home, Callum took the wheel of the pickup. Jody settled back, content to let him drive. The truck had been her father's and had never suited her.

"Tell me something," he said. "Are you happy here?"

"In Everett Landing? Sure," she said.

"Always have been?"

"Yes."

"Always will be?"

"Probably." As long as she had something special and wonderful to hold on to, Jody added silently. Like two adorable little boys. And a trip to Paris that she'd never forget.

"You enjoy being a rancher?" he probed.

"I like carrying on my parents' work. The Wandering I meant the world to them." That had been clear from her father's will, which had left Jody copious instructions for running the ranch, as if to make sure she didn't rush to unload the place.

"What about teaching?"

The question made Jody's throat tighten. She'd adored her classroom and the challenge of helping her second graders master new material. "I miss it."

"Will you ever go back?"

She hadn't allowed herself to think in that direction. "It would be disloyal to give up the ranch."

"You mean you're going to spend the rest of

your life playing Dale Evans even though you always wanted to be a teacher?'' he said. ''When we were in college, you used to dream about decorating your classroom.''

''Things change,'' Jody said. ''This is not your problem, Callum.''

''Okay, I'll back off. For now.'' He steered around a pothole in her driveway. ''Let's talk about getting married.''

Her heart performed a ballet leap. ''Have you made a decision?''

''Only in the preliminary sense.'' Maddeningly, he stopped talking while parking in the garage. After the engine cut off, he climbed out and started to come around.

Jody exited by herself, too impatient to wait. ''What do you mean, you've made a preliminary decision?''

''There's no sense in embarking on a marriage of convenience unless we're sure we can handle it,'' Callum said. ''Do you agree?''

''I suppose so.''

Walking toward the house, he matched his stride to hers. ''We weren't very convincing yesterday during our jam session.'' He opened the side door, which she'd left unlocked as always.

''What does music have to do with marriage?'' Lifting her long skirt, Jody stepped over the sill.

''I wasn't referring to the music. I meant our lack of restraint.'' Callum paused in front of her.

At such close quarters, his nearness made her skin tingle.

"What lack of restraint?"

"The part where I grabbed you."

"It was just a kiss." She was getting good at lying, Jody reflected ruefully.

"Like this?" His touch on her arm was all the warning she had before his lips gently explored hers.

Jody's tongue tasted fire. She drew it back, and then dared the flames once more. Only when she heard a groan and realized she didn't know whether it was hers or Callum's did she wrench herself away.

"You see the problem." His eyes had a hooded appearance. "We can't keep our hands off each other."

"My hands were nowhere near you," she protested weakly.

"How can we spend a lifetime as platonic mates if we can't spend a single day simply being pals?" he asked.

"Who says we can't?" She was ready to fight her own instincts, Mother Nature itself and him, too, if necessary.

Callum drew himself up. "I take that as a challenge. Since the kids are gone, how about if we use this afternoon as a test?"

Jody usually took Sundays off, so there was no

work to interfere. "It's a deal. Anything special you'd like to do?"

"It's warm. We could go swimming." The animals' water tank doubled as an informal pool.

An image of Callum in minuscule trunks quickened Jody's breathing. "I don't think swimsuits are such a good idea."

"Who said anything about swimsuits?" He grinned.

She forced herself to stay calm. "Let's go riding. That ought to cool your ardor, City Boy. I plan to change into jeans, and I'd recommend you do likewise."

"You're the boss." With a casual salute, he strolled toward his room. She allowed her gaze to linger on his taut rear end beneath the silky blue suit.

What was wrong with her? They hadn't even started, and she was already giving in to temptation! Jody chastised herself, and hurried off.

Dressed for the outing, they met in the kitchen, packed sandwiches and headed for the barn. Callum saddled his horse adeptly. He hadn't forgotten much from his high school days, when he'd worked on ranches during the summer to help earn money for college.

"I should have put you to work the minute you got here," she teased.

He held up his unscarred hands. "I'm out of

shape. The only kind of animal I can wrangle these days is a mouse. The computer variety.''

"Let's see what sitting around in a desk chair has done to your riding seat.'' Jody swung onto her favorite mare, Flicka. "I'll race you to the windmill.''

"Wait!'' He was still arcing onto his saddle as she pressed her knees into the horse's flanks.

From the barn, Flicka sped past the big house on Jody's left and the corral chutes to her right. As they shot up the hillside, she heard Callum's gelding, King Arthur, thundering behind them.

"Go, girl!'' she shouted close to the horse's neck. Warm sun bathed her back as Flicka hit her stride and they chunked over the grassy slope, the reverberations of the hoofbeats welding them into a single determined entity.

"Beep beep!'' Callum called as he pulled alongside.

Atop the tall horse, he resembled a cowboy from a John Wayne movie, slim and hard and born in the saddle. Callum had the gift of looking at home anywhere, Jody reflected.

Was there any chance he really could feel at home on a ranch? He already had many of the basic skills. Maybe he, like her, was ready to consider a change of careers.

If she didn't snap out of her daydreams, she was going to lose the race. "Hit it!'' she commanded Flicka, and flattened herself against the horse. Inspired, the mare flew past the gelding and reached the windmill first by half a stride.

"I win!" After the horses slowed, Jody raised one fist in a victory salute.

"You do indeed. I'll even forgive you for the head start, since my horse is bigger." Callum had always been a good sport. "That was exciting."

"You're a good rider," she conceded.

"It comes back to me." He tilted his face to enjoy the sunshine. "This is almost beach weather."

"Don't you miss the seasons, living where it's summer all the time?" Jody asked as the horses walked side by side. "To me, springtime is extra glorious because it comes after a cold, dark winter."

"Don't exaggerate," he said. "This is Texas, not Montana."

"It snows here!"

"Just enough to keep things interesting." At the top of the hill, he reined to a halt and surveyed the patchwork panorama below them. Green fields and rambling fences, meandering cattle, stands of trees and a distant ribbon of highway sprawled to the horizon.

"Welcome to my place of business," Jody said.

"You've got an even better view than I do," Callum said. "This beats skyscrapers, hands down."

Her heart leaped. Maybe there was hope, after all.

A sense of peace stole over Jody as she gazed across the land where she'd grown up. Here, to the ranch, she'd retreated when the popular high school girls snubbed her or she failed to get a date for a dance.

It had been her refuge five years ago, too. Jody had given up her rented house in town and returned, pregnant and defiantly independent but scared, too. Her parents had offered support, and the ranch had reassured her with its permanence.

It was different living and working here twenty-four hours a day, though. This past year, sometimes she'd felt confined and out of touch with the world. Maybe that was why she yearned to fly away to Paris.

"I wish I could read your mind," Callum said.

"I was just thinking." Jody didn't want to go into detail. She hated revealing her vulnerabilities, because doing so made her feel weak. "You wouldn't understand."

"Try me."

"No, seriously." She relaxed in the saddle, letting Flicka graze. "You couldn't wait to leave this area. To me, it's the center of the universe."

King Arthur, who could get edgy if he sensed any insecurity in his rider, calmed enough to join the mare in grazing. It was a tribute to Callum's skill in the saddle.

"This area is beautiful but I never felt like I really fit in here in Everett Landing," said the man beside her.

Jody let out a disbelieving hoot. "You were the most popular guy in school, except maybe for the football team!"

"That's a big exception." He chuckled. "Besides, you're biased."

"The kids wouldn't have voted you Most Likely to Succeed if they hadn't liked you," she pointed out. "I didn't get voted anything."

"What would you have liked to be?" he asked.

Most likely to have Callum Fox fall in love with me. "Most likely to teach school," Jody said, sticking close to the truth.

"I was flattered, getting voted an honor like that," Callum said, "but if you view it a different way, it meant I was being voted Most Likely to Leave Town."

"That doesn't mean they wanted you to leave!" she protested. "I can't understand why you say you didn't fit in."

"Let's ride," he said. "I think better on the go."

Jody clucked to Flicka and they moved forward. She was glad Callum had arrived in time to enjoy the spring wildflowers and the bright new grass.

Since he'd worked on ranches himself, he probably also noticed that some of the fence posts needed replacing, which was an endless job, and that one of the pastures might be a bit overgrazed. Gladys had suggested hiring another full-time hand and buying new equipment, but it would mean taking out a large loan. Jody wasn't ready to face the risk.

"I guess the place where I felt most out of place was in my own family," Callum mused as they rode. "My parents were wonderful people, content living in a small town and running a store. They never understood why I was so eager to head off to college and see the world."

"They were proud of you." Jody had dropped by the feed store occasionally after he left, eager for news of his activities.

"I know, and I loved them a lot," he said. "I wish I could have been the son they expected. It was hard on them, having their only child live so far away. But I took after my restless grandmother."

Jody recalled his mentioning once that his father's mother had been a painter from Chicago who arrived in town to capture the Texas landscape and ended up marrying a local man. "She must have found something special in Everett Landing."

"I suppose she did, although she stopped painting after a while," he said. "I think she romanticized the place to herself, and by the time she figured out that she'd boxed herself in, it was too late. But I'm just guessing. She died when I was little."

"Did she paint the landscape in your parents' living room?" Jody had admired it when she visited there.

He nodded. "She had quite a talent and a great imagination. Dad was nothing like her."

"Your father had his own gift," Jody said. "He always had a kind word or a joke to brighten my day. You're more like him than you realize."

She wondered if she'd said the wrong thing, because Callum changed the subject and began asking for details about the ranch. Or maybe he simply wanted to know more. He listened intently as she described how much she'd learned the last year as the cycle of seasons rolled past, from summer haying to winter repairs and spring calving.

While she talked, Jody felt both satisfaction and the heavy weight of responsibility. With her students, she'd been able to measure their progress, and she could count on a paycheck. A ranch struggled to survive. She no sooner finished a chore than it needed doing again, and there was always the risk of a natural disaster or other financial setback.

She tossed her head, letting her hair billow on the breeze. This was the life into which she'd been born, and she'd put down roots here.

Even so, she hoped right down to her bones that soon she and the boys would be kicking up their heels beneath the spires of Notre Dame. Although she might lack Callum's daring, once in a while she got restless, too.

"YOU'RE HUMMING," he said approvingly. Callum enjoyed the way Jody often hummed or sang under her breath as if a musical current ran through her veins.

She blinked in surprise. "Was I?"

He let the melody reverberate in his memory before identifying it. "It's 'Under Paris Skies.'"

"Oh." She blushed.

All the while she'd been rhapsodizing aloud about her life as a rancher, she'd been dreaming of Gay Paree. "I understand how it feels to wish you were somewhere else," Callum said.

"I don't wish I were somewhere else!"

"You never wish you were in a classroom?"

"That's cheating," she told him. "I was able to indulge my dream for a while. Maybe I'll do it again when I get too old for physical labor, although standing in front of kids all day isn't exactly easy."

"When we were in college, I half expected that you'd decide to come to California, too," he said. "You seemed interested in the challenge of working in a larger school district, and you used to pepper me with questions about everything from Disneyland to the movie industry, as if I had some secret fount of knowledge."

"I was just curious because you were going there," Jody said. "I wasn't interested for myself. I've always known where I belong."

"You've always known where you felt safe," Callum corrected. An unexpected thought occurred to him. *The place you've always belonged is with me.*

That didn't make sense. They'd spent so many years apart that in some ways they hardly knew each other. Yet in other ways, it felt as if no more than a few months had passed since they'd attended college together.

"Let's have our picnic over there." Jody pointed out a stand of trees. "There's a stream through the middle. It's one of my favorite spots."

"I'm sold."

Inside the dappled grove, they set the horses free to graze. With their reins draped on the ground, the well-trained animals wouldn't wander far.

There was no need for words as he and Jody spread a blanket on the ground and helped themselves. In addition to the sandwiches, they'd packed carrots and cookies, which vanished swiftly.

"Is my hair a mess?" Jody asked as they relaxed afterwards. She wore it loose, the way he preferred.

"A little tangled maybe." Callum plucked a twig from one curly strand. "Hold on." He retrieved a folding comb from his pocket and, moving closer, began to work through her tangles.

"You don't have to do that." Despite her words, Jody didn't pull away.

"I don't mind." Sitting behind her, he slid

closer until she fit between his upraised knees. "You smell like roses."

"I smell like my shampoo."

"Could you be a little less romantic?" he teased.

"We're supposed to be testing our ability to remain platonic friends," Jody reminded him.

How could a man remain platonic with a softly built honey of a woman grasped between his thighs? Callum knew better than to even hint at his response to her, though, or Jody would whisk out of his grasp so fast she'd take the comb with her.

He searched for a neutral topic. It wasn't easy, because he kept picturing her in the shower, shampooing her hair with her arms raised and her full breasts thrust prominently the way she'd done after they made love. Correction: after the first time they made love and just before the second time.

"Do you think I should cut my hair?" she asked.

"It's beautiful this way."

"It's messy and it makes me look like an idiot," she said. "The reason I wear it all one length is because Louise can cut it."

"You don't look like an idiot," Callum said. "I know actresses who would kill to have hair like yours."

"You're lying!" Even with her back turned, she radiated disbelief.

"With the split ends trimmed off," he amended.

"I do not have split ends!"

Callum laughed close to her neck, and felt her quiver in response. "I made that up. Seriously, you have lovely hair. Lovely everything else, too."

"No, I don't. I could lose some weight," Jody said.

"What?" To him, her womanly figure had always been the standard to which he compared all others. "You're built just right."

"I don't look like a model, and don't lie to me about it." Although he couldn't see her face, Callum imagined the way her lips must be twitching as she awaited his response.

"I agree. You don't look like a model." He played the comb lightly against her scalp, doing his best to tantalize her. "If I put my arms around a model, all I feel are bones."

Her shoulders drooped. "You put your arms around them a lot, don't you?"

"Hardly ever. Let me show you what I mean." Setting the comb aside, he stroked Jody's cheek and trailed the back of his hand along her jawline. When the tension eased from her muscles and she issued a small sigh, Callum bowed his head until his nose grazed her neck. "There's no one else I want to be this close to."

"Me, either," she whispered.

He collected her in his arms. Although his body tightened instinctively, Callum didn't want to rush.

Every moment with Jody was precious, he mused as he kissed her earlobe.

The breeze sifted around them, filled with the scents of fields and trees. From nearby came the rustling of the horses as they fed. Callum didn't remember when he'd known such utter peace.

His arm brushed the swell of Jody's breast. Her nipple hardened and he rubbed his wrist up and down against it.

She arched her back, thrusting her breasts harder against his arm. That, he gathered, was a definite Go.

As Callum unworked the buttons of Jody's blouse, it occurred to him that this whole platonic business didn't appear to be much of a success. He didn't mind in the least.

CHAPTER SIX

IN TWENTY-NINE YEARS of hard living, Jody had accumulated her fair share of wisdom. For the chance of making love to Callum again, she tossed it all to the wind.

Her muscles grew heavy as his fingers opened her shirt and smoothed down the bra straps. When he cupped her bare breasts, exquisite sensations spread all the way to the spot between her thighs.

His palms squeezed her before easing down to stroke her ribs and waist. Jody heard his breathing intensify and his heart pound in counterpoint to her own, creating their own private music.

She turned her face until their lips met. Gently, Callum tipped her chin upward and introduced his tongue into her mouth. It probed her with the tantalizing sweetness of a flute.

Freed from her inhibitions against touching him, Jody gave herself over to exploration. Silvery blond hair drifted between her fingers, a startling contrast to the prickliness of Callum's jaw. She nibbled on his neck and then, after prying open the buttons on his shirt, rubbed her nude torso against his sculpted strength. Together they swayed to a subtle, intensifying beat.

Rising on her knees, Jody rubbed her cheek across the top of Callum's head. His hands smoothed her jeans down her hips.

They should stop, she thought distractedly. Maybe in another century or so.

Callum fondled the curve of her bottom. "Magnificent," he whispered.

There's too much of it, Jody wanted to say, but that wasn't true. At this moment, she relished her feminine curves because they gave him pleasure. And he gave it back to her in waves as he tasted her.

Jody released a small cry, like a clarinet tone that gets lost in a soaring symphony. How did she dare to open herself to Callum this way? Yet how could she do anything else?

When she almost couldn't bear any more pleasure, he laid her on the blanket and stripped off his pants. What a beautiful sight he was, even better than in memory, with sunlight and leaf-shadow highlighting his splendidly toned body. Best of all was the tenderness on his face and that grin of pure, unabashed happiness.

She loved everything about Callum, from his long legs and taut masculinity to his exuberance. She wanted to urge him on, and yet…

"Wait." Jody rolled over.

"I'm not sure I can."

She reached for her jeans and, from the pocket, produced the protection she'd brought in case of something she hadn't wanted to admit was possible. "Remember what happened the last time we did this?"

"Thank you for thinking ahead." He reached for it, unfolded it and slipped it onto himself. The sight of him so ready for her carried Jody past a moment when her good sense almost reasserted itself.

Callum rolled her atop him, lifting her easily. She gripped him with her knees and they came together in a fierce thrust that vibrated through her like the clash of cymbals.

Callum gasped. "You're beautiful."

"You," Jody whispered.

He gave her a puzzled look. "What about me?"

"Gorgeous." That one word encompassed it all. The man electrified her, as he had from the first moment she'd seen him. He was the wild clarion call that stirred her long-suppressed sense of daring.

Callum rocked his hips rhythmically, moving himself into her and out, slowing the tempo and then speeding it again. Atop him, Jody floated into a dimension ruled by sheer sensation.

Just when she thought she might actually levitate, he shifted away and slid her onto her back.

As he rose above her, cool air replaced him between her legs. The absence was intolerable.

Jody wrapped her legs around him, determined to take charge. She drew him downward, wriggling and arousing him with a dance into which he joined eagerly. She could read the joy on Callum's face as he lost his battle to prolong the exquisite agony of delay.

When he entered her again, it was with the wild abandon of a conductor bringing a symphony to its crescendo. Jody writhed against him, giving herself to his power.

Callum's mouth closed over hers. Their tongues entwined as the climax seized them both. It roared through her, a thrilling tangle of melodies and percussion that she wished would never end.

The last note reverberated into silence. Jody lay spent, eyes shut, as Callum stretched out beside her. She wanted nothing more than this.

Gradually the caress of the breeze, the chirp of a bird and the nicker of a horse transformed paradise back into a ranch. Callum changed from her dream man to the boyfriend she couldn't keep. Before long, he would be flying away from her arms.

Maybe she would be flying away, too, to that fantasy known as Paris. But it could never be as perfect as this, Jody thought.

For a foolish while, she lay hoping to hear Callum say *I love you*. That would be the ultimate magic.

It occurred to her, when the words didn't come, that they'd just banished any possibility of a marriage of convenience. What could they substitute? More years of silence and separation?

Curious about Callum's reaction, she peeked at him. On his nose sat a butterfly, its black-and-yellow wings undulating. He stared at it cross-eyed, and she laughed. Disgruntled, the insect caught a current and bumbled away through the air.

"Only you would have a butterfly land on your face," Jody said.

"Bugs like me. What can I say?"

Apparently horses liked him, too, because King Arthur, tired of grazing, ambled over to him. Callum reached out and scratched the gelding's ears. "We should pick up the boys soon. I don't want them to think we've forgotten them."

Jody realized to her surprise that she hadn't given a moment's thought to her sons all afternoon. How ironic that it was Callum who'd remembered.

"I think you're bonding with them," she said. "They've taken a liking to you, too."

"Jeremy's the most resistant." He pulled on his underclothes.

"I'm surprised you noticed." Although reluctant to end their idyll, she reached for her clothing, too.

"They have distinct personalities." Callum shrugged into his shirt. His chest gleamed in a ray of sunlight, and Jody wished he wouldn't cover it. But he did. "I can't wait to see how they develop. It should be a fascinating process."

"I'm sure it will be." She wanted to share the miracles with him day by day. First, though, they had to figure out how they were going to handle this relationship. "Where do we go from here?"

"They're at the Curly Q. We can take my car if you like," he said.

"I didn't mean literally," Jody said. "You proved your point. We can't have a marriage of convenience. What are the other options?"

"One thing at a time." He stretched lazily. "What happened just now was fantastic. It's going to be a while before I can think clearly."

There was no arguing with that, Jody reflected. As for herself, she wasn't sure she could ever think clearly where Callum was concerned.

THE TWO ADULTS cooked dinner while the boys watched a videotape. When the meat was browning, Callum slipped his arms around Jody and nuzzled her neck, but otherwise he behaved himself. He had to set a good example for their sons.

After the meal, they sat around the table and

played Go Fish. Callum, who normally reveled in winning any game he attempted, found it was more fun to yield to the boys. The odd part was that, while Ben had accepted him more readily, it was Jerry who kept asking him for help while his brother turned to Jody.

They were in the middle of their second game when Jerry got a huge grin on his face. "Anybody got any kings?" he called.

"No fair!" Ben said.

"Give me your kings!"

Callum intervened before a fight could erupt. "Sorry, Benjamin. If your brother asks for a king, you have to give it to him."

"But he hasn't got any kings!" Ben answered. "I just drew my third. Mommy has number four!"

Callum and Jody exchanged glances. The rules of the game must have escaped Jeremy. It was understandable, at his age.

"Let's see." Callum examined the boy's hand. Sure enough, he didn't have any kings. "I'm sorry, son. You have to have a card before you can ask for the ones that match."

"I want the kings! The kings are best." Storm clouds gathered in his son's blue eyes, darkening them to a smoky gray.

Is that how I look when I get angry? Callum wondered, but brushed the thought aside. "Aces are the high cards, Jerry."

"I want the daddies!"

"The daddies?" Callum asked.

"That's the kings." Ben was in agreement with his brother for once. "The queens are the mommies."

"You mean the mommies are second best?" Jody asked with feigned hurt. Or maybe it wasn't entirely feigned.

"They're the best cards, too," Ben said diplomatically. Jerry nodded.

"If kings are daddies and queens are mommies, what are the jacks?" Callum asked.

"They're us," Jeremy said. "You know, boys."

Jody spread her hands in amazement. "I have no idea where they got this notion."

"The tens are girls," Ben added.

"Hold on." Jody folded her arms and glowered. "The tens are below the jacks. This is a sexist hierarchy."

"What's that?" Ben asked.

"Your mom's right," Callum said. "Kings and queens are equal in this house and so are jacks and tens." After a moment's thought, he added, "Just not in card games."

"I want the kings," Jerry said doggedly.

"I had them first!" His brother stuck out his tongue.

The next minute, cards tumbled to the carpet as

Jeremy lunged at Benjamin. It took both adults to untangle them.

"Now what?" Callum asked as he threw Jerry over his shoulder.

"They both get time-outs," Jody said. "Jeremy for attacking his brother, and Benjamin for sticking out his tongue and provoking him. You go that way and I'll go this way." Holding Ben's hand, she marched him toward her bedroom.

"Well, big guy, I guess it's you and me," Callum said.

"You're hurting my tummy." When this didn't bring an immediate response, Jerry added, "I might throw up."

"Down my back?"

"And into your pants. I did it to Mommy."

"I'll bet she loved that." Callum set the boy on his feet. "Okay, kid, march!"

The little guy's stubborn expression hadn't softened by the time they reached the boys' room. "How do these time-outs work?" Callum asked.

"You have to go away." Jerry's mouth quivered.

"Is there any rule that says the daddy can't stay here with you and have a time-out, too?" Callum asked.

Jeremy shook his blond head. As the boy plopped onto his bed, a slow smile warmed his features. "I guess I won."

"How's that?"

"You're the king and I got you."

Callum lowered himself beside his son, bending so as not to bump his head on the upper bunk. "What was this fight really about?"

"Ben says you like him better than me." Jerry wiggled around on the quilt as if unable to hold still. It might, Callum suspected, be a condition endemic to four-year-old boys.

"Where did he get that idea?"

"You let him play with your 'puter."

"Only because he invited himself into my room."

"Can I play on it?"

On the point of agreeing, Callum remembered that this was supposed to be a punishment. "Not until you've served your time. You attacked your brother, remember?"

"Can I play later?" Jeremy asked.

"You bet." He supposed he ought to leave now. The last thing he wanted was to interfere with Jody's discipline program. "I don't know about this household, but where I grew up, the rule was that time-outs also included a hug. Is that true here?"

"Yes. Unless I'm mad," his son said.

"Can I have my hug now, in case you get mad later?"

The boy considered the question solemnly.

"Okay." He threw his arms around his father's neck.

Drawing Jerry onto his lap, Callum hugged and rocked him. It took a moment before he realized that this rush of tenderness was love, a different kind of love than he'd ever experienced before. He wanted to protect this little boy so fiercely that he would do anything, give anything, sacrifice anything for his sake.

When the boy started wiggling again, Callum released him. "I'll see you later."

"Okay." Jeremy beamed.

In the front room, Jody said, "You'd better go see Ben. He feels neglected because you went with his brother."

"They're amazing."

"I'm a little jealous," Jody admitted. "Although I know that's ridiculous."

"I'm the new toy. Of course they find me more interesting, temporarily," Callum said. "But they'd be lost without their mom. So would I."

The words slipped out before he had a chance to reconsider. Well, so what? He'd meant it.

Ben kept him entertained with tales of adventures at the Wiltons' ranch. Later, after the twins apologized to each other, they took turns at the computer and Jody then read them all a storybook. Her animated face and voice cast a spell over Callum.

When the twins were asleep, he went to his room to work on the laptop. It was rare for him to spend a whole day, even a Sunday, without accessing the Web site and reading his e-mail. Tonight, however, he couldn't concentrate.

Hoping another cookie would help, he wandered into the kitchen. Music reached him from Jody's room. Oh, to heck with work, anyway, he thought, and went to pay her a visit.

She lay on the king-size bed where he'd hugged Ben earlier, reading a novel while country music played on the radio. Beside her on an end table lay a monitor, which he realized must be tuned to the boys' room.

With her hair spread across the pillow and her inviting curves outlined by a silky nightgown, Jody might have been a seductress from an exotic tale. His own private Scheherazade.

"Hi," she said, bookmarking her place.

"Want company?" Callum sat on the edge of the bed. "If you're not too tired, maybe we could…"

"Shut up and kiss me," said the most enchanting woman in the world, and she pulled him down beside her.

This time, there was less urgency to their love-making and more sweetness. They amused each other slowly, teasing and talking. Callum wished he could extend this intimacy forever, but at last passion overcame his resistance.

When they'd finished, it was a luxury to sleep beside her all night, to listen to her breathing and feel the subtle electricity of her skin. He wanted to spend every night this way.

Toward morning, Callum dreamed that he was riding home after a long day on the range. Jody emerged from the barn to greet him, a little girl clinging to her skirt. The boys, grown into pre-teenagers, waved from a corral where they were training horses. He drifted awake with a profound sense of yearning.

He glanced toward the other side of the bed. Empty. Jody must have arisen early to start her chores. She couldn't afford to linger in bed on a Monday morning.

Monday! Callum sat up straight. He was missing the weekly staff meeting, and he'd promised to call his secretary about rescheduling his appointments. With April almost here, the copy was due for the July issue and the Web master would be changing the site soon.

Of course, Tisa could run the operation for a while. She did her job efficiently and with flair. No one had Callum's gift for the stylish and the eye-catching, though. When celebrities called, they asked for him personally. Some of the major advertisers did, too.

Enthusiasm powered Callum through his morning routine. When he'd showered and changed, he was relieved to find Gladys's daughter, Louise, ready to take the boys to town for their half day of preschool.

He gave each boy a hug, distracted for a moment from his preoccupation with work. Once they'd left, Callum powered up his laptop, picked up his cell phone and got to work.

He came alive as he immersed himself in activity, his mind ticking off a dozen details at once. The adrenaline rush made him forget his surroundings for hours.

By lunchtime, last night's dream had almost disappeared. It came back to Callum only when he looked out the window and saw Jody and her hired hand marking off a large rectangle toward the back of the house. Judging by the stumps of cornstalks, they must be planning to clear and replant the vegetable garden.

The cycle of life on a ranch had a nostalgic familiarity. Callum understood the satisfaction of seeing crops grow and herds increase. Although operating a modern ranch required sophisticated knowledge of everything from cattle prices to tax laws, would it be outside the realm of possibility for him to stay here and learn to run the Wandering I with Jody?

A shudder ran through him. That man riding

home in the dream could never be him. Not for long, anyway. He loved Jody and the boys, but he didn't want their closeness to deteriorate into broken promises and resentment. There had to be a better solution.

Callum went to fix lunch. Jody must be starving after a morning of hard physical work. Ranching didn't suit her, he thought, even though she was doing a conscientious job. She belonged in a classroom.

He set to work fixing a large *Nicoise* salad with leftovers and some purchases he'd made in town. Boston lettuce, ripe tomatoes, thick slices of potato, hard-boiled eggs, tuna, black olives, capers, anchovies. The names of the ingredients fitted into a mesmerizing rhythm while he worked.

He was mixing the vinaigrette when Jody came in. "That smells wonderful."

"As good as chalk dust?" he asked impulsively.

"Is that a joke?" Her nose wrinkled. "Because it isn't funny."

"It's not a joke." Callum took her hands in his. Turning them over, he inspected the scarred and calloused palms. "You're doing a great job. Your father would be proud of you. But this isn't right."

A frown settled across her face. "What you mean is, it isn't what you want me to do."

"That's partly true," Callum conceded. "I want

you and the boys to move to L.A. so we can be together.''

''You want to have your work and us, too,'' Jody answered. ''Well, this is my work. That land out there is my office, and I have a staff, too. You can't ask me to toss them aside any more than I can ask you to toss your magazine aside.''

''One of us has to move,'' he said.

She pressed her lips together. He imagined he could hear what she was thinking: *It won't be me.*

Darn! She'd always been stubborn. But then, so was he.

''Let's eat,'' Jody said. ''I'm grumpy on an empty stomach.''

He had to win her over, but he'd already played his trump card by mentioning her teaching career. He knew she'd be happier teaching in a classroom than oiling farm machinery any day of the week, if only she would allow herself to admit it, but for some reason she'd refused. What else did he have to offer?

For once, Callum Fox had run out of ideas.

CHAPTER SEVEN

AFTER LUNCH, Callum took a cell phone call and disappeared into his room. Too edgy to return to work, Jody sat at the piano and rippled through a show tune, then another and another, while her thoughts played over their conversation.

He'd asked her again to come to L.A. The scary part was that she'd been tempted to agree.

Here at the ranch, she fit into Callum's arms and matched him in their verbal sparring. She was his equal. In California, she would be just one more woman seeking his attention, and not the most beautiful one, by far.

She'd also meant what she said about the boys having emotional ties to the home where their grandparents had helped raise them. True, during the past few days she'd been surprised at how quickly the pair had taken to Callum. Perhaps they needed a father more than she'd realized. Still, something was missing.

As her fingers moved across the keys, Jody was finally able to pinpoint what troubled her so much. Despite his invitation, Callum still held back. He hadn't said he loved her. He hadn't asked her to marry him.

He might love her a little, but not enough to sustain a lifetime. The omission confirmed her belief that he wasn't truly committed to her. And if it didn't happen here in Texas, it certainly wasn't going to happen in the land of temptation.

Hearing his footsteps in the kitchen, she dropped her hands to her lap and let the silence enfold her. The moment she glanced up, she saw the news in his expression.

"You're going home," she said.

Callum blinked. "I didn't know you could hear my conversation."

"I didn't have to." The mixture of emotions on his face told Jody everything. Especially the hint of relief playing around his mouth. "It's obvious. You're eager to be gone."

"I've got my work cut out for me. One of our major advertisers is threatening to take his business to a rival publication." Callum's long legs carried him down the steps toward her. "While our advertising director's been out with an injury, our competition seized the chance to wine and dine our client."

"And you're the only one who can turn him around." Jody understood the impact of Callum's charisma.

"I don't want to leave until we resolve our situation." He sat beside her on the bench. "Jody…"

To her dismay, tears clouded her vision. Defiantly, she said, "Don't try to snow me. You're relieved. Go on, deny it."

He couldn't. Callum might seem glib at times, but he was honest. He proved it by admitting, "In a way, I am. Not because it means leaving you and the boys. I hate that part."

"What's the part you like?" Jody forced the words through stiff lips.

"Do you remember my senior year in college, when Dad had his first heart attack?" Callum asked.

"You went ballistic." He'd left campus the moment he got the news, skipping classes to stay at his father's bedside until his recovery was assured. "You did everything you could for him and your mom."

"Until then, I'd taken them for granted, the way kids tend to." In the warm midday light filtering through broad windows, Callum's eyes had a faraway glaze. "I was thrilled that he got better. But not entirely for selfless reasons."

"You were worried about the feed store," Jody remembered. "I told you your mom could run it."

"Not alone. I wouldn't have let her. You know she had chronic health problems." A shadow fell across his clean-cut features, perhaps from recalling her death soon after their graduation. "During that whole period, I had a recurring nightmare where I was locked in a room and couldn't find the door. After a while, I realized there was no door."

"You felt trapped," she summed up. "You were afraid you'd have to give up your dreams to run the store."

He nodded. "I realized that later."

"Is that how you feel about the ranch? Like you'd be trapped if you stayed here?" Until this moment, Jody hadn't wanted to admit to herself how much she was hoping Callum would either sell the magazine or find a way to run it from the ranch.

"There's a part of me that loves this place." His hands closed over hers. Although they were sitting very close, he hadn't touched her until now. "That part of me wants an idyllic life here with you and the boys."

"You'd hate it." Her voice came out flat, making a statement she desperately wished weren't true.

"I could do it," Callum said earnestly. "For a while. Then I'd get testy and difficult, and I'd be a total pain in the neck."

Jody couldn't deny it, because he was right. The nonstop action of city life, the acclaim of talented people and the thrill of achievement were as essential to Callum as security and close friends were to her. Fate must have laughed when it made them soul mates, because they could never live together.

"I don't want us to become enemies. That's what would happen if I stayed here." Callum swallowed hard. "We have to find a way to stay close and share the boys."

"You can visit them here until they're old enough to fly out west by themselves," she said. "As for staying close, I don't see how that's possible."

"I'm sorry the marriage of convenience idea didn't work." His smile was tempered by regret. "Maybe we should have tried harder to keep our hands off each other."

"It was a lost cause from the start." Jody didn't regret making love with Callum yesterday. She would always cherish the memory.

"When's the boys' birthday?" he asked.

"August fifteenth."

"I'll come back then," he said. "Sooner, if I can."

"Fine."

That was it? Everything smoothed over and an appointment made as if these past three days had been simply an interlude? Jody wanted to rage, except that it would be useless. Callum had to go. And she had to let him.

She found the strength to stand up calmly and

say, "I'd better go watch for the boys. Louise will be bringing them home any minute."

The rest of the afternoon passed in a blur. Callum explained his departure to Ben and Jerry and promised to return for their birthday. Although the boys protested, before long they went out to play with the puppy, which was eager for attention.

She didn't ask what he was going to do about her being a finalist in the contest, even though she knew that was the reason he'd come to Texas. He didn't say anything, either. Maybe he needed to consult the rules or talk to his managing editor or figure out some alternative. Jody decided to leave that up to him.

It amazed her how fast he could pack, make a plane reservation, kiss them all and drive away. She knew he was eager to fix the problems at work. She wished she felt the same enthusiasm about vaccinating her calves, but it was simply one more chore to be accomplished.

Despite the distraction of hard labor, the next few days proved difficult emotionally. Jody cried often, and knew her friends worried about her, especially Gladys and Bo, who dropped by to check on her.

Ben and Jerry got excited when their father called to say he'd arrived safely and missed them. The next day, he e-mailed a photo of his office so they could see where he worked, along with shots he'd taken of them at the Wiltons' ranch. When he spoke to Jody on the phone by herself, he asked how she was doing and she told him "Just great" with hardly any irony.

A few days later, Callum reported that he'd persuaded the advertiser not only to sign a long-term contract but also to sponsor a cable TV series in conjunction with the magazine. The man had one condition: that Callum himself host the show.

"You'll be fantastic," Jody said, and meant it.

On Friday, she went into town to do some grocery shopping and collect the boys. As she was about to leave, the preschool director said, "Congratulations."

"For what?" she asked, but another parent called the woman's name at the same time and distracted her.

At the grocery store, several more people congratulated Jody. She wondered if the contest winner had been named earlier than expected. Too embarrassed to admit she hadn't checked the magazine's Web site, she simply thanked everyone.

Could she possibly have won the trip to Paris? It didn't seem likely, given Callum's conflict of interest. Perhaps a winner had been named and the magazine had decided to give the other finalists consolation prizes. A new wardrobe or a smaller trip would be nice, too.

As Jody drove onto the ranch, Gladys waved from horseback and called, "Good for you!"

She waved back, but the forewoman was too far away to engage her in conversation. Besides, she'd be able to access the Web site in a few minutes and get the story herself.

After settling Ben and Jerry for quiet time in their room, Jody logged onto the computer in her office. The *Family Voyager* site was a collage of enticing headlines and lively photos, including one of Callum shaking hands with the advertiser. His sunny image leaped off the screen.

She couldn't stay angry with the man. He was like a force of nature. How could she have believed she could capture him any more than she could hold the wind in her hands?

Tearing her attention away, Jody scrolled down to the latest developments in the contest. There was more information about the finalists, but no reference to a winner. If people hadn't been congratulating her about the contest, what had they meant?

Outside, she found Gladys releasing Elsie and Half-Pint into a grazing area near the house. "They're getting along just dandy now," the forewoman said before Jody could question her. "You're doing a lot better job than your daddy thought you would. He told me once that you were a born town girl."

"Wait a minute." Her father hadn't believed she

was suited to being a rancher? "I thought my parents were counting on me running the Wandering I. Dad went on and on in the will about how to handle everything." Jody had read the document many times for guidance. "If he expected me to sell it, why did he bother?"

"What your father expected and what he wanted, well, I don't know if they were the same." Removing her baseball cap, the forewoman wiped the sweat off her forehead.

"Don't pussyfoot around!" Jody said. "Did Dad want me to run the ranch or not? You were a witness to the will. You must have some idea."

Gladys leaned against the fence. "You want me to level with you?"

"You bet!"

"Your father told me he figured you'd insist on running the place because you're so stubborn," she said. "As best I can remember, his words were, 'Once she gets an idea in her head, Gladys, she won't let it go. She's a schoolteacher, not a rancher, but just you watch.' He left you those instructions because he figured you'd need the help."

Jody struggled to absorb the implications. "What did he want to happen to the ranch?"

"He didn't say."

It wasn't like Gladys to act so cagey. "Why didn't you tell me this before?" Jody demanded.

Her forewoman wedged the cap onto her head. "Because, you see, Louise and I..." She broke off to clear her throat.

"You and Louise what?" Jody prompted.

"We're both ranchers by nature," Gladys said. "But she knows how hard it was for me to find anyone that would hire me, so she's studying transcribing although she doesn't give a darn about it. As for me, I'd like to buy the place if I could work out the financing, but I doubt any bank would take a chance on me. In any case, it wasn't my place to tell you what to do."

In other words, Jody thought, she could have arranged a year ago to sell the ranch to Gladys and carry the financing herself, but her forewoman had been too ethical to take advantage of the situation. "I'm glad you told me this."

"Don't worry about it," Gladys said. "I'm glad you're running the place. Just as long as you don't sell it to some male chauvinist, I'm happy. I'm sure Bo and I will get along fine."

"What's Bo got to do with it?" she asked.

"You mean you're not going to let your husband be involved with the ranch?" Gladys asked.

Jody wondered what on earth she was talking about. "What husband?"

"You and Bo," said her forewoman. "The other day in town, he said you two were engaged."

This was getting weirder and weirder. "When was this?"

"I was at the drugstore restocking our supplies and some of those ladies who've got nothing good to say about anyone started pumping me for information about Callum."

"Oh, great." Every town had its busybodies. Everett Landing was no exception.

"Melody Lee, that old witch who always looks like she's sucking a lemon, said wasn't it too bad you couldn't hold on to a man and how glad she was you weren't teaching school anymore and corrupting the children with your loose ways. You know how she is." Gladys shook her head. "Well, Bo overheard and he said, 'A lot you know. The fact is, Jody sent him packing because she and I are engaged, only we haven't announced it yet.'"

"Bo said that?" She had to smile at the image of her friend flying to her defense. "I appreciate the impulse, but it's not true."

"It's not?" Gladys let out a snort. "It sure did shut up those gossips."

"No, it didn't." Jody sighed. "They must have told everyone in town. That's why people kept congratulating me. What a mess!"

"It's not so bad," the older woman said. "It wouldn't hurt if Callum heard that rumor himself."

"Don't you dare!"

A piercing whistle from the barn drew their attention to Freddy, who was signaling for Gladys's help with a stubborn horse. "Got to go, boss-lady. I'll see you later," said the forewoman.

"Thanks for telling me about Dad. And about Bo."

"My pleasure."

Jody marched into her office and dialed the newspaper. Bo's secretary put her through.

"Jody!" His voice rose half an octave on the end. It sounded as if it were in danger of breaking.

"I heard we're engaged," she said. "It came as kind of a surprise."

He issued a choking noise. "I meant to tell you about that."

"When?" she asked. "On our wedding day?"

"I'm really sorry." Bo sounded so miserable that she took pity on him.

"I appreciate that you were trying to help. Gladys told me about Melody and her remarks," Jody said. "Couldn't you have said something less extreme?"

"We could make it true," said her friend. "We could get engaged. Married, even. I mean, if you want to. I'd sure be honored."

Although she'd set aside any notion of marrying him after Callum returned, Jody allowed herself to toy with the idea once again. Having a husband would protect her and the boys from gossip. And with Bo, she could truly have a marriage of convenience.

She doubted that was what he had in mind, however. It certainly wasn't what she wanted or needed. "Thank you, but I'm afraid I'm not in love with you," she said. "Besides, it would break Evelyn's heart."

"Evelyn?" he asked in confusion.

"The waitress at the Downtown Café."

"Oh, that Evelyn," Bo said. "I eat lunch over there two or three times a week. She's so pretty, I figured lots of guys ask her out."

"Bo, you're the one she wants," Jody said. "Callum said it, so it must be true."

"Callum found out that Evelyn likes me?" He sounded baffled but not displeased. "That's amazing. I mean, a woman like her could have anybody."

Jody supposed she should be offended that a man who'd just proposed to her was flattered by another woman's interest. On the other hand, since she'd rejected him, his ego deserved massaging. "You should ask her out."

"Are you matchmaking?" Judging by his tone, the prospect amused him.

"I like happy endings," Jody said. "If I can't have one for myself, I'd at least like to see one for you."

"How'm I going to explain my chasing another woman when I'm engaged to you?"

"Tell people the truth," she said. "It hurts less in the long run."

"You're a wonderful woman. If Callum can't see that, he doesn't deserve you," Bo said. "I guess I'd better take your advice. If I eat dinner at the café tonight, I can ask Ella Mae to spread the word that I spoke in haste."

"Oops. I just remembered, I volunteered to help at the charity bazaar at church tonight," Jody said. "I guess that means I'll get lots of opportunities to set the record straight."

"I could stop by and help." His statement lacked enthusiasm.

"Go to the café," she said. "I'm a big girl. I can take care of myself."

By the time she hung up, the boys were awake. Jody had no more time to think until much later. As it turned out, Gladys's revelation about the ranch had given her plenty to chew on.

By Callum's usual standards, the week had been a triumph. On Friday afternoon, the entire staff celebrated the plans for the cable series. He sent out for champagne and chocolates, and everyone was having such a good time that an hour later he ordered pizza so they could party into the dinner hour.

It was a lot better than going home alone to his empty condominium. Despite its prized beach view—at an angle from the balcony—and trend-setting decor, he now found the place less than satisfying. There was no one to play cards with and no one to accompany his trumpet playing. The steady boom of waves and the mutter of passing cars were no substitute for childish shouts and womanly laughter. He even missed the smell of manure from the barn.

Until last week, he could have sworn no one in L.A. looked like Jody. Now he saw her every-where. A ripple of brown hair going into an ele-vator had pumped adrenaline through Callum's veins only this morning, and yesterday he'd quick-ened his stride on the sidewalk to come alongside a shapely brunette in jeans and a bandanna. Each time, his spirits had plummeted when he angled into position and saw that, of course, it wasn't her.

"You can't be having much fun, standing over here wearing a lost-puppy expression." Tisa paused in front of him. Around them, he realized, the room was emptying as co-workers finished their pizza and departed for the weekend.

"Sorry. Am I putting a damper on things?" he asked.

"You know, I've met a lot of men who think they're the center of the universe," the managing editor told him. "You're the only one who actually comes close to being it. This whole place feeds off your energy. When you're down in the dumps, we all start to sag.''

Callum couldn't summon enough energy to enjoy the compliment. "I miss my family."

Tisa folded her arms. "I never thought I'd see you lovesick, Callum Fox. That Jody must be one fine lady.''

"I asked her to move out here. She turned me down," he said.

"When did you start taking no for an answer?" asked the editor.

She had a point. Still, Callum knew that, where Jody was concerned, applying pressure might simply backfire. "I'll think about that."

"I hope you get it together before we all sink into a major depression." Tisa flipped shut a box holding half a pizza. "Take this home and eat it. That ought to help."

"Thanks. I haven't had time to get to the supermarket in days."

The beach area was filling with people in a party mood, Callum saw as he drove home. Young couples wandered along the sidewalks, scanning menus posted outside restaurants. From the condo next door, music blared through open windows. As he closed his garage door and circled to the front, he caught the smell of spilled beer mingling with the briny sea scent.

One of these days he ought to buy a house in-land with a yard big enough for a dog, Callum thought. He might even find a horse property in one of the canyons that ringed L.A.

What on earth was he thinking? He didn't have time to take care of a horse, or a dog, either.

In the kitchen, he munched on pizza while calculating how many times he'd phoned Jody since Monday. Once to report that he'd arrived. Again on Wednesday to tell her about the cable show. In between, he'd e-mailed photos. She didn't seem to mind the intrusion, and it *had* been two days. He decided it wouldn't be intrusive to call again.

His mood lifting at the prospect of talking to her, Callum rapid-dialed her number. His heart gave a sharp thump when he heard a female voice, until he realized it wasn't hers.

"Reilly residence," said a familiar Texas twang.

"Hi, Gladys," he said. "Is Jody around?"

"She went out," said the forewoman. "I'm baby-sitting."

Although he always enjoyed talking to the boys, Callum's spirits nose-dived. "Do you expect her back soon?" Surely she couldn't be out much longer. It was nearly nine o'clock in Texas, and ranchers kept early hours.

"I don't expect so," Gladys said. "I don't suppose you've heard the news."

"What news?" He hadn't been gone long enough for anything major to change, surely.

"About her and Bo. It's all over town that they're engaged."

"You're joking, right?" Jody hadn't shown a trace of interest in the man!

"She can hardly get out the door without someone congratulating her," Gladys said. "Folks around here think it's a great idea."

"It's a terrible idea," Callum said. "She doesn't love him."

"He's crazy about her." That much was true, he supposed. How could a man help falling for Jody? "And the boys need a father."

"They already have a father!" he said. "I won't allow it."

"I can't see that it's up to you," Gladys answered in a maddeningly calm drawl. "You're not here, if I may point out the obvious."

"I'm going to be," he said. "I'm coming right out. Don't tell Jody. I don't want to give her time to marshal her arguments."

"My lips are sealed," said Gladys.

At his request, she put the boys on the phone. Callum managed to concentrate long enough to enjoy their anecdotes about their games and the puppy. He assured them that he loved them and promised to see them before they knew it.

As soon as they hung up, he got on the Internet and booked the first available flight.

CHAPTER EIGHT

RUNNING THE Rototiller was hard work. Sweat trickled between Jody's breasts, darkening her T-shirt as she pushed ahead, determined to finish the job this afternoon. The garden needed proper tilling to bear enough vegetables not only for eating but also for canning.

Behind her, the boys followed at a safe distance, collecting rocks and debris in buckets. The dirt smears on their faces testified to their enthusiasm.

She supposed she could have assigned Freddy to push the machine, but she relished accomplishing the hard task on her own. Maybe her father had been right that she wasn't cut out to be a rancher, but he'd been right about her stubbornness, too.

Over the roar of the motor, she heard the boys shouting, so she turned it off. As the rumble died, Ben and Jerry were calling, "Daddy! Daddy!"

Impossible. Jody turned and stared. How could Callum be here? Yet there was no mistaking his grin, so bright it eclipsed the sun, as his sons pelted toward him across the yard. Tailored slacks and a soft jacket outlined the lean stretch of his body when he lifted first one and then the other overhead.

Too overwhelmed to react, Jody stood like a tree stump, waiting for this sophisticated apparition to acknowledge her. She hated being so disheveled but it couldn't be helped.

After setting the boys on their feet, Callum let them tug him forward. At the edge of the dirt, he stopped to frown at her. She didn't think he was really angry, but something must have put his nose out of joint.

"What?" she demanded.

"You are not going to marry that man!"

"Excuse me?"

"You don't love Bo. He could never make you happy." Callum folded his arms. "Furthermore, I refuse to let another man raise my sons. They're mine and you're mine." He blinked as if surprised by his own words. "Not that I'm trying to boss you around. Well, yes, maybe I am. Break off the engagement. I'm not leaving till you do."

Jody's mind performed a rapid search of possibilities and hit on the obvious. Gladys must have told him about the sham engagement. Shame on her! And hoorah, too.

Apparently Callum had flown all the way to Texas to demand that she jilt Bo. Double hoorah!

Unfortunately, once he learned the truth, he'd go straight home.

Jody decided not to let him off the hook yet. "It's not every day an old maid rancher gets a proposal of marriage."

"You're no old maid. And there's no reason to run down the aisle with the first man who asks you!" Callum snapped.

"Don't be ridiculous," Jody said. "I have no intention of running at my own wedding. I might trip over my gown." The boys stared from one to the other of them, trying to understand. Since this wasn't an appropriate conversation for them to overhear, she said, "Why don't you kids go tell Gladys that Callum is here? I think she's in the barn."

"Okay." Ben turned to his brother. "Race you."

"Loser!" said Jeremy, and took off running.

"I don't understand," Callum said when they were alone. "Why are you doing this?"

"Bo asked me to marry him," Jody said. "He also told some people in town that we were engaged because he was trying to spare my reputation after you left. But I said no."

For several heartbeats, Callum didn't move. Finally, he said, "You're not getting married?"

She shook her head. "No, although I was tempted."

"Why?" he said.

"I told you. Because he asked me."

He waited as if expecting more. When it didn't come, he said, "That's it? You were tempted to marry Bo because he asked you?"

"It's more than you'll ever do." To Jody's chagrin, her voice trembled.

"But I asked you to move to L.A.," Callum said. "You and the boys."

"What kind of commitment is that?" she demanded. "You want me to uproot my entire life so I can be your girlfriend? No, thanks."

"Whoa." He spread his hands to halt her.

In the past, she'd avoided confrontations from fear of alienating him. Well, she was finished letting fear run her life, and she didn't intend to stop talking until she was good and ready.

"California is your turf, not mine," Jody said. "You have your work and your friends. What about me? In case you hadn't noticed, I'm not the type to hang on some guy's coattails. I don't want to be part of your entourage, Callum."

"What entourage?"

"All those women who think you're wonderful and those celebrities who invite you to their parties." She barely caught her breath before raging on: "You're going to be an even bigger deal once you're on television. Maybe when they drop by your house, your pals will mistake me for the housekeeper. Won't that be fun?''

He looked so bewildered she almost felt sorry for him. ''Is this because I haven't asked you to marry me?''

''You're really slow on the uptake,'' Jody said.

''But in L.A., people don't worry about things like that,'' he said.

''About things like what? A wedding ring?''

He nodded.

''I'm not from L.A. I'm from Texas.'' As an afterthought, Jody threw in, ''And so are you.''

''Good point,'' said Callum. ''Wait here.''

Without another word, he walked past the screened porch and disappeared around the chicken coop. Jody was so furious she wanted to scream, except that she didn't see what good that would do. She was debating whether to turn the Rototiller back on and take out her frustrations on the hard ground when the boys dashed toward her.

''We can't find Gladys,'' Ben said, plowing right through the dirt.

''Where's Daddy?'' Jeremy trailed in his wake.

''I don't know,'' Jody said. ''He's kind of a funny guy sometimes.'' An outrageous guy, she wanted to add, one who never made her forget she was alive.

If he were here right now, she'd slap him and then she'd hug him. Or maybe the other way around. Of course, once she hugged him, she might not feel like slapping him anymore.

"I see Daddy!" Jerry crowed. "I see him first!"

"I see him second!" cried Ben.

Callum swung through the afternoon carrying a big bunch of wildflowers. He raised them above his head, clasped both hands and gave a victory salute.

Okay, so I love him, Jody thought, her heart swelling. *I must be the most foolish woman who ever lived.*

He marched right through the freshly turned soil. In front of Jody, he dropped to his knees, extending the flowers. She took them as gently as if they were made of glass.

"Daddy, your pants will get dirty!" Ben said.

"Too late." Callum chuckled. "Well, now that I'm here, everybody gather around." They drew closer. Jody could hardly breathe. "First of all, I love you, Ben. I love you, Jerry. And I love you most of all, Jody."

If a tornado had struck at that moment, she wouldn't have stirred.

"If you would do me the honor of becoming my wife, I'd be the happiest man in the world," he said. "I'll sue anybody who claims he's happier than me."

"I was wrong," she said. "You're not a Texan anymore. Definitely from California."

The interruption didn't faze him. "I've given it a lot of consideration while I was picking these flowers and I'm willing to move the magazine to Dallas," Callum said. "That's as close as I can get and still have access to a major airport and the kinds of facilities we need. Maybe we can buy a ranch within commuting distance. What do you say, Jody? Will you meet me halfway?"

"You'd give up the West Coast for me?" she asked.

"I used to be afraid of getting trapped," he said earnestly. "But I've changed. Setting the world on fire doesn't mean much if there's no hearth fire waiting for me at home. Not that I expect you to become my hausfrau when you look so cute behind a plow."

"I look like an idiot," Jody said. "I'm just stubborn, that's all. I was never cut out to be a rancher. I've already decided that as soon as we can arrange it, I'm going to sell the ranch to Gladys. And since I'm going back to teaching, I might as well do it in Los Angeles."

"Really?" Hope lit Callum's face. "Does that mean you'll marry me?"

"I will!" Jerry said.

"Me, too!" said his brother.

"That makes three of us," Jody said.

"You mean it?"

"I love you," she said. "I'll sue anybody who says I don't."

Callum's shout of happiness wiped away the memory of all those lonely years without him. As he drew Jody and the boys close, she could see that it had been her own anxieties that had held her back. She could have left with him after college or five years ago, but each time she'd feared that she would lose him once they reached the big city. Well, she'd nearly lost him anyway. It was long past time to take a chance.

When he released them, he was covered with dirt and utterly unconcerned. Jody brushed him off and then noticed the hopeless condition of her own shirt. "I'm going to change into clean clothes and then we'll celebrate."

"What about the garden?" Callum asked.

"I'll deal with it later," Jody said. "I was mostly doing it as a favor to Gladys, anyway."

He handed her his jacket. "Take that inside for me, will you? I'll finish for you."

"But…"

"Never say I refused to do a favor for your forewoman," he told her. "Besides, I like playing with noisy machinery."

The motor roared to life and clods of dirt filled the air. Jody beat a hasty retreat while the boys stayed to cheer for their father.

Gladys was going to be delighted at the results

of the trick she'd played on Callum. As for herself, Jody knew that, as the wife-to-be of the publisher, she would have to withdraw from the Mother of the Year contest. Under the circumstances, she didn't mind one bit.

It seemed to be a good day for making dreams come true, all the way around. As carefree as if she were still a girl in high school, Jody went into the house.

LOVE IS IN THE AIR

Jill Shalvis

PROLOGUE

There is nothing more special than a mother/child relationship, which basically makes being a mother the best job in the world. I don't need an award for that, but I'm applying for the Mother Of The Year award anyway. It's not because I'm the greatest mother on the planet—although I do think I've done a great job—but simply because my daughter is the best daughter out there. I figure that means I've done something right. Let me tell you about her.

Kylie Birmingham is kind and giving. She takes care of everyone around her without complaint, including me, her grandmother, and an entire airport, and trust me on this, that's not an easy job. She's hardworking, dedicated and yes, okay, she's also stubborn as all get-out, but that's because she cares so much.

So please consider me for Mother Of The Year. If I win, I plan to use the trip to take Kylie on vacation, which she desperately needs. In Paris I can spoil her for once. I can ply her with wine and food and culture. I can make sure she laughs and smiles. She really needs that. And a nice French man as a bonus...for me.

You're probably wondering why Kylie works so hard. She's running her deceased daddy's airport, which she loves more than anything, but as with just about everything Kylie is passionate about, she's developed tunnel vision to the point of ignoring all else, such as *life*.

So in conclusion—an essay has to have a conclusion, right?—please award me Mother Of The Year so I can take my wonderful, deserving, overworked and endearingly curmudgeonly daughter to Paris, and give her a life. *Thank you!*

CHAPTER ONE

ONE OF THESE DAYS Kylie Birmingham figured she'd slow down. But as she ran, gasping for breath, toward the maintenance hangar with a cell phone to her ear, a can of sealant in one hand, a wrench in the other and the radio at her hip squawking, she knew it wouldn't be soon.

She lived her life running through her airport, or so it seemed. The crux of being her own boss, she supposed, and of being the boss of thirteen-and-a-half others, as well—the half being Patti the custodian because she was pregnant. Kylie didn't count the baby as one half, she counted Patti that way, since she spent every afternoon sleeping in the storage closet while pretending to check supplies.

The radio squawked again. Dispatch needed her. Kylie's extremely wealthy and extremely spoiled rotten client in the lobby needed her. Her head mechanic needed her. Her secretary needed her. Her accountant needed her.

Kylie's head pounded, and she realized what *she* needed—a vacation.

Paris would do. Yes, Paris with its teeming crowds and bustling streets, Paris with the mind-boggling architecture and museums she could lose herself in, with the bakeries she could get happily fat in…oh yes, Paris, wild and romantic Paris, would do perfectly.

She'd never really take a vacation. Too frivolous, too time-consuming…and neither frivolous nor time-consuming were exactly part of her nature.

Her legs pumped the quarter mile distance between the front lobby and the third hangar of the small, private Orange County airport. The late-summer heat didn't bother her, nor the fact that she hadn't eaten since six that morning, but then again, stamina had never been a problem for Kylie.

Time, however…time was a problem, a big one. With so much work to do, there was no wild and romantic *anything* in her life, much less fantasizing about a trip to Paris.

"Kylie…are you listening to me?"

The voice came from the cell phone permanently planted to her ear. It was the sweet little voice of the biggest tyrant she'd ever met. "Yes, I'm listening," Kylie said. "As my accountant, I always listen to you, Lou."

"That's *Grandma* Lou to you," her grandmother said. "And I need your checkbook. I think I forgot to balance the thing last month…and maybe the month before…I don't know. Anyway, the bank is calling, and…''

Kylie's stomach fell to her toes. As she'd learned six months ago, it had been an incredibly stupid idea to hire her grandma after Grandpa had died. But the four foot four inch, eighty-going-on-sixteen Lou had blinked those rheumy baby blues, claiming poverty and boredom, and that she'd be dead in a week if someone, anyone, didn't give her a job. And because Kylie, like her father before her, collected the needy, she'd folded like a cheap accordion on talent night.

The radio at her hip was still crackling with tension as the three people in her dispatch continued to argue over who was going to work the late shift tomorrow night. Their second richest client was coming through at midnight and required some tie-down assistance. Cocking her head, Kylie listened as the tiff upgraded to mutiny, which was nothing new. Bringing the radio to her mouth, she panted for air as she slowed down. "I'll be there in two minutes. Fix this before I get there and heads won't roll." Empty threat, and they all knew it. She couldn't have found another linesman, dispatch or mechanic in this puny, one-horse hellhole to save her life, but it was *her* hellhole and she'd make it work.

She always did.

"*Well.*" Her grandmother huffed a bit in her dainty little voice over Kylie's cell phone. "No need to get your panties in a twist. Fine, then. I'll handle this situation myself.''

"Grandma, I was talking to—"

"That's *Lou* to you."

Dial tone.

The cell rang again before Kylie could toss it in a ditch. Warily, she glanced at the caller I.D. and sighed.

"We have a situation in the front lobby," Daisy, her secretary—and mother—reported.

A chip off Lou's block as another sweet, little, dainty ex-socialite, Daisy had lost all her money dabbling in day trading. She couldn't file, couldn't answer a phone without disconnecting someone and couldn't find the engine compartment of an airplane to save her life.

Yet another pity hire.

Funny though, the only person Kylie pitied at the moment was herself. "What's the situation?" She pictured two planes coming in at the same time, or a computer failure. Maybe a plane hadn't been tied down properly and was hurling itself down the slight hill toward the hangar designated as the lobby, because nothing, absolutely nothing, would have surprised her today. "Mom?"

"I've been answering the phone all morning and I need aspirin. Do you have any?"

Kylie stopped, leaned against hangar number two and thunked her head back against the metal wall. Eyes closed, head tipped up facing the sun, she decided *she* was the one who needed aspirin. She loved her mom with all her heart, she did, but for once, just once, she wanted her mother to be the mother.

"Maybe I should leave early."

"But mom, the phones—"

"No problem, I figured that all out weeks ago. I just call line one with line two, then put them both on hold." Daisy's bubbly laughter tinkled in Kylie's ear. "That way the phones are both busy and you don't miss any calls! Ingenuous, huh?"

Kylie resisted the urge to slit her wrists. "How often do you do this?"

"Why, whenever I need to go home early. Just a couple days a week, I suppose. Oh, and guess what I just did, honey?"

Kylie was afraid to guess, honest to God she was.

"I picked up my favorite magazine this morning, and besides having that hunky Harrison Ford on the cover, it had a contest form for some Mother Of The Year award. You'll never guess what I'm going to win."

Kylie choked back a laugh because it would probably be a half-hysterical one. *Mother Of The Year?* Wouldn't that be *Kylie,* who'd raised everyone around her?

"A trip to Paris!" Daisy laughed. "Isn't it too perfect?"

Busy streets, lots of wine, no anxieties...no

mother or grandmother to drive her off her rocker. "Perfect," she agreed.

"I know! Everyone deserves their dream, honey, and I know yours is Paris. So when I win Mother Of The Year—which, of course, I will, as I've done a fabulous job with you, if I say so myself—I want you to come with me!"

The sun felt good on Kylie's face. If only she could stand here all day instead of going inside and facing the chaos. "Mom, if I wanted a trip to Paris, I'd go."

"No, you wouldn't. Because ever since your father died you've taken it upon yourself to run this place just because it was *his* dream."

It was Kylie's dream, too, to kept the airport afloat, to see it prosper.

All she needed was a miracle.

Both she and her dad were practical, single-minded, goal-oriented, orderly, *sane* people, who had shared this weakness for the impractical, chaotic, unorderly, bankruptcy-bound airport. Maybe because in the air, they found true freedom, or because there was just something about walking through a hangar full of planes knowing you could hop in one and be anywhere you wanted to be. Whatever the reason, the airport had been her dad's one passion, and she'd inherited both his love for the place...and the debts.

"You know, if you'd only get married, you'd

feel more relaxed. Grandma said a nice boy just moved in across—"

"No," Kylie said quickly. Relationships didn't work for her. She only had room in her life for one problem area—the airport. Everything else had to be, well, easily managed, practical.

Men were not easily managed or practical, not for her.

Her mother and grandma shared the opposite approach. Men were like candy, to be gobbled up. They often tried to impose this lifestyle on the reluctant Kylie in the form of blind dates from hell. "I don't need a date," she reiterated.

"Yes, you do."

"No, I don't."

"Yes, you do."

"No, I—" She broke off, refusing to argue with the one woman no one on the planet could win an argument with. "So there *isn't* an emergency up there?"

"You work too hard, Kylie. You care too much, you give too much. You need to get something back, and this trip—"

"*Mom.* Is there an emergency up there?"

"Of course there is. I told you, I need aspirin!"

"Okay, fine. I'll be there as soon as I put out the fire in dispatch, deal with Grandma, and—"

"There's a fire in dispatch? Why didn't you say so? I'll call 9-1-1."

"No!" Kylie lowered her voice with effort. "Don't call 9-1-1, I have it covered."

"Well, if you're sure, honey."

"I'm sure. Gotta go, Mom. *Don't* call 9-1-1. I repeat, don't call 9-1-1."

"You don't have to shout, Kylie Ann."

She could feel her blood pressure rising. "You know what, Mom? Take the whole afternoon off. On me."

"Oh, honey, really?"

"Really—" She hadn't finished the word before her mother disconnected. Picturing her mother racing for the door, and bulldozing over clients in her hurry to get out, Kylie managed not to thunk her head against the wall again.

BY LATE THAT NIGHT Kylie had handled each and every crisis, including dealing with the fire department, who'd come roaring out, sirens and lights flashing, due to her mother's call.

Because of course she'd called 9-1-1 before heading out.

But for now, everything was good. She was head-deep into the engine compartment of a Cessna, with good old-fashioned rock music cranked up to head-banging volume on the radio, singing to her heart's delight as she worked. The airport was empty, shut down for the night, and she was in her favorite state.

Alone.

Yes, maybe she'd rather be in Paris, but this wasn't so bad either. She stood in her airport— *thank you, Dad*—surrounded by her favorite things...airplanes. Airplanes couldn't talk back, couldn't screw up the bank account, couldn't leave early to get their nails done and their hair bleached.

She felt lucky, even with the debt weighing her down. After college she'd worked at other private airports to gain experience, always knowing she'd end up back here. She'd just never imagined she'd be here without her father, the only man to ever really understand her.

Wearing overalls stained with grease, her old clunky work boots and a backwards baseball cap on her short mop of dark hair, she felt perfectly content. Even—get out the record books—relaxed.

"Hey, babe."

And just like that, with those two simple words uttered in that unbearably familiar, husky and, damn it, sexy voice, she shot from content to tense in a heartbeat.

McKinnon.

Peace shattered, an automatic snarl appeared on her mouth. "What do you want?" she asked without turning around.

"Hmm. That's quite a question."

A tall, dark shadow fell over her, but she didn't need to turn her head to see the long, leanly muscled form of Wade McKinnon, owner of McKinnon Charters, not when that very form was seared on her brain from what she had aptly named The Unfortunate Incident.

The Unfortunate Incident had occurred last New Year's Eve, at their annual airport bash where all the employees used the holidays as an excuse to party hard and work little. Her mother, ever so helpful, had spiked the punch, which, Kylie told herself, was the one and only reason she'd been caught beneath the mistletoe by Wade in the first place. Technically, he wasn't even an employee, he merely leased space for his operation. But she'd been caught.

Caught and kissed.

That the kissing had been instigated by her in a vodka-induced giggly haze really burned her butt, but Wade had done his fair share of the kissing that night, too, and he'd been damn good at it.

The jerk.

She'd kissed experienced guys before, and had occasionally followed her hormones. Okay, twice. She'd followed her hormones twice. That's how she knew they happened to be in perfectly fine working order.

They seemed to be exceptional in this man's presence.

"What do I want..." Stepping closer into the meager light of her single hanging bulb in the nearly empty hangar, Wade stroked his jaw thoughtfully.

Against her will, the sound of his fingers against

the day-old growth of beard made her knees wobble. Damn it, he looked mouthwatering, with his dark hair cut pilot-short, his tanned, rugged face with the laugh lines fanning out from his deep blue eyes.

The face of a fallen angel, her grandmother had said on the day he'd shown up with a signed lease and a crooked, wicked smile.

The "angel" flashed that smile now. "You know what I want, Kylie. Same thing I've always wanted."

Her stomach quivered, which she ignored. He wore black jeans, a black shirt shoved up past his forearms, and was quite possibly the sexiest man on the planet, while she was covered in grease and overalls, had her hair stuffed beneath a hat and didn't have an ounce of makeup on. His "interest" was laughable, but that was okay. She knew what he meant when he said he wanted her.

He wanted her airport, and in the year that they'd known each other, he'd made her three official offers, two of which she turned down flat. The last one, made the week before, was such a good one she'd nearly passed out. That offer would solve her every problem. It'd fix the debts her father had wracked up before dying while testing an untried, handmade aircraft. It'd solve the problem of feeding and caring for her mother and grandmother, something her father had always told her would fall to her if something happened to him.

And it'd solve the whole Paris fantasy, as she'd be able to go. And maybe never come back.

"You agreed to give me two weeks to think about it."

"I'll give you your two weeks." He cocked his head, his sharp eyes missing nothing. "Working again? Or should I say still?"

"Smith wants his plane first thing in the morning. Since you know damn well I can't afford Doogie's double-time pay, here I am." Her head mechanic was expensive, but good. But she was even better, and far cheaper.

"You're going to kill yourself with your pace, Kylie," Wade said softly.

Why was it that whenever he said her name it felt like a caress? Probably because she hadn't had sex in this millennium. "Don't you have your own life to worry about?"

"Yep." Another flash of the grin that could, and did, melt bones. "Heading out to Doogie's birthday bash as a matter of fact."

She turned back to the plane. Doogie had a fondness for airplanes, parties and girls. In that order. There'd probably be girls jumping out of his cake.

Looking as good as Wade did, she had no doubt he'd be fighting them off by the end of the night. They'd be falling at his feet by the dozen.

"So come with me," came that sensuous voice right in her ear. "Protect me."

Ah, hell, she'd spoken *out loud*. Jerking upright,

she smacked the top of her head on the engine. Stars exploded in her head and she ground her back teeth. "I don't really care what you do, or who you do it with."

"Really?" He stroked a finger over the tender bump on her head. "Then why are you bringing it up?"

Right. Why was she bringing it up? Oh, yeah. Because she was an idiot.

"Come on, Kylie. Come with me to the party."

His eyes were deep, and the most unusual shade of deep blue. When he looked at her, her body wanted to say yes to him, yes to everything, especially if it involved an orgasm. "No," she said, listening to her head; and buried herself back into the engine compartment. Men were not her thing, she reminded herself. She had enough trouble in her life at the moment. "Go away."

"Such sweet talk." He sighed, a frustrated sound. "Good night, Kylie. I'd say don't work too hard, but you would just to be difficult."

She waited until the sound of his footsteps faded away to let out a shaky breath. She'd done them both a favor, he just didn't know it, that's all. She wasn't a girly girl. Pretty hairdos and fancy clothes and all stuff female was one big collective mystery.

Then there was the serious case of nerves that hit whenever she thought of him. It had nothing to do with the fact he could buy her airport. Or that he had eyes that made her...yearn. Bottom line was, Kylie, so fearless in everything else, felt terrified of adding yet another person to her list of people to be in charge of. She was hardly managing as it was, and she couldn't add another living soul.

She knew it was a pathetic attempt at self-preservation, but at the moment it worked for her.

A trip to Paris would have worked better.

CHAPTER TWO

WADE MCKINNON'S alarm went off at 6:00 a.m., startling him into near cardiac arrest and bringing back flashes of the military life he didn't feel like facing at such an ungodly hour. Groaning, bleary-eyed, he knocked the clock to the floor and put his pillow over his head.

But before sleep could claim him again, he remembered.

He had to get up. He was no longer a wild, irresponsible nobody. Shocking as it was, he'd pulled himself out of the gutter. He now actually had a reason to get up in the morning. The Air Force had had a big hand in knocking sense into him, and as a result, he'd managed to put his experiences from it to good use by starting his own charter company. He was even—and he was just getting used to this after five years—successful. Hugely so. Unbelievably, he could actually do whatever he wanted, when he wanted, the only irony being that he was often too busy now to do just that.

Surging out of bed, he got into the shower,

drank a gallon of coffee straight up, and went to work.

Walking through the private airport never failed to make him smile. God, he loved it here, in this dinky, falling apart, old place. A year ago he'd moved his charter business from Oregon to Southern California because he'd gotten tired of the rain, and he'd never been sorry.

Of course that might have something to do with Kylie, the lean, mean fighting machine who owned the airport. Man, he loved a kick-ass woman, and there was no doubt, Kylie was kick-ass. She was rough and tough and battle-ready, and in sharp contrast to her curmudgeonly nature, was so hauntingly beautiful, he could never take his eyes off her.

She did her best to hide that beauty, with her dark hair in its ragged cut he suspected she did herself, little to no makeup, and coveralls over the taut body he wanted beneath his. But to Wade, it was all in the eyes, and hers, deep jade ones, gripped him every time she laid them on him.

It wasn't often a woman got under his skin, but she'd crawled in there at first sight and had never left. She'd laugh hysterically if she knew. Then she'd go back to work and forget about him. All she did was work, and it drove him as crazy as the memory of kissing her did.

The hangars were filled with airplanes, new and

old. The smell of fuel and warm summer morning filled the air, and he inhaled deeply. With both the east and west doors open, the wind whipped through at a good enough clip to nearly rip his donut right out of his hand. Couldn't have that, so he popped the rest in his mouth and dusted off his fingers.

He had an early flight taking some movie star to Moro Bay for a photo shoot. Which meant he'd get to sit around on the bluffs and kick back for a few hours before flying her home.

Oh yeah, life was good.

Moving toward the lobby, he figured he'd just check in with Daisy and see if his client had arrived yet. He wondered if the photo shoot was a bikini one....

"But, Kylie, he's such a nice boy," he heard Daisy say.

"Oh, please." Kylie's voice was strong and determined, just like every other part of her, and Wade grinned. She and her mother were behind the reception desk, their backs to him as they put up the schedule for the day.

"Honestly, Kylie," Daisy tsked. "The least you could do is go out with him once!"

"No," Kylie said firmly. "I am *not* going out on any blind dates, especially one you set me up on. No offense, Mom, but I don't have the same taste you do."

Daisy put her hands on her hips and jabbed her dry-erase marker in her daughter's face. "I always set you up with nice boys. Keith. Justin. Steve. You should have married Steve."

"*Seth,*" Kylie corrected. "And I couldn't have married him even if I'd wanted to. Grandma chased him off, remember?"

"Well, who would have guessed he'd be afraid of one little old lady?"

"She told him I was desperate for a husband and that he fit the bill!"

"She was just kidding. He had no sense of humor."

"Mom." Kylie rubbed her temples. "I'm not going to get married, okay? It's not for me."

"Just because a few relationships didn't work out?"

"Because *none* of them ever work out. Let's face it." She lifted her arms, exhibiting her coveralls and favorite baseball cap, not an ounce of femininity anywhere, and beautiful in spite of it. "I'm not exactly marriage material."

"Nothing a brush and some makeup wouldn't fix," Daisy sniffed.

"Mom." With a little laugh, Kylie shook her head. "Why should I bother? Look at you, you're the epitome of a woman...."

Daisy smiled and preened, patting her perfect hair, her pretty sundress. "Why, thank you."

"And you can't keep a man, either. You've had how many boyfriends since Daddy died?"

"Well, who's counting?" Daisy muttered.

"Three. And each broke your heart. Grandma's been married five times. *Five!* And each time nearly destroyed her."

"That's because she wasn't smart enough to marry someone with money the first time."

"Well, I'm not interested, with or without money. Even you and Daddy had issues."

"Because he thought he had to pamper me, and take care of every little thing."

"He *did* have to."

"Only because, sweet as he was, he was also..." Daisy winced apologetically. "Look, he was anal, okay? Completely and totally anal."

And so was Kylie. That fact was written all over her mother's face. Well, she'd rather be anal than the opposite. "All I'm saying is, for all I've seen, love is a pain in the a—"

"Kylie Ann Birmingham! Watch your language."

"Love doesn't really exist, Mom. Admit it."

Daisy threw up her hands. "I give up trying to convince you. But at least try to have fun once in a while. Anything, Kylie, but try something."

"I don't need it."

"Really? What if it was Wade asking?"

Wade's ears perked at that. The conversation

had been hugely interesting so far, but was getting even better now.

"First of all," Kylie said. "He dates anything in a skirt, so he's certainly not going to give me a second glance, and second..."

"Yes?" Wade pushed away from the wall and moved toward the front desk, smiling when Kylie whipped around, her eyes wide. "Second?" he asked sweetly.

Daisy grinned. "Well, hello, Wade."

"Hello, Daisy." He cocked his head at Kylie. "Oh, and your 'first of all' isn't quite accurate. I've dated women in pants before. Not in coveralls, though..." He ran a finger down her arm, grinning when she glared at him. "And you never finished. Second of all...?"

"You had a client." Deliciously flustered, she shoved some paperwork at him and changed the conversation.

"Had?"

"She cancelled because the wind scared her."

He glanced out the wall of windows. "It's hardly blowing."

"Yeah, well, she cancelled. Probably was worried the wind would disturb her hair. Now if you'll excuse me, I have to go test that plane I worked on last night, the owner will be here soon."

When she brushed past him, he took her elbow,

smiling when she whipped around, practically growling in his face.

What was it about him that put her so on edge? The same thing that made him want to keep touching her? He'd learned a lot about her in this very fascinating conversation. "Who's riding shotgun?"

"No one."

"I will."

"I don't need—"

"I will," he repeated. He had no idea what the hell he was doing, he now had the morning free. He could go into his office, shut the door, open the windows, kick up his feet and take a nice snooze.

Instead he wanted to be up in the air. With Kylie. He figured it had nothing to do with those big, expressive jade eyes and everything to do with how she'd tasted. It had been nearly six months since their one and only kiss and he couldn't quite get the memory out of his head.

Maybe she'd give him another taste, and then they could each go on their own merry way.

Yeah. *That's* what he wanted. To go on his merry way. Alone.

KYLIE PILOTED. Wade watched. It was a first for him, sitting passenger side with a woman in charge. And she *was* in charge. She flew the same way she did everything else, with utter intensity, a serious expression, sure and firm hands, her dark glasses hiding her every thought.

The sky loomed large in front of them, brilliant blue with lazily floating puffy white clouds. Incredible. Being up in the air, as always, exhilarated him as nothing ever had.

"So." Wade leaned back to enjoy himself. "Do you make love with the same abandon when you fly?"

Her hands jerked, and so did the plane. Craning her neck, she stared at him. "What?"

"I bet you do."

For another long heartbeat she was silent, then she shook her head and turned forward again. "You're insane. That explains everything."

"We had such a connection that night. Do you remember?"

"No."

"Christmas Eve."

"New Year's Eve," she corrected, then rolled her eyes when he laughed.

"You *do* remember, and you've ignored it ever since."

An interesting blush crept up her face. "I don't remember anything."

He shook his head. "Coy, Kylie? After you've practically crawled up my body?"

"I most definitely did not crawl up your body."

"Don't tell me I need to remind you who kissed who."

She hissed out a breath. "Okay, so I kissed you. I was wondering what it would be like, that's all."

"And?"

"And nothing. Wondering gone."

"Are you telling me that kiss quenched your thirst?"

She shifted in her seat and broke eye contact.

"See?" he said. "You want more, too."

"Giving in to simple urges isn't always the answer," she said primly.

"Baby," he said on a laugh. "There's nothing simple about my urge for you."

"Stop it."

"I can't. I'm still curious. You're so tough on the outside."

"I'm tough all the way through."

"Nah." He grinned when she glared at him again. "Know what I think?"

"If I say yes will you shut up?"

"I think that your toughness is a shield. That you're really soft and sweet, with a heart of gold."

That made a laugh tumble from her lips. "Right. And you know me so well."

"Otherwise why would you let Daisy destroy the office on a daily basis? Or let Lou near your books?"

"Because I'm clearly mentally incompetent. Watch out, it could be contagious."

His mouth quirked. "You care about your family very much."

"They're family," she said simply.

"Some would just let them make their own way."

"Their own way?" She shook her head. "My mom and grandma would get lost on their way there."

"Exactly. I've been watching you for a year now. Even more so in the past six months."

"Should I be concerned you're stalking me?"

"Look, just admit it. You're really one big softie who collects people to take care of so you don't have to take care of yourself."

She stared at him, then laughed. "I do not collect the needy."

"See? I didn't say needy. *You* did."

She sighed. "How about we just don't talk period."

"Sure, soon as you tell me why you'd rather bury yourself in work and raise your mother and grandmother than live your own life."

"Shut up. I have to check out the plane, and that requires listening. To the *plane,* not you."

"The plane is perfect."

"How do you know?"

"Because you worked on it."

Startled, she blinked her huge green eyes at him.

Oh yeah, he had her attention now. "You might run the airport," he said, "but you're the best mechanic out there. You're also not a bad pilot. So…now that we have all business out of the way, and you don't want to discuss kissing or making love, how about—"

She turned back to her flying. "I don't want to sell you the airport."

"I wasn't going to bring that up, but now that you have…you're out of money."

Her jaw went tight. "Not quite."

"I'm not greedy, sell me half. We'll be partners."

"I'm not *that* desperate."

He shrugged and leaned back. "Fine. We'll talk about something else." Glancing behind them at the roomy cabin, which was luxurious and empty, he smiled. "Ever heard of the mile-high club?"

Having just taken an unfortunate sip of soda, she choked.

"Guess you have," he said innocently, while his insides churned and tightened at the adorably flustered expression on her face and unwilling speculation in her eyes that his question caused. "Want to join it together?"

"Does 'not in your lifetime' mean anything to you?"

He laughed. "So you're not ready for that."

"No!"

"Maybe next time then. Just think of how good it'd be, you and me, more of those mind-blowing kisses, added with—"

"Stop!"

He could see the pulse at her throat beating like a desperate little chick. She was trying so hard not to let him see he was getting to her, and for some reason, that softened him.

"I mean it," she said, eyes dark, lips wet from where she'd nervously licked them. "Stop."

Whether she admitted it or not—and he was far closer to the not—she wanted him. For now, that was enough. *For now.* "Stopping," he said, and smiled.

"Uh, Kylie?"

She was in her office, swamped with paperwork and getting none of it done due to a particularly naughty daydream that involved, damn it, the mile-high club. With a sigh, she picked up the radio. "Go ahead, dispatch."

"Have you looked at the phone lines lately?"

Kylie glanced over and saw all phone lines flashing wildly.

Ah, hell. Her mother had sneaked out again. "Thank you," she said, feeling a headache coming on as she made her way to the lobby and the front desk.

"Kylie, Kylie!" Oddly enough, Daisy *was* there, waving at her, beaming from ear to ear, apparently utterly unconcerned about the phones. "You'll never guess! I did it!"

Oh God. "You did…what exactly?"

"I got the call saying I did it. I mean, of course I did it, who wouldn't think so?"

"Mom…what are you talking about?"

"I'm a nominee for Mother Of The Year! I sent in that essay, and the magazine picked their finalists from across the country, and I'm one of them!"

This was difficult to wrap her mind around. Her mother—whom Kylie took care of—was up for Mother Of The Year.

"Get ready, honey, because I'm going to win us that trip to Paris yet!"

"The phones, Mom. You can't just—" With a sound of exasperation, she picked up the receiver and pushed line one. "Birmingham Airport."

"*Orange County Post.* We'd like a quote from a Kylie Birmingham."

Kylie looked at her mother as a bad feeling came over her. "About?"

"About the front-page article we printed on her mother being a national nominee for Mother Of The Year."

With a wide smile, Daisy held up the newspaper. "See?" she whispered.

Yep, there it was, right on the front page for the whole world to see.

> ### Our Own Daisy Birmingham!
> ### National Mother Of The Year?
> ### You Bet!

Kylie didn't know whether to laugh or scream. "Hold on." She hit line two. "Birmingham Airport."

"This is Flora's Florist. We have a delivery for a Daisy Birmingham."

"What?"

"They're from the retirement center where she volunteers as bingo manager. We just want to make sure someone is there to receive before we bring the arrangement over."

Kylie sank to her mother's chair and set her head down on the desk.

Daisy just smiled.

Kylie groaned.

"Hello?" said the florist. "Hello? Hello?"

CHAPTER THREE

WHEN KYLIE GOT UP the next morning, she'd convinced herself the publicity had died down. After all, her mother wasn't a celebrity, Kylie wasn't a celebrity and where they lived was little more than a one-horse town.

Why would anyone care about a silly little contest? Yes, today would be just fine. And indeed, when she got to work, the place was blessedly quiet.

Perfect.

Relieved, she went to her office and shut the door, determined to do something about the mountain of paperwork threatening to overtake her desk.

She worked through lunch, and was well on her way to having a deliriously good day due to lack of interruptions when Lou ambled in.

"You need money in the checking account," her grandma announced. "Quite a bit of it."

"A new lease is supposed to come through today. Some guy wants to park his two Learjets here for six months, and I'm just waiting for his call. Once that's finalized, we'll get a hefty deposit. Oh, and we sold a lot of fuel this week, so—"

"None of that is going to help you."

Kylie frowned. "Why not?"

"Well, because I'm mailing the bills." Lou lifted a shoulder. "So you'll need to do something today. Okay, then, luvie..." She clapped her hands together. "Gotta run."

It boggled the mind how quickly one old lady could destroy Kylie's brain cells. "Maybe you can wait until next week to go to the post office."

"Okay, dear. You're the boss."

Oh yeah, she had a headache now. A huge one. She watched Lou dance toward the door.

Suddenly Kylie realized the phones were flashing like crazy again. Damn it. With a sigh, she made her way to her mother's desk. "Mom, I've told you, you can't just tie up the phone like that!"

"Oh, I'm not the one doing it." Daisy smiled sweetly. She leaned close. "The press is here," she whispered. "They want to talk about what a great mom I am. Oh! And in an hour, the local television news is coming as well."

"But the phones—"

"I know, isn't it awful?" Daisy hit a few of the buttons, then shook her head. "Definitely, there's something amiss. I tried to take care of it a while ago, but I couldn't figure out what I did wrong...."

"A while ago..." Kylie let out a breath. She

was going to blow up. Just *poof,* blow up. "Are you saying the phones are down, and have been for...*a while?*"

"That's what I'm saying."

Goodbye new client.

"So are you ready to talk to the press?" Daisy asked. "Maybe get your pic taken?"

"No!" Kylie pressed her fingers to her temples and turned in a slow circle, going still when she saw Wade standing there, smiling at her.

"Good afternoon," he said. "Need some help?"

"Yeah, I need someone to shoot me and put me out of my misery." She pulled her cell phone out of her pocket and ignored the flutter in her tummy at just the sight of the man she hadn't been able to stop thinking about since their plane ride. Nothing an antacid wouldn't cure.

"What are you doing?" her mother asked.

"Calling the phone service, which you might notice I have on auto dial." She rolled her eyes when her mother just sniffed in irritation.

"*I* am not messing up the phones," Daisy said. "The repair man told me the problem is on your roof."

Or under it, Kylie thought crossly. Why was it so hard to be her? All she wanted was the airport running smoothly and good help to ensure that. She wanted to take care of Daisy and Lou. Simple. She'd be completely happy, just as her father had been. But somehow, it'd seemed easier when he'd done it.

"He said to check for a bird's nest on the roof."

That had been last week's problem.

"Or a squirrel chewing the line."

Which had happened the week before, but the line to the repair department was busy, which meant Kylie was on her own. "I'll be on the roof," she said, her mood not improving when Wade followed her outside. He looked good today, though she'd bite her tongue before admitting it. Having just come back from flying a charter, he had his aviator sunglasses shoved up on his head, a leather jacket tucked beneath his arm and a soda in his hand. He wore his pilot's uniform—dark blue trousers and a stark white shirt with his logo over the breast that inexplicably made him look tall, dark and official.

Everything about him made her heart beat fast, and all she could think about was doing what he'd so brazenly suggested the other day—getting some. With him. In the air.

She had the feeling he would know exactly how to make her feel good, too. She'd probably, if her breathing problems from just looking at him were any indication, even have an actual orgasm. "Why are you following me?"

"I worked for the phone company one summer. Maybe I can help."

She came to the back wall of hangar number one, where high above her was the phone box. There was already a ladder there, due to the problems she'd been having over the past few weeks, problems she now knew were directly related to her mother's "help." With a testing shake of the ladder, she started to climb.

"Why don't you let me—"

"I've got it," she said over her shoulder, and promptly forgot about Wade as she got to the top of the ladder and surveyed the phone equipment. Nothing obvious, no bird's nest, no chewed wires from the squirrels. Climbing onto the roof, she sat and contemplated the situation. Basically, she had a phone system that didn't work, she had a grandma who didn't care about work and a secretary/mom who'd rather be in the paper and go to Paris than secure her future.

Oh, and she had an airport about to go under from lack of funds. Yep, it was official. Her life was in the toilet.

"Kylie?"

With a sigh, she lay back on the roof, studying the clouds overhead. It was a gorgeous day. "I'm still here."

"I'm coming up."

"Don't." If he did, he'd look at her with those eyes, the ones that made her melt. Then she might get a little desperate and ask if there was some sort of club involving sex on a roof. "I've got it under control. I've nearly got it handled."

"Do you? Because from here it looks like you're taking a nap."

With a roll of her eyes, she pushed to her feet, moving more completely out of view.

And promptly sank through the old, half-rotten roof up to her hips, which, thanks to her daily morning habit of two old-fashioned chocolate-glaze donuts, stopped her from falling all the way through.

"Kylie? What was that crash?"

The sound of my ego hitting the earth at the speed of light. "Nothing," she managed in a perfectly calm voice, wriggling her feet to make sure she hadn't paralyzed herself. Actually she was wedged in nicely between the rotten roof and the supports. She couldn't fall any farther, but neither could she pull herself out. She imagined the attic, which they used as storage space, and the view she presented to anyone in there looking up. Luckily, as all her employees were incredibly lazy, no one would be in there.

"I'm coming up," Wade said again.

"No," she replied, sounding slightly less calm now. But damn it, she didn't want him to see how stupid she'd been to walk on the one weak spot on the entire roof. "Why don't you go fly your last charter for the day."

"How do you know I have one more?"

"Uh…" Because if anyone was stalking anyone, she was stalking *him*. Every morning she looked his schedule over, checking the weather, memorizing where he'd be flying, picturing him out there… "Daisy mentioned it."

"Are you sure you don't need help?"

Oh yeah, she needed help, but she wasn't ready to admit it to him. "I'm quite sure. But…thank you. Thank you very much."

WADE WENT. He did so because he knew damn well what Kylie had done, and knew she'd never admit to needing anyone, much less him. But at least she was still ornery as hell, so he figured she couldn't have hurt herself too badly.

Damn her. He went up into the attic to verify for himself that Kylie was really good and stuck, and yep, there were her two long legs dangling through the rafters.

Too bad she wasn't wearing a dress.

Then he cancelled his charter. A first. That he cancelled it for a woman really bit. He went back outside, but waited a good half an hour first, until the building cleared out and everyone had gone home. He waited an extra half an hour just because.

Then he climbed the ladder until his head was

level with the roof. "Still here?" he asked of the woman half-in and half-out of the building.

She'd been studying the sunset, but turned her head to look at him through narrowed eyes.

"Ready to admit you need help?"

"Oh, has hell frozen over?" she asked sweetly.

He grinned and, reaching out, brushed a stray tendril of hair off her cheek, tucking it behind her ear. He loved the feel of her skin, so soft, and he loved the scent of her. No fancy perfumes for Kylie, heaven forbid, just the irresistible scent of shampoo and woman. Because he could, he leaned in, pressed his face to her hair, inhaling deeply.

Interestingly enough, she shivered. "What are you doing?"

"Smelling you. You smell good. Are you cold, Kylie?"

"No."

"Ah." He climbed up the rest of the way and carefully sat right next to her. On the unrotten spot, of course.

She was frowning, his Kylie. "What does that mean, 'ah'?"

"It means if you're not cold, you shivered because of me touching you." He tucked another wayward strand of hair behind her other ear and goose bumps appeared on her arm. Stroking a finger down that arm, he watched her eyes go dark. She bit her lower lip.

"Admit you need my help," he said softly.

"No."

He danced his finger down her neck, over her throat, to her racing pulse. She trembled, and unbelievably, so did he.

"Look at us," he whispered. "Both shaking from just a simple touch...we should give this a go."

"I'm...not into you."

"Really? What was that kiss about then?"

"It was about the spiked punch. And anyway, it was a long time ago. It wouldn't happen now."

"Hmm." He ran that finger over her collarbone and her nipples beaded.

He went hard as a rock. "So you're saying I could kiss you now and you'd feel nothing."

"R-right."

Bracing his feet of the roof molding, he wrapped an arm around her and tugged, until she popped free...and ended up in his lap. The now filthy, curvy, hot Kylie squirmed like crazy, trying to scramble out of his arms, but he put his mouth to her ear and said silkily, "I dare you to sit still for another kiss."

"Don't be stupid—"

"I dare you to sit still," he repeated. "And not respond."

She stared at him.

"Double dog dare you," he whispered, tracing

a finger over the dust on her jaw. "Come on, Kylie. Prove to me there's nothing here to wonder about."

She swallowed hard.

"What's the matter, you chicken?"

"Of course not."

"Well, then." He leaned close enough to drown in her annoyed yet curious-in-spite-of-herself gaze. "Remember now, hold still. No jumping my bones. No showing how badly you want me, or I get to claim a prize." And when her eyes flashed, he bit back his grin and put his mouth over hers.

CHAPTER FOUR

AT THE TOUCH of his mouth to hers, Kylie thought, Oh. My. God. The man had the most amazingly perfect kiss on the face of the earth. Tender, warm, firm…just right.

Completely beyond herself, she let out a helpless little sound because she wanted more, more, more, and what did he do?

He pulled back! Pulled back and shook his head at her. "No sound," he whispered gruffly. "Don't want me to get any ideas, right? And no touching," he added, unwinding her arms free of his neck—how had they gotten there?—and holding them at her sides. "No talking, no nothing." His voice sounded thick and raspy, as if he was having trouble breathing. "Because if you're not careful, I'll think you want this, really want this." And before she could slug him in the belly for laughing at her, he'd put his mouth back on hers.

The gentleness was gone now as he dove in, hot and hard, claiming, possessing, using his lips, his tongue, his teeth…. She struggled to free her arms and wind them around his neck, her hips arched to his, but his hands held her immobile.

He pulled back again, staring down at her with fathomless eyes, his mouth grimmer than she'd ever seen.

She opened her mouth, to say what she had no idea, but he put his fingers over her lips, shaking his head. Then he pushed her off his lap and went down the ladder, disappearing into the night.

Guess I passed his little dare, she thought dimly, hot as hell in the cool night. When had night come anyway?

Damn it.

Damn *him*.

THE NEXT DAY Kylie hadn't even opened the glass doors to the airport lobby when two reporters stepped out in front of her and shoved a microphone in her face.

Beyond them, inside, she could see her mother behind the reception desk, laughing. And one Wade McKinnon in front of that desk standing there with casual ease, also smiling.

What were they laughing at?

Even from here she could see the speculative gleam in Daisy's eyes…no doubt she was going to try to set Kylie up with him.

She should have stayed in bed.

But in bed she couldn't be at the airport. Surrounded by everything that was such a comfort.

Besides, in bed, she'd lie there thinking about the night before, being in Wade's arms, his mouth on hers, driving her right out of her living mind.

And maybe she'd forget why she couldn't add one more person to her load.

"Kylie Birmingham?" Reporter number one stepped even closer. "Tell us how you feel about your mother's essay, about the heartbreaking way she wrote about you."

Kylie blinked in surprise. "I..." *Should have read that essay, apparently.*

Daisy happened to glance up and catch her eyes. Was it Kylie's imagination that her mother flushed guiltily? No, it was not. And it wasn't the reporters that made her mother do so, her mother loved reporters.

Which left Wade McKinnon.

They were plotting something. The thought was confirmed when Daisy broke eye contact first.

The tall, sexy man who kissed like heaven didn't so much as glance in Kylie's direction, but he was still smiling. Conspiratorially.

Oh, yes, they were most definitely up to something.

"Ms. Birmingham? About your mother? Can you tell us about your relationship? Does she require your help to run this airport?"

Ha! "No comment," she said. "And no pictures," she told them when one lifted a camera. Looking at her mother, she stalked into the lobby. She strutted right up to them in midlaugh and pointed at the both of them. "Stop it."

Wade, looking vexingly scrumptious in his pilot's uniform, just cocked a brow.

"Stop what, dear?" Daisy asked. "Did you sleep well? Because you have black circles beneath your—"

"I'm a big girl, just so you both know. I'll make my own plans when and where it suits me."

"Well, of course you will," Daisy clucked. "How about breakfast? I have an extra bagel—"

Kylie crossed her arms. "I'd like to know what you two were talking about."

Wade, apparently amused, didn't comment.

Daisy rolled her eyes and pushed a mug of something hot towards her. "Herbal tea. It'll help you relax. You could use a gallon."

"I don't need to relax—"

"We weren't talking about you," Daisy said, lifting the mug to Kylie's lips.

She drank, but would eat her own tongue before admitting the stuff actually tasted good. Then her mother's words sank in.

"That's right," Wade said when her cheeks went hot. "We weren't talking about you. Contrary to popular belief, there are other things to talk about.''

''You…weren't trying to make him go out with me?'' Kylie asked her mother.

Daisy laughed. ''Oh, right. As if anyone could make this man do something he doesn't want to do.''

Wade smiled sweetly—*sweetly!*—when both women looked at him.

Right. No one made Wade do anything. She needed to remember that. He might want to kiss her stupid. He might want to buy her airport. But he didn't want to go out with her, because really, how ridiculous would *that* be?

''We were discussing quarterly taxes,'' Wade said, still sounding amused. ''They're due tomorrow.''

Ah, hell.

Her stomach sank. ''I need to get Lou on the forms,'' she said to herself, her mind racing. Did her grandmother even have the forms? Had she gotten all the financial stuff together to fill them out? Had she—

''*Relax*,'' Wade said in her ear. He'd pushed away from the wall and now stood so close she could see the yellow specks dancing in his eyes. She could smell the soap he'd used that morning. She could feel his warm breath on her cheek.

And was vividly, vibrantly, unhappily aware that

her body wanted to curl into his, that he looked good enough to gobble up in one bite.

"Lou can handle it," he said. "Don't get all worked up so early in the day, it's not healthy."

What wasn't healthy was her body's response to him.

"Your grandma can handle it," Daisy confirmed, and pushed the tea on her daughter again. "She always talked about going back to college to finish up her accounting degree."

Grandma loose on a college campus? Terrifying.

"Now if you'll excuse me," Daisy said. "I have a massage appointment this morning."

"Mom—"

"Just kidding." Daisy laughed. So did Wade. "But I do have work, so if you kids'll stop standing around my desk and making me look bad for the boss…"

"No problem." Wade took Kylie's arm before she could escape, before she could finish obsessing over the quarterlies. *Dad, how did you do it all?*

Wade led her outside and toward the maintenance hangar. Halfway there they passed by a beauty of a Learjet. Standing in front of it was one of their more wealthy customers, Jimbo Stanton. Standing in front of Jimbo Stanton was Lou, flirting with the sixty-something-year-old customer.

"Lou!" Kylie refrained from wrapping her fingers around her grandma's neck, and instead gestured her over. "Can I see you for a moment?"

"Sure." Lou walked saucily toward them, making sure Jimbo watched her walk away.

He did, with his tongue practically on the ground.

"What are you doing?" Kylie growled when she got closer.

"What does it look like?" Lou patted her hairdo. "I'm trying to get a date. You remember what a date is, don't you, Kylie?"

Wade laughed and Kylie groaned. "Don't you have work to do?" she asked. "Accounting work?"

"All caught up."

"How about the quarterlies?"

"Well, darling, I would, but I just did them last night."

"Are you sure?"

"I'm quite sure."

"And then there's the checking account situation—"

"Balanced," Lou said proudly.

"Are you positive?"

"Of course, I'm positive. I've done this before, you know. Now shoo, scat, vamoose, you're cramping my style." Without looking back, she sashayed toward Jimbo.

Kylie was overcome with impending doom. She was failing, miserably.

"Hey," Wade said. "It can't be that bad."

"As long as I'm wearing rose-colored glasses."

He took her hand and pulled her away. They walked alongside the tarmac for about a hundred feet before they walked down the alley between hangars two and three toward maintenance.

She was just numb enough to actually let him lead her.

"Pretty day," he said.

It was, but it'd be prettier if their hopefully new client called. She glanced at the cell phone. She'd given him this number in case there was a problem with the phones again.

No missed call.

Wade moved closer, and before she realized it, she had the cool hangar wall at her back and the big, bad, sexy pilot at her front. "Your mother is right," he said, running his hands up her sides. "Tension is spilling right out of you."

"That's because you're standing in my space," she retorted, both the words and her breath backing up in her lungs when he spun her around and put her hands on the wall. "What—"

The word turned into a moan when he pressed close, pressed his fingers into her shoulders, massaging right where she felt most of the tension, at the base of her neck. "Wade—"

"Do us both a favor and be quiet a moment."

Oh, man, did he know what he was doing. Those fingers were magic, pure, unadulterated magic, as they dug into the knots in her shoulders, her biceps, her neck. She wore a sleeveless faux-silk blouse, and he wasn't shy about slipping his hands beneath the material to work more of that magic.

Within two minutes her legs were Jell-O. Her hands slipped from the wall, and he tsked, putting them back up. "Hold still."

Hold still. If she so much as arched her back, her bottom found a snug home at the vee of his trousers. She knew this because she did it. Then his hands danced all over her and she couldn't breathe. Hold still? She couldn't!

"If you'd only admit you liked this," he whispered into her ear, causing a set of delicious shudders to race down her spine. "I could do it for you whenever you tense up. Which is all the time."

She spun around, not realizing until that moment just how close they were. Her chest brushed his, so did her hips. His eyes darkened, and his hands slid from her shoulders to cup her face. "Kylie?" His thumb slid over her lower lip, making it tremble open. "Do you like it?"

Definitely, a woman more in charge of her sexuality would do just that, admit it and then take more, take all of what was offered, whatever that might be. But Kylie wasn't that woman. She knew what she wanted, and what she wanted was her life simplified. Wade wouldn't do that, he'd complicate it.

Yes, in the deep dark of the night, she could admit the airport needed more help than she alone could give it. She needed a partner.

But in the light of day, she wasn't willing to let go yet. And then there was Wade himself. She told herself she wasn't interested. She needed more than a single smoldering look.

A single smoldering look, which at the moment, was consuming her, making her a little sweaty, a little tingly, a little dizzy even, so she put her hands on his arms for balance.

He stared down at them, then looked at her.

Oh my, he had hard muscle beneath his shirt. Her fingers squeezed, testing, her knees quivering again when nothing gave.

"Kylie…"

Fascinated, utterly unable to help herself, she squeezed him again. "Yeah?"

"You're…touching me."

She was. She couldn't stop. "I'm sorry."

"No, I like it," he said in a voice that sounded a little ragged. He gripped her when she might have pulled away. "I like it a lot."

Suddenly her entire body forgot its own pledge. It was humming, craving, yearning, and when she looked up into Wade's face, his mouth slowly curved into a wry smile.

"Say the word," he said huskily, with one more trace of the pad of his thumb over her mouth. "Just say the word and I'll touch you back. I'll be quite happy to touch you back, Kylie."

She almost went for it. She certainly, suddenly, desperately, wanted to. But she just realized something else...Wade stood there, looking at her patiently. *He understood her enough to know she required patience.* Buckets of it.

And that, she decided, was the worst part of the morning. Not the reporters, or the pictures they'd almost gotten. Not her grandmother looking for a date amongst the clients.

But Wade knowing her so well.

CHAPTER FIVE

KYLIE WENT BACK into the lobby, with Wade not far behind. He had a flight—she knew because once again she'd peeked—and would be gone the rest of the day on a charter to Santa Barbara.

Good.

She needed the rest of the day to recover from the feel of his hands on her body. In less than two minutes he'd dissipated most of the stress tension in her neck, replacing it with a different sort of tension altogether.

One that wouldn't be easily assuaged by working on an airplane engine.

When she stepped into the lobby, Kylie automatically braced herself for the worst. Her mother had probably single-handedly destroyed the phone system again, or somehow managed to break down dispatch.

"Honey!" Daisy called, waving her over. "I just reheated your stress-relieving tea, come and get it." She held out the mug, then swept a stray strand of hair off her daughter's face. "You seem a little pale," she murmured. "What's the matter?"

Nothing, except every hormone she had was on full alert. "I'm fine."

"Okay, but drink your tea, you need some color in your cheeks." She patted her hair. "I was thinking about going a shade lighter to celebrate. What do you think?"

"I'm going to my office."

"But what about my hair? I don't want to look too old."

Kylie looked at the woman who wasn't quite fifty and looked two decades younger. "Mom, you look like my only slightly older sister."

"Oh, honey. Really?"

"Really."

Daisy grinned. "You're such a good daughter. Now about you...I don't suppose you have a hairbrush and lipstick lurking under all that mess on your desk? Because now might be a good time to find them."

That "mess" was their livelihood. "Yeah, right, mom. Lipstick on my desk. Funny stuff." Kylie went to her office. In the center of her desk sat a little pot of daisies. There was also a little sack lunch with a sticky note attached that said "eat me."

Her mother.

And her heart sighed. *You're a good daughter,*

her mother always said, but suddenly Kylie saw the flip side. "You're a good mother, too," she whispered in the empty room.

But she still didn't look for a hairbrush or lipstick.

WADE FOUND IT amusing how Kylie took all the press over the next few weeks. She glowered, scowled and grumbled her way through the days when it came to anything contest related, and yet seemed to thrive on running the airport. Watching her in charge—flying, wrenching, all of it, turned him on.

But then *Family Voyager* magazine wanted a spread in their next issue with all the nominated mothers and their children. Kylie appeared to look forward to that about as much as one would a root canal. On impacted molars. Without drugs.

Wade hadn't mentioned his offer to buy the airport, and knew that even though she was up against the wall financially, she wouldn't bring it up, either.

But oddly enough, that was okay, because he was distracted with something else, something disturbing.

He wanted Kylie more than he wanted the airport.

They were night and day, he and Kylie. He knew that, and yet they shared so much. They were both bullheaded, and far more likely to walk into a fight rather than away from one.

They also had both worked hard for their dreams, and had a passion for flying.

And they both figured love would never play a serious part in their lives.

He had a bad feeling he was wrong there, and was man enough to admit it. But he was also man enough to let Kylie figure it out for herself.

With his help, of course.

For two weeks he'd been running into her as often as possible, timing their entrance into the maintenance hangar down to the second, so that he could brush a hand low on her spine as he held the door open for her. Or squeeze past her in the lobby, making sure to touch her hip, to flick the bill of that baseball cap she wore in favor of doing something with the short mop of hair he so loved.

It worked, too, he could tell because her breath would catch, or she'd stare at him wide-eyed, a little bewildered, as if she didn't quite know what to do with him.

Which made them just about even, as he didn't know what to do with her, either. Correction—he knew exactly what he *wanted* to do with her, which was toss her in his bed and follow her down to have his merry way with her hot little bod.

Beyond that, he had a sinking idea he knew what

else he wanted...and since it involved more than he'd ever wanted before, he decided to dance around that for a while and concentrate on the lust aspect.

And getting her into his bed.

On the day of the scheduled magazine photo shoot for Kylie and Daisy, he found Kylie in front of the vending machine in the deserted mechanics office. She had her hands on her hips and a frown on her pretty face. Before he could say a word, she kicked the machine.

A candy bar fell out. "Now *that's* more like it," she muttered, and tore into the chocolate.

"Skip breakfast again?" he asked mildly, smiling when she whirled to look at him. "I should tell you, that snarl on your face makes me want to shove you up against that wall and kiss it away."

She turned her attention back to the machine. "I'd do just about anything for that Babe Ruth bar in there."

He nearly swallowed his tongue. "Anything?"

"Maybe even give you that kiss of my own free will."

For that he'd do a lot more than buy her a candy bar, but when he pulled change out of his pocket, she snickered. "Oh, like *that's* going to work."

He didn't care if he had to tear apart the entire vending machine with his bare hands, he was going to get her that candy bar, and she was going to give him the promised kiss. He was already hard just thinking about it. The money dropped in, he pushed the button, and like magic, the requested candy bar came out.

She stared at him in such utter surprise when he handed it to her, that he nearly grinned. "Now about that kiss," he murmured, stepping close.

With a narrow little laugh, she backed up a step, hit the back of her knees on a low table in front of the couch, and sat down on it hard. "But…that machine never works, not without a well-placed kick and three times too much money."

"So you were lying about the kiss?"

Her eyes narrowed as she tipped her head back to look up at him. "I never lie."

"Didn't think so." Sinking to his knees before her, he took her hands and wrapped them around his neck and said, "Give me your best shot then."

She tried to tug her hands free, but he held them in place. "Are you welshing on your promise?" he asked.

Her mouth was only inches from his, and it was open. Most likely with shock. Or maybe just plain irritation. But her lips were bare and full, and since her tongue darted out to lick them, also wet. "Fine," she said. She squeezed her eyes tight, puckered up, leaned in a little bit…and waited.

And waited.

Finally her eyes flew open. "What are you waiting for?" she demanded.

"*You* promised to kiss *me*."

Irritation definitely swam in those eyes now, and once again she leaned forward, puckered tight as a drum. But this time her mouth touched his, even if it was the light, chaste kiss of a friendly cousin.

When she pulled back, she smiled. "Duty complete."

"Duty?" He laughed. "You afraid of a simple kiss, Kylie?"

She looked away. "I'm not afraid of anything."

"Liar."

"Okay, fine!" She yanked her hands back. "But kissing you is never simple. It makes me..."

"What?" He put his hands on her hips, squeezing gently. "It makes you what?"

"It makes me..." The expression on her face assured him she was holding back.

Big surprise there.

But then the radio at her hip squawked. Daisy's voice broke the mood. "Kylie Birmingham, you're behind schedule. Get your tush up here and get dressed and spritzed up for the photo shoot."

Kylie leaned her head back and studied the ceiling. "You know everyone at the airport can hear her talk to me like that," she said to Wade.

"There's nothing wrong with her loving you."

"Yeah." With the sigh of someone holding

the weight of the world on her shoulders, she moved away.

"Going to get dressed and spritzed up?"

"Suppose so."

He eyed her baseball cap and coveralls. "Do you even know how to do that?"

"Shut up, McKinnon. *What?*" she said when he surged to his feet and stopped her with a hand to her wrist.

"For the record?" he said quietly. "You scare me, too."

KYLIE WENT to her office, and everyone waiting there had a bomb to drop. Daisy held up a fitted, flowery sundress. Lou held up a piece of mail and looked guilty and since the dress gave Kylie hives, she addressed her grandma first. "What have you done now?"

Lou smiled a bit guiltily. "Uh…maybe you're too busy to go over this."

"Spill."

"You're being audited."

"Because?"

"Because your number was up? I don't know."

Kylie closed her eyes, but her mother shook her, then shoved the dress in her hands. "Get this on. We'll deal with the audit after the photo shoot."

"Oh, don't worry," Lou said. "Wade said he'd take care of it."

"Wade?" Kylie asked.

"Turns out he's got an ex-girlfriend who works high up in the IRS. In fact, he's probably talking to her right now."

Why did that make her *more* grumpy? With a sigh, she started to strip. "Come near me with that thing," she warned her mother as she hefted a curling iron, "and I'll have to get mean."

Daisy just shook her head, then came after her anyway.

Lou unzipped her makeup case, which was the size of a bowling ball bag.

"Oh, no," Kylie said with a laugh, backing up. "No way."

"Yes, way. You look like death warmed over. At least use blush." Lou pulled out a bright red blush powder with a brush the size of Kylie's head.

"Mom," Kylie said, panicked.

Daisy sighed again. "Oh, leave the girl alone," and then it was Lou's turn to sigh.

"Fine. But don't complain to me when you look horrid in the photos." She proceeded to put two big red circles on her own cheeks. Then she pulled out a siren-red lipstick, carefully and thoroughly lining her lips before kissing the air and smiling proudly. "See? I look great. You should really let me help you."

"No, thanks."

Lou sniffed.

Kylie could deal with Lou's attitude, and she'd deal with Daisy's, too. She could deal with shoving herself into a long, thin, spaghetti-strapped sundress, and even with applying a little mascara. She could deal with being overworked and underpaid, and she could deal with an audit.

But when she was all done dolling herself up, when she'd walked out of her office, when Wade had turned toward her, dropping his jaw and the file he held, she realized the one thing she couldn't deal with.

The way he looked at her as though she was pretty. As though she was hot.

Her knees wobbled, infuriating her. Yep, she could deal with just about anything…except him.

CHAPTER SIX

WADE STOOD in the lobby, stunned into silence by the vision heading toward him. She wore a long, flowery sundress that hugged her curves and a tough-girl grimace on her lips. Attitude screamed with every swing of her hips. Her eyes blared irritation and impatience, and when they landed on him, uncertainty was added to the mix. Her lips shined with some light glossy color he wanted to eat right off, her hair lay gently around her face, framing the bite-me expression he'd come to count on.

And that body...he'd never really realized how mouthwatering it was.

He wanted to devour her.

An equally made-up Daisy followed Kylie toward where the magazine photographers had set up at the far end of the lobby. Being a slow business day, with no scheduled incoming flights, every employee in the place stood around, ogling their boss.

Wade understood, because he stood there, too, his own news completely forgotten, watching the photographer try to coax a natural smile out of Kylie. She was as stiff as a board, and though he doubted anyone else saw past her orneriness, he did. She felt uncomfortable in the limelight, and probably would have given her last penny to get out of it.

Feeling an unexpected surge of sympathy, he moved in close. "Excuse me," he said, pushing his way through. "Got a message for Kylie. Excuse me."

She visibly braced herself, most likely waiting for a comment on her looks, but she was going to be disappointed. He didn't need the makeup and fancy clothes to see that she was the sexiest, most hauntingly beautiful, most amazing woman he'd ever met. Undoubtedly, he could see the real Kylie far better in her everyday clothes, but this was a nice change. *Real* nice. "I have something that just might put a genuine smile on your face," he said in her ear.

"Today *nothing* could put a real smile on my face."

He let his lips brush the sensitive skin beneath her ear, his entire body tightening when she shivered. "Really?" he wondered. "How about the audit is indefinitely postponed?"

Pulling back, she narrowed her eyes. "Yeah?"

"Yeah. Where's my smile?"

"You probably agreed to sleep with her."

He lifted a brow. "Would that bother you?"

"Not in the least."

He just looked at her, and she let out a snort. "Okay, yes, it'd bother me. Happy?"

"Oh yeah." He stroked her jaw. "But it was just a phone call, Kylie." He stepped back just as she let out the genuine smile he'd wanted to see, and the photographer snapped the shutter.

Wade leaned in one more time. "And all you have to do for me in return? Smile like that. At me."

Then he wisely vanished before she could smack him.

TWO NIGHTS LATER Kylie was alone, once again buried in engine work on a customer's plane. She stood on a ladder, stretched out, trying to reach a particularly unreachable bolt.

Behind her, the radio was turned up as high as it could go so she couldn't think for a change.

Normally this would fulfill her, as she loved nothing more than a late night by herself buried in an airplane.

But normal no longer applied to her life. She'd had to charge the fuel for their tanks this morning, because she hadn't had enough money in the accounts to cover the purchase. The new client had never materialized, and though she had a lead on two more, if they didn't call soon, it might be too late.

It was entirely possible she was going to have to sell the airport. That burned. But she finally had to admit her love for the place wasn't enough. It needed more than she could give.

Wade could give it. She'd read his proposal, she knew what he planned. With his marketing savvy and fancy connections, he'd have this place hopping in no time.

Damn him.

She didn't begrudge him his success, she just wanted it for herself, too. Did that make her a bad person? Probably.

He hadn't kissed her again.

Her fault. She didn't want more kisses. Hell, she could hardly concentrate now with the power of the last one still messing with her head.

Damn it, she couldn't reach the bolt. Wriggling just to the point of no return on the ladder, she realized she had the wrong size wrench. Of course she did.

Suddenly the right size appeared at her hip, extended to her by no other than the tall, dark, enigmatic man she'd been thinking about.

"Hey." He shot her a crooked grin that destroyed her from the inside out. "Need any help?"

Oh, boy. Loaded question. Yes, she needed help easing the tension strung tight inside her. Yes, he could ease that tension with just a touch, a kiss. And no, she wouldn't let him. "I'm fine."

"Uh-huh."

"What does that mean?"

"It means you make everything so damn difficult. Why can't you admit, just once in a while, it's okay to lean on someone?"

"I don't need—"

"I know." He tossed up his hands, then shoved his hands through his short, spiky hair. "You don't need anyone. Well, I think that's stupid."

She blinked. "Are you calling me stupid?"

He stared at her. "How can you be so smart, driven and beautiful, and yet so absolutely pigheaded at the same time?"

"I— You think I'm smart and driven?"

"Maybe," he said, eyes still flashing. "And maybe I also think you're sexy as hell, too."

She just stared at him, because he'd done what few had—stunned her.

"If you'd only take a single solitary breath from the whirlwind that is your life," he said, knocking the air from her lungs by hauling her off the ladder. "You'd see that not everything is about work, or about taking care of someone." Squeezing her

hips, he held her still before him. "It's about relationships. Like ours."

While she gaped at that, he stepped back and
pointed at her. "And I don't need taking care of,
so you can drop that excuse right now. I'm not one
of the needy you collect. Hell, I'm even downright
easy. I put the toilet seat down, the cap back on
the toothpaste and believe it or not, I can even
dress myself." He lifted his arms out to exhibit
that fact.

She could only stare at him. "There's no us."

"You don't think so?"

She let out a long breath. "Even if there
was…what does it mean?"

"Why don't you come to my place and find out?
Tomorrow night."

"That's a really bad idea. What would we do?"

"Tell you what, babe." He ran a finger over the
grease spot on her cheek, and her heart fluttered.
"You can decide when you get there."

WADE SET UP KYLIE'S seduction carefully. Food
was key, Kylie loved food, the junkier the better.
He'd ordered an extra large, extra loaded pizza,
and put on a loud rock CD to go alongside the
food. He had candles, too, lots of them. Probably
not her style, but he needed something to keep her

off balance. Off balance, she was uncertain and adorable.

Plus, he figured he had a better shot that way.

He hadn't even been sure she'd come, so when he heard her arrive, he took a deep breath and moved to the window to be certain it was her. Who else could it be? She drove an ancient old Jeep that she'd rebuilt herself, and far before it appeared in front of his house, he heard it clunking up the street.

Looking harassed, a bit tired and more than a little ready to rumble, she stalked up the driveway, holding a folded newspaper like a weapon.

He opened the door just as she leaned forward to knock, and for whatever reason, his quick appearance seemed to have startled her into a tumble.

Right into his arms.

"Well, hello," he said, enjoying the feel of her in his hands. "That step's a doozy, huh?"

In his arms she never failed to do a very ego-satisfying melt, which he could unequivocally say went both ways. He'd been around the block a few times in his life, and no one had ever created this combustive sexual tension within him. Sex with Kylie would be mind-blowing, toe-curling, heart-pounding. He just knew it.

"Back off," she told him. "You're going to get dirty." Pulling away, she tugged at the straps of her overalls. She wasn't kidding about getting dirty, with the smudges all down the front of her and on the tip of her nose, she'd obviously been working on an airplane. She wore her favorite cap over her mop of hair, and the usual scowl.

But beneath it was a touching amount of nerves and an unsureness that broke his heart. "Come inside."

She wrapped her arms around herself. "I'm not dressed for that."

"Then why are you here?"

She lifted the newspaper. "Because of this."

"Well, come in if you're going to hit me with it."

"Fine." She stepped inside. "Nice place," she said in such a begrudging way he had to laugh.

"Thanks. I think."

She looked around at the cabin-style house with the high vaulted wood-beam ceilings, at the wood-planked floors covered here and there with throw rugs, at the large but comfortable furniture, and then narrowed in on the music and candles. "What are you up to?"

"Nothing."

"You're always up to something, and we both know it."

She walked away from him, to the far side of the living room. She opened his French doors and stepped out into his backyard. He followed her to the edge of his pool.

Coming up behind her, he put his hands on her shoulders. Tense as usual. "What's the matter, Kylie?"

With another sigh, she spread out the newspaper, then pointed to the article on her mother. "You're in here."

"Am I?"

"You said, and I quote, you think Daisy did a superior job raising 'the amazing' Kylie. That 'they balance each other out and complete each other.'" She looked at him. "I know those reporters are pulling words out of a hat, but—"

"No."

"What do you mean, no?"

"I said what they said I did."

"You...said it? You talked to the reporters? About me?"

"Yes."

"But you knew that would bug me."

"What I knew was, you weren't telling them anything, and they were going to make it up. And you *are* balanced by your family."

"I don't need you to protect me. I told you, I take care of myself."

"Uh-huh. And you're doing such a good job of

it, too." He touched the black circles beneath her eyes.

Kylie had been spoiling for a fight, for a release of the building tension within her, since she'd read the paper. In truth, it was why she'd come, because she knew he'd give it to her, and whether he knew it or not, he just had.

"You're stubborn as hell," Wade said, stoking her temper nicely. "But you are everything I told the reporters. You're amazing, Kylie."

She had no idea why that last really got to her, but it did, and before she gave it another thought, she shoved him into the pool.

CHAPTER SEVEN

THE TALL, gorgeous, *obnoxious* man hit the water. Kylie felt a surge of satisfaction that was quickly washed away by…remorse. She really shouldn't have done it, but her other choice had been to kiss him and she couldn't do that.

Wade surfaced. He tossed his hair and water out of his face, narrowing dark blue eyes on her.

Remorse turned into a nervous giggle. "Oops," she said. "Sorry."

Water dripped off his nose. "You are not."

"You're right." Tension eased, she leaned over the edge. "Maybe you'll stay out of my life now, and—"

He moved like lightning, grabbing her hand and tugging her in.

The water muffled her scream. The night had been cool, but the water that rushed over her was warm. Still, the shock of it held her immobile for one moment.

Long enough for Wade to haul her close. "Chicken," he taunted when she sputtered and gasped for air. "Trying to scare me away with temper." His hands tightened. "Guess what, Kylie? I don't scare easily."

His hands were creating this delicious and confusing state of chilled heat. His face was so close she could see the fading sunlight dancing in his eyes.

And the yearning in them.

Oh, God. He wanted her, she could see it. "Let me go, Wade."

"I can't."

Fine. She'd simply get away from him on her own. But she'd lost her hat. Her shoes were weighing her down, and her arms were held at her sides by the man holding her close.

"Now." He lowered his forehead to hers. "I meant what I said. You are amazing. And if Daisy had anything to do with that, then she's amazing, too."

She stared at him, in that usual state of confusion he always put her in with his proximity. Plus, he was holding her so effortlessly she had the most horrifying urge to nestle her face in his throat. "Let me go," she said again, in a barely there whisper.

"Kylie…"

A light breeze rippled over their wet bodies as they drifted in the water in each other's arms. Kylie was grateful for the fence around his yard. She couldn't touch the bottom of the pool, but she knew Wade could as he danced them in a slow circle beneath the dusk sky. The sound of the water lapping against the edge was rhythmic, hypnotic. The feel of his warm strength lulling. She breathed him in, the faint scent of man and hunger, and when he drew her closer, she went.

She told herself it was because she felt chilled and he was so warm, but that was a big, fat lie. She went because she wanted to, and because in his arms some of the emptiness inside her started to dissipate. And when he kissed her, his mouth soulful, his tongue deep, any lingering emptiness vanished.

That was why, when he unhooked her overalls and pulled them off, that she let him. Let him strip her completely, and watched as her clothes drifted away in the water. A few bolts from her pocket sank to the bottom of the pool like stones.

Wade pulled off his shirt. Good Lord, he was beautiful, all hard angled planes and tough, sinewy muscle, with smooth, sleek, tanned wet skin. Oh yes, and he was hard everywhere, except the soft, crinkly patch of chest hair between his pecs, which she reached out and tangled her fingers in.

And tugged.

"Closer?" he murmured, and when she hummed her affirmative answer, he wrapped his arms around her tight—so tight she lost herself. When he kissed her this time, she kissed him back. His mouth was firm, demanding in a way that was so vintage Wade. The fist on her heart tightened. As always, and without a word, he commanded her the way no one else could.

Beneath his hands, her body came alive. There was no other way to describe it. She came to life, responding to his talented, greedy fingers and mouth in a way that might have scared her if he wasn't right there with her, lost right alongside her.

The rest of his clothes fell away, too. She stared down at his erection and quivered at the sight. "Ridiculous," she panted, even as she reached out and touched. "This is ridiculous."

"You're supposed to swoon at such a sight, not use words like *ridiculous*."

She let out a half-hysterical laugh. "I meant the situation, not you. You…you're…"

"Huge? Impressive?" he teased, his smile faded when she stroked him and looked up into his eyes.

"Perfect," she whispered, and wrapped her legs around his waist. His hands cupped her breasts, his thumbs rasping her nipples, his most impressive hard-on nudging…

Then he wasn't just nudging, he'd slid home with one full, oh-so-perfect thrust and she couldn't remember what was ridiculous about the most sensual, erotic experience of her life. She had the tile at her back, the giving, warm water surrounding them, the darkening night upon them, and Wade deep inside her.

"Okay?" he asked, and when she could only stare at him, he let out a groaning laugh. "I'll take that as a yes."

"Yes," she managed. "Very…yes. Wade?"

"Yeah?"

"Stop talking."

"I can do that." Then thankfully, finally, he began to move.

Later she would remember her hoarse cries, her soft whimpers and wordless demands. She'd remember how she sank her fingernails into his tight butt and made him go harder, faster, and later, much later, she would blush in the middle of whatever she was doing when she remembered.

But for right now, there was no later, there was nothing but this. He was so familiar, and yet a complete stranger. Every kiss, every taste, every touch felt new and thrilling, and just when she thought she would die if he ever stopped moving inside her, he said her name in a ragged, husky voice so filled with awe and longing, she was lost. Simply lost. She didn't have a chance of holding back, even if she'd remembered to, and with a small cry and a trembling that rippled through her entire frame, she broke into a shattering climax. Vaguely she heard his guttural moan, felt him shudder in her arms right with her.

Reality returned slowly, in the same easy sloshing waves of the water lapping over them. They lay on the steps in the shallow end, breathing ragged, staring up at the now night sky. She wondered at the tight ache in her chest, and the delicious sensation between her thighs…and at the need to have him again.

Definitely, time to go home and lick her wounds. She sat up and remembered she was naked. She wondered at the flash of embarrassment, when a moment ago she hadn't been able to get naked fast enough.

Wade sat up, too, and reached for her. "Regrets already?"

Yeah, she had regrets, but man oh man, did he look good. "Wade—"

"I should tell you," he said, unusually solemn, snagging her wrist, looking right into her eyes. "I love you. I love you, and I have for some time."

If she thought it'd been hard to breathe with his mouth on her while he'd been buried deep inside her, it was impossible now.

"Did you hear me?" he asked. "Should I say it again?"

"No! It's…it's just the sex talking." She scrambled up the steps of the pool, weaving like a drunk on the deck. Still very naked. Dripping. Shocked. *He'd used the L-word!* "You can't l-l—"

"Love you? Why not?"

"Because I can't...do it back. My life..." She lifted her hands, and had to let out a laugh. "My life is crazy enough, I can't take on one more person—"

"I already told you, no one takes care of me but me." Calmly, he retrieved her shirt, her overalls, then stepped out of the pool, too, standing there in all his leanly muscled—and nude!—glory, water pooling at his feet.

"Fine." She snatched her clothes from him. "You take care of yourself, and I'll take care of myself, and we'll just forget this happened and—"

"And what?" All that glorious male specimen moved closer. Very close. Very unconcerned about the nudity. "We'll go on our merry way and forget that we just rocked each other's world?"

She shoved her legs into her wet overalls, which meant her foot got stuck halfway in and she had to hobble around or fall on her ass. Her bra was still floating in the pool so she skipped that, too, and shoved her arms into her still inside-out shirt.

"Kylie—"

"I am leaving now."

"But—"

"Bye."

She got all the way home before she realized she'd forgotten her boots, too.

KYLIE WALKED into her office the next morning and found her bra and panties, dry and neatly folded, on her desk. No note.

None required, she thought grimly, staring at the plain white, serviceable bra and panties as she sank to her chair. The sexiest, most intelligent and startlingly intuitive man on earth fancied himself in love with her.

Her own little miracle, that.

And her own nightmare.

"Good morning, honey." Daisy, dressed in a pink suit with matching fingernails and toenails, and a little matching purse, smiled sweetly as she entered. As usual, every hair was in place, and she looked incredible.

A feat her daughter had never managed.

"Do you have a minute?" Daisy asked.

"No, actually, I—"

"Don't ask her if she has a minute," Lou scolded, coming in behind Daisy, looking just as spectacularly put together as her daughter, though her finger and toenails were cherry red. "She never has a minute."

"Grandma—"

"Be quiet, and welcome to This Is Your Sucky Life."

Kylie blinked. "What?"

Lou shut the door. "What happened last night?"

Kylie's stomach dropped. "Nothing." *Besides hot and wild sex in Wade's pool.* "Why?"

"Because your bra and panties got here before you did."

Kylie grabbed the underwear in question and shoved it in her drawer. "I...lost them."

"At Wade's house?" Daisy smiled kindly when Kylie frowned. "Should we have the birds and the bees talk again, honey? Because—"

"Mom!" Kylie scrubbed her hands over her face. "I remember the talk. Jeez!"

"So do you love him?"

"Love him? What are you talking about?" But she knew, God help her, she knew.

She had no idea what Wade saw in her, she was a tomboy who forgot to comb her hair half the time, she was grumpy and ornery, and she didn't have a soft spot to her.

And yet he loved her.

A serious problem, because she didn't know how she felt in return. And yet if this stomach-in-her-toes, heart-on-its-side, can't-eat-can't-sleep feeling meant she loved him back, she didn't know how she could live through it.

"Sit down, dear, you're looking pale." Lou pushed her into a chair. "Here's what's wrong. One, you work too hard. Two, you don't smile enough. Three, you have people who love you, and you snarl at them instead of loving them back. Four, you have the most gorgeous hunk on the entire planet mooning after you and it takes you six months to notice—"

"Grandma. What is this?"

"I told you, I'm giving you the quickie version of This Is Your Sucky Life." She turned to Daisy. "Tell me the truth, she's the mailman's child, right? You adopted her. You didn't really have this alien."

Kylie groaned and covered her face.

"What your grandma is trying to say, is that it's okay you made love with Wade," Daisy said. "We know you love us, and we think maybe you love him, too. It's okay to love people, Kylie. It's okay to lean on someone once in a while—"

"Lean on someone?" Kylie started to laugh, then realized she was close to tears and bit her lip. "Mom, it's just that I can't handle someone else leaning on *me*."

"Why I ought to take you over my knee!" Lou said. "Sure, you run the business. And sure you're more mature than we are. And okay, yes, maybe you're even smarter, but Kylie Ann Birmingham, this taking care of people crap goes both ways. Who makes sure you actually eat once in a while? Your mother. Who makes sure you actually laugh once in a while? Who makes sure you stop and smell the flowers? Me, thank you very much.''

Kylie opened her eyes and looked into the two pairs of baby blues watching her so anxiously despite the levity in her grandma's voice. They cared. They cared deeply. Why had she ever doubted that? ''Look, I—''

''Just say you're sorry and that you've been an idiot,'' Lou said. ''Go on, say it.''

''Okay, maybe I've been a bit of an—''

''Idiot,'' Grandma filled in helpfully.

''Idiot,'' Kylie agreed, rolling her eyes.

''No doubt there,'' her grandmother agreed. ''A *complete* idiot. Now. Forget about us and go get your man.''

Go get her man. Yeah. Shocking, but she liked the sound of that. But first she turned to Daisy. ''Mom. I love you. I know I don't say it enough, but I really do.''

Daisy's eyes filled.

''Yeah, yeah. Love, love, love.'' Lou pushed Kylie toward the door. ''You have a man to catch.''

"I love you, too, Grandma."

Lou's eyes filled, as well. "If you're going to go soft now, you're wasting it on the wrong person," she said, her voice suspiciously wobbly, and shoved Kylie out of her own office.

Kylie smiled, her heart feeling…light. Then her own office door shut in her face, and just as it did, she heard her grandma say, "I love you, too, even if you are an alien."

CHAPTER EIGHT

WADE WOKE UP ALONE. He'd woken up alone a thousand mornings before, but this morning, for the first time ever, it didn't feel right.

Kylie should have stayed. Should have been in his arms all night, blinking sleepy, sexy eyes at him. Then he'd have shown her what mornings were good for.

If he knew her, and he was quite certain he did, she'd ignore him today. She'd bury herself in work and pretend nothing was different.

When everything was different.

He walked from his office, braced, knowing he'd be facing a ten-foot brick wall when it came to Kylie, and dreading it. Damn it, if *he* could face his feelings for her, then she should have to do the same.

And she did have feelings. He didn't care what she admitted out loud, he'd made love to her now, he'd seen how she looked at him, how she'd lost herself in his touch.

If nothing else, she wanted his body. Good news, but it wasn't enough.

Walking through the maintenance hangar, he sighed heavily, disgusted with himself, because since when hadn't lust been enough for *him?*

Since now, apparently. Since Kylie.

And then he noticed, someone had opened up one of his planes. With a frown, he headed toward it and stepped onboard.

And nearly swallowed his tongue.

Kylie stood there…in a *dress.* And not any regular dress, either, but the knock-'em-dead, formfitting, flowery number from the photo shoot. Her hair had been styled, her lips glossed, and when she saw him, she…smiled.

She didn't ignore him, didn't snarl at him, she simply kept smiling.

"I'm…sorry," he said, his voice a little hoarse. "I think I've entered the wrong plane." He turned away, and she let out a little laugh.

"Wade…"

He turned back to her. "My God, Kylie, you look beautiful."

"It's the same dress because…" She laughed again. "Well, it's the only one I have." She held a file, and suddenly she shoved it at him. "Here."

He realized she had music on, not her usual hard rock, but something soft and romantic. She had a cooler opened with sodas in it. And she had a look to her face…. If he didn't know better he'd think she was trying to seduce him. "What's this?" he said, opening the file.

Inhaling deeply, she clasped her fingers in front of her. "It's a proposal." She took a step closer, nearly tripped on her heels, swore roughly, then forced a smile. "For you."

Watching this rough and tumble woman trying so hard to be soft and sexy made him want to both laugh and grab her. Grabbing her won out, and he reached for her, but she stepped back. "It's a proposal," she repeated. "For the very thing you've wanted."

Blankly he stared down at the file, remembering only that he wanted her. But Kylie wouldn't fit into this file.

"I've learned something about myself these past weeks," she said quietly, her fingers turning white as she twisted them together. "I need people in my life. I need you in my life. And I'm ready to admit it out loud."

Shocked, he stared at her. Was she saying what he hoped she was saying? "You...need me?"

"I need your expertise, I need your business savvy. I need you, the airport needs you. I'm just sorry it took me so long. So..." She drew another deep breath. "Will you buy into the airport as you've wanted? Will you become my business partner?"

When he didn't answer, Kylie let out a slow breath. "Did you change your mind?"

"On what, Kylie?"

Why was he looking at her like that, she wondered, his eyes all dark and inscrutable? His mouth grim? His body language looking as if maybe he wanted to strangle her? "On...being my business partner."

"Yes. Yes, actually, I did change my mind. I don't want to be your business partner."

What? *What?* How could he do this to her? Taking the last step between them, she stabbed his chest with her finger, hard. The sinewy strength of him didn't give an inch, so she stabbed harder. "You've been after me all year for a piece of this place, and now, suddenly, when I'm the one asking, you don't want a part of it?"

"Kylie—"

Oh, but she wasn't done. She stabbed him again. "You wanted this. You said so—"

"Now," he said, and grabbed Kylie. He settled his hands on her waist and whipped them both around so she was the one backed to the closed door. "We were discussing something very important."

"No, I was discussing and you were rejecting."

"Not rejecting. Negotiating."

"What kind of negotiation is no, Wade?"

"I don't want to be *just* your business partner,"

he said, still holding on to her, still making her
yearn and burn with just his hands and his eyes.
"I want to be your husband."

"You…" The air whooshed from her lungs. Her
heart stopped. "Oh my God."

"Yeah. So…Kylie Birmingham, will you marry
me? For better or worse, through sickness and in
health, through grumpy moods and business deals
and meddling relations?"

Kylie opened her mouth, then shut it. Then
opened it again. "You never said anything about
marriage," she managed to whisper through the
terrible burning in her throat.

"I just did."

"Yeah." She cleared her throat, then lost her
breath when Wade ran his hands up her body to
cup her face.

"I love you," he said quietly. "Does that
help?"

It did, if the hope and joy and heart-thumping
desire pumping through her meant anything. "I
think so." Suddenly feeling light and carefree, she
slid her arms around his neck. "Know what?"

A small smile curved his mouth. "What, baby?"

"I love you back."

His eyes softened, and so did his mouth as he
gently, tenderly set it to hers. "So the answer is
yes?"

She opened her mouth, but someone pounded on the door.

"Go away," yelled Kylie.

"But that's what I need to tell you, I have to leave early!"

At Daisy's voice, Kylie rolled her gaze heavenward. "Mom, I'm a little busy, can't you give me a few more minutes here?"

"Honey, I just found out I didn't win the trip to Paris."

Oh, damn. "Mom, I'm really sorry," she said through the door. "I know how much it meant to you, but—"

"Never mind, it doesn't matter. That's what I wanted to tell you, I just found a hell of a deal on a travel site on the Web. Your grandma and I are leaving today. Can we have two weeks off?"

Kylie looked into Wade's laughing eyes. "You know what? Go for it."

"We'll wait until they get back to go on our honeymoon," Wade whispered, and her heart soared.

"You're taking me to Paris on our honeymoon?" she whispered back.

"Is there anywhere else?"

Laughing, Kylie leaned away from the door and hugged him. They were still hugging and kissing when the door opened behind them.

"Oh my," Daisy said. "I'm sorry."

"Mom, we're getting married."

"You're..." Daisy looked faint. "Can you say that again?"

Kylie grinned, feeling a little faint herself. "We're getting married."

"You wouldn't tease an old woman, right?"

"You're not old, and I'm not teasing you."

Daisy looked to Wade for confirmation, and he nodded. She hugged them both, sniffling loudly. "So you can take care of my baby while I'm gone," she said to Wade.

Kylie shook her head. "Mom, I can take care of myself."

"I'll be glad to take care of her," Wade said, squeezing Kylie gently.

The reporter was behind Daisy, with tears in her eyes. "That's so beautiful."

Kylie thought so, too. She looked at Wade. "You know, that all happened so fast...do you think you could ask me again? Just so I can hear it one more time?"

The reporter lifted the tape recorder. "Oh, no need! I got it all on tape. You can listen to it whenever you want. In fact, you can listen to it all the way to Paris."

EPILOGUE

Contest Winner Announced!

Margaret Milford of Buffalo, N.Y., the mother of two-year-old quadruplets, has been chosen *Family Voyager's* Mother of the Year! She wins a trip for two to Paris, along with a five-thousand dollar shopping spree.

"My husband and I are dancing the macarena!" Mrs. Milford said after being notified of her selection. She was picked by the editors of *Family Voyager* from among nine finalists.

A tenth finalist, Jody Reilly of Everett Landing, Texas, withdrew after marrying *FV* publisher Callum Fox—click on *Wedding Festivities* to see photos of their hometown ceremony.

Mrs. Milford said she's planning to leave the quads, Mary, Max, Molly and Manny, with her mother-in-law. "Sam and I want to rekindle our romance on the trip. We might also catch up on our sleep, although I wouldn't count on it."

FV photographers will accompany the couple to Paris. You can follow their adventures on this

Web site, and read about them in our print edition.

Congratulations to the Milfords!

* * * * *

*Harlequin Duets invites you to turn
the page for an exciting preview of
YOU'LL BE MINE IN 99
by Jennifer Drew*

*Along with THE 100-YEAR ITCH
by Holly Jacobs, this special 100th
anniversary volume offers two terrific
tales by a duo of Duets's acclaimed
authors. With two volumes offering
two special stories every month, Duets
always delivers a sharp slice of the
lighter side of life and especially
romance.*

1

JOEL HAD A BAD FEELING. Katy was efficiently handing out the pageant rule sheets, but there was no reason to believe she was a contestant herself.

She had assets all right, taut thighs that strained against the material of her worn jeans, breasts that swelled against the hornet logo on her bulky sweatshirt, a pleasing oval face with great cheekbones and sapphire-blue eyes that radiated good humor. Yep, Katy Sloane had potential, but she was also a genius at hiding it. Her round glasses, which seemed to constantly slip down on her nose, were better suited for an octogenarian. Her hair was black and thick, carelessly held back by a yellow rubber band. He couldn't see a trace of makeup.

She reached the end of the line of contestants—at least twenty hopefuls—then glanced up and met his gaze.

He'd gotten a shock once trying to fix a faulty toaster. Looking directly into her eyes gave him same jolt without being painful or scary. Her shimmering eyes mesmerized him. They were easily the deepest and richest blue he'd ever seen, even with the distraction of too thick, shaggy eyebrows.

He shook his head, tried for a casual smile, and discovered his mouth was hanging open like a slobbering basset hound's.

"Would you like one?" she asked in a voice as smooth as satin.

He realized she was holding out one of the rule sheets.

"Oh, no thanks. Well, maybe I will look at one. If you have enough, that is."

"Is your girlfriend thinking of entering?"

"Girlfriend?"

He dated women and sometimes slept with women, but he hadn't called anyone a "girlfriend" since he'd reached six foot two and finally scrounged a few dates in high school.

"Oh, no, I was just curious. I'm here for the centennial." Two long weeks of the preparations and events, he remembered without enthusiasm.

"Do you have relatives in town?" she asked.

In Cleveland he'd write her off as nosy, but here in Hiho she probably thought she was being friendly—and she was. With a smile like hers, she could ask him anything, and he'd probably be happy to answer.

"Not exactly." He grinned because he was suddenly enjoying himself. "My great-great-grandfather had something to do with founding the town.''

"Are you Hiram Hump's descendant?'' She looked and sounded delighted.

"Guilty.''

He couldn't imagine why she seemed so enthusiastic until he remembered how little happened in small towns.

"Mr. Hump, I'm so happy to meet you.''

She reached out to shake his hand, but all her remaining rule sheets fluttered to the gym floor. They both bent to retrieve them at exactly the same instant, and their heads collided with a resounding thump.

He didn't actually see stars, but he was knocked on his backside. He probably looked as silly as he felt, and it didn't help his dignity any when she started pulling on one of his hands with both of hers to help him up.

"Oh, Mr. Hump, I'm so sorry!''

"Please, I'm Joel Carter. The Hump name died out when my grandparents had daughters but no son.''

He managed to scramble up with all the dignity of a baboon in a tutu.

"I always did have a hard head. Are you sure you're all right? I can get you a cold cloth,'' she offered.

"No, I'm fine.''

To demonstrate, he bent over and tried to gather up the fallen papers. He scooped up most of them but felt disturbingly light-headed. When he straightened, the yellowish-white cement-block walls of the gym seemed to be swirling.

She was quick to notice him wobble. She took his hand and led him to the nearest bleacher, then insisted he sit and hang his head between his legs.

"So you don't faint," she said, keeping her soft, cool hand on the back of his neck. "I can't tell you how sorry I am."

They'd attracted a crowd, but she shooed them back.

"Give him some air. This is Hiram Hump's descendant, our guest of honor," she announced to everyone within hailing distance.

He had a flashback to the third grade when Ben Juke had smeared a peanut butter sandwich all over his face while half the school watched and laughed. Even when she released her viselike grip on his neck and let him sit up, he felt like an idiot.

Several women clucked at him sympathetically, but kindness didn't help. The centennial guest of honor had given the town something to talk about.

HARLEQUIN® *Temptation*

*Legend has it that
the only thing that can bring down a Quinn
is a woman...*

Now we get to see for ourselves!

The youngest Quinn brothers have grown up.
They're smart, they're sexy...and they're about to be
brought to their knees by their one true love.

Don't miss the last three books in
Kate Hoffmann's dynamic miniseries...

The Mighty Quinns

Watch for:

THE MIGHTY QUINNS: LIAM
(July 2003)

THE MIGHTY QUINNS: BRIAN
(August 2003)

THE MIGHTY QUINNS: SEAN
(September 2003)

Available wherever Harlequin books are sold.

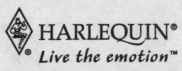

HARLEQUIN®
Live the emotion™

Visit us at www.eHarlequin.com

HTMQ

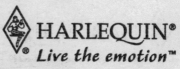

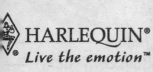

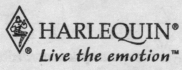

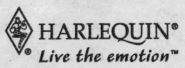